BULLETS DON'T ARGUE

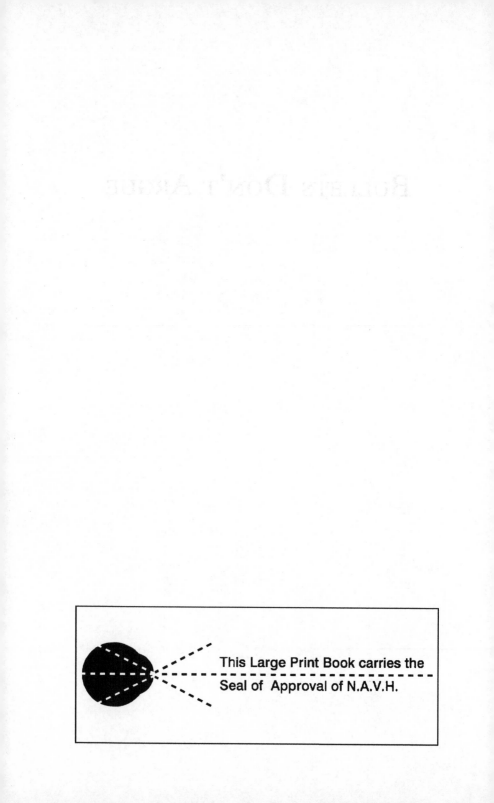

A PERLEY GATES WESTERN

BULLETS DON'T ARGUE

WILLIAM W. JOHNSTONE
WITH J. A. JOHNSTONE

THORNDIKE PRESS
A part of Gale, a Cengage Company

LIBRARY OF CONGRESS CIP DATA ON FILE.
CATALOGUING IN PUBLICATION FOR THIS BOOK
IS AVAILABLE FROM THE LIBRARY OF CONGRESS

ISBN-13: 978-1-4328-7099-7 (hardcover alk. paper)

Published in 2020 by arrangement with Pinnacle Books, an imprint of Kensington Publishing Corp.

Printed in Mexico
Print Number: 01   Print Year: 2020

Bullets Don't Argue

CHAPTER 1

Emma Slocum paused, thinking she had heard something outside the cabin. She tucked the blanket back over the sleeping baby in the crib her husband had built. It was late, past time when she had expected her husband to be home. He was often late to come home at night, but this was later than usual. Pausing again when she heard what she was sure was the sound of a horse approaching the cabin, she went at once to the door. "Dan?" she called out, wondering why he didn't go straight to the barn to unsaddle his horse as he usually did.

"It ain't Dan," Possum Smith answered her, "and we got to get outta here just as fast as we can."

She recognized the rider then as he approached the cabin, leading two horses, one of them saddled. Confused by his alarming statement, she asked, "Possum? Where's Dan?"

7

"Dan's been shot," Possum said, as he stepped down from the saddle, "and we've got to get movin', 'cause he's comin' after us."

Stunned by his frank and unemotional tone, she questioned, "What are you talkin' about? Who's comin' after us? Possum, where's my husband?"

"Emma, he ain't comin' home. Dan's dead, shot by that yellow, low-down dog, Jack Pitt. And you gotta get your stuff together while I hitch up the wagon! Just grab whatever you can't do without, 'cause I don't know how much time we've got before Pitt figures out where I went. Grab all your clothes and anything you need to cook with, 'cause we ain't comin' back." Horrified, Emma was caught in a fit of shock, unable to move, while her brain struggled to make sense of what she was hearing. "Emma, you and your baby are in danger!" Possum pleaded when he saw her confusion. "You've got to move!"

"Dan's dead?" she gasped, not willing to accept it, even though she had feared this day might come. "It's that damn money, isn't it? Where are we going?" she asked frantically.

"I don't know," Possum answered impatiently, "just away from here. Now hurry!"

Pitt had never been to Dan's cabin, but he knew it was somewhere along this creek, and it wouldn't take him long to find it. Finally impacted by the gravity of the situation, Emma spun around quickly, trusting that he was telling her the truth. Fearing for her and her baby's safety, she hurried to do as Possum had instructed with no time to grieve her husband's death.

Possum ran to the shed and corral that served as a barn and hitched the two horses there up to the wagon. When that was done, he took a pitchfork and went to work on a pile of hay in the corner of the shed until he uncovered a canvas bag. After a quick look inside it, to make sure the contents were still there, he shoved it under the wagon seat. Then he took another look around to see if there was anything else he might need. Nothing more than a coil of rope, an axe, and a short-handled shovel caught his eye, so he threw them in the wagon, as well as the canvas cover for the wagon bed. Unwilling to take any more time, he climbed up into the seat and drove the wagon up to the front door of the cabin. A pile of blankets and bedding told him that Emma was following his instructions. He jumped down from the seat and threw the items she had gathered into the wagon. Then he went inside to help her gather more. When they had loaded all the pots and pans and what food supplies she had, there was only room for one more item. It came down to a choice between the one rocking chair and the baby's crib. She was reluctant to leave the crib that Dan had built, but on Possum's advice, she decided to take the rocking chair. "That young'un's gonna grow outta that crib before you turn around twice, and you can rock him to sleep in that chair," Possum said.

He helped her up on the wagon seat, then handed the baby up to her. Before leaving, he went back inside to make sure the fire in the fireplace was dying out. As he explained to Emma when he climbed up into the wagon, it was an abandoned shack when Dan had found it. So he thought it only right to make sure it was still standing when the next drifter found it. With his two horses and Dan's extra horse tied to the back of the wagon, Possum gave the horses a slap of the reins and they crossed over the shallow creek and headed out toward the road, a quarter mile away.

A big full moon had already lifted above the far horizon by the time they struck the road to Dodge City. Possum was anxious to head south on the road in case Jack Pitt decided he might have gone to Dan's cabin instead of his own shack east of town. Right now, he wasn't sure if he was happy to see a full moon or not. It made it easier to avoid some of the rough spots on the well-traveled road, but it might also make it easier for Pitt to pick out his tracks, if he did come this way, looking for them. He glanced over at the frightened young woman frequently, somewhat amazed that she was now quietly accepting this nightmarish interruption in her evening.

Even though she had seemingly accepted this invasion into her home, Emma was not at all ready to dismiss her husband's sudden death so easily. She and Dan had not known Possum Smith for very long, but she trusted the usually mild-mannered old man, who had been part of a three-man partnership with her husband and Jack Pitt. Possum was certainly older than either of his two partners, but it was difficult to guess his age, and he never volunteered it. From the age lines in his weathered face, and the long gray braid of hair resting between his shoulder blades, it was obvious that he had ridden many trails in his life. She trusted him because Dan had trusted him. It was Jack Pitt that both Dan and Possum had been wary of, and now their distrust had evidently been justified. From the very beginning, Emma had feared that the money was going to bring bad luck in some form, but she was not prepared to deal with it when now it had arrived in the form of her husband's death. "Should we have turned the money over to the authorities?" she suddenly asked Possum. "Maybe we should do it now."

"No, no," Possum was quick to reply. "It's been too long, and we'd be held accountable for our share and Pitt's share, too. We shoulda known Pitt wouldn't keep our agreement not to spend any of that money till it had all blown over. Now he's wantin' to take our share. I knew it was bound to happen. Dan did, too. We both shoulda skipped town as soon as we found it." He turned his head toward her and added, "Besides, you're gonna need that money now that Dan's gone. And the bank ain't gonna miss it."

He turned his attention back to the horses, encouraging them to maintain the pace he had called for. *Should have known better,* he thought, *trying to help the law.* He thought back on that day when the bank was robbed, and he had volunteered to join the sheriff's posse. He and Dan had decided, "What the hell . . ." They sure as hell weren't busy doing anything else, so they joined half a dozen other volunteers and chased after the two bank robbers. West along the banks of the Arkansas River, they had raced, steadily closing the distance between them and the outlaws until they split up. He and Dan and another man, Jack Pitt, broke off and chased the robber south of the river. They caught up with the outlaw when his horse stumbled over a small gully and broke a leg. The rider was tossed, landing on his back. When the three possemen pulled up to him, he was still flat on his back. Possum ordered him to put his hands up, but before he had gotten the last word out, Jack Pitt shot him. "He was goin' for his gun," Possum remembered Pitt saying. That was his introduction to Pitt. He knew now that it should have been a warning as to the kind of man he was. There was a long moment of conscience upon finding the canvas money bag. With no one to witness it, Pitt immediately suggested they should keep it. "We can say there wasn't no money on him," he said. "Ain't no way anybody can say there was."

Possum remembered the glances he and Dan had exchanged. It was obvious that both of them were hesitant to go along with Pitt's suggestion. After all, it would make them as guilty of robbery as the man Pitt

13

had just killed. At the time, however, a sack full of money was too much to turn their backs on. Times were tight and money was scarce. There was also the possibility of getting the same medicine the dead outlaw had received from Pitt, had they not agreed to his proposition. So they had hidden the money and carried the outlaw's body back to join up with the sheriff and the rest of the posse.

Pitt did most of the talking when they reported back to the posse, telling the sheriff that they had been forced to shoot the outlaw when he refused to surrender. He told him that the man they chased wasn't carrying any bank money. And when they found out that the second outlaw had been killed as well, Dan and Possum were even more encouraged to keep quiet about the money they had hidden. A canvas bag, filled with money, was found with the man the sheriff had killed, so they assumed it was the whole sum stolen. Possum remembered the grin on Pitt's face when they realized there was no one to say the outlaws had two sacks of money, no matter what the bank said.

The three-way partnership started out all right, with all three men riding back together to the spot south of the Arkansas where they had buried the money. The money was counted and divided into three separate piles of eleven thousand, three hundred dollars each, more money than any of the three could imagine earning by honest means. They agreed then to go their separate ways, but to refrain from spending any of the cash until there was time for the robbery to become old news. Feeling a trusting kinship with young Dan Slocum, Possum had decided to hide his share of the robbery with Dan's. They agreed it a good idea to avoid Jack Pitt, especially since witnessing his lack of hesitation in killing the helpless outlaw. It wasn't long, however, until Pitt sought them out.

Thinking back on it now, as he kept the horses to a fast walk, Possum blamed himself for possibly causing Dan's death. The fault lay in the easy friendship that had resulted between them, when it might have been better had they not associated with each other at all. Had they not been sitting at a table in The Trail Driver, having a drink, they would not have run into Jack Pitt. And Dan would still be alive. It had been this feeling of guilt, and not his share of the money, that had caused him to come for Emma and the little one. The decision to be made now was, where should he go?

He decided he would talk it over with Emma when they stopped to rest the horses.

As near as he could estimate, they had traveled close to ten miles, maybe a little more, when they came to a small creek. Thinking he would not likely find a better place to rest, he drove the horses about forty yards up the creek where he stopped the wagon. While Emma took care of the baby, Possum unhitched the horses and led them down to water. He left them to graze on the grassy bank of the creek while he gathered some limbs for a fire. He had a healthy flame going when he looked up to see Emma coming back from the trees after having answered nature's call. "We'll have to rest these horses for a little while," he announced when she approached the fire. "I thought a little fire might go good right now, and I've got some coffee in my packs, if you want some."

"That would be good," Emma said. "Tell me about Dan," she was finally able to ask.

"Well, it was just bad luck," Possum said. "We was just havin' a drink while we talked about startin' us up a cattle ranch somewhere away from here, now that we had some money. Jack Pitt walked in. We wasn't expectin' to run into him. He said he was

16

gonna head for Wichita, so we didn't know he was still in Dodge. He was half drunk and talkin' crazy about me and Dan takin' more'n our share of the money. Well, Dan told him to quit shootin' his mouth off about the money before somebody heard him." Possum paused, as if reluctant to go on. "It was just like it was with that outlaw we caught up with, Pitt drew his .44 and shot Dan, without any warnin' a-tall. I reckon he realized what he had done then, so he ran out the door." He shook his head slowly. "I'm powerful sorry, Emma, I reckon Dan had no business foolin' with people like me. He shoulda been home with his family."

Emma sat, calmly listening to Possom's accounting of her husband's death. It was a sad, heartbreaking story to hear, but there were no tears in her eyes, just a feeling of sorrow that she had become accustomed to. Her life had been defined by bad choices, choices that seemed to always result in disappointment and regret. She had never truly loved Dan Slocum. He was a good man and had stepped up to take her out of a bad situation. She gratefully said yes to his proposal of marriage. Dan was the youngest son of Zachary Slocum, owner of one of the biggest cattle ranches in North Texas,

17

so she gladly accepted the opportunity for a good life for her away from Butcher Bottom. It was not to be, however, for Zachary Slocum was not happy when his youngest son wanted to wed a girl from Butcher Bottom, a small settlement of poor farmers. There resulted a clash between father and son that ended with Dan and his bride striking out for Kansas. "I reckon we'd best decide where we're headed," Possum said, breaking her silence.

She had no place to go, other than to return to her home. She had Dan's share of the stolen bank money, but she had no idea what to do with it. "I don't know of anyplace I can go except Butcher Bottom," she said. "That's the only place where I know anybody."

"Butcher Bottom," Possum repeated, "that's in Texas, ain't it?" He had heard Dan refer to it, but not in a complimentary way. "Well," he sighed, "if that's where you need to go, I reckon I'll try to get you there in one piece. Or maybe two pieces," he added, with a glance at the baby.

"You ain't got no obligation to take me all the way to Texas," Emma said. "I reckon I'll just have to drive this wagon myself."

"No such a thing," Possum replied at once. "I can't let you start out all that way by yourself. What if you broke a wheel or somethin'? No, ma'am, I'd best take you to Texas." He wasn't all that enthusiastic about the idea, especially since they would be carrying all that money, but he couldn't escape the feeling of guilt he had for Dan's death. "I might not know exactly how to find Butcher Bottom, but Dan's talked some about what part of Texas it's in. We'll get there, all right." He shrugged. "I reckon we can just follow the Western Cattle Trail back down to Texas, then somebody oughta know where Butcher Bottom is. If they don't know that, they might know where your daddy-in-law's ranch is, if it's as big as you say."

"You have my thanks, Possum," she said humbly, "and I'll pay you some of Dan's share of that bank money for your trouble." She was more than willing to pay him for the expense of the trip. He was getting along in years, but having him along was a sight better than traveling alone.

"No such a thing," Possum said again, making an effort to cheer her up. "I'd like to see Butcher Bottom." His almost-white whiskers parted enough to permit a smile.

John Gates pulled over close to his brother and commented, "Looks like somebody's havin' some trouble." He pointed to a wagon jacked up on the far bank of the river with the left rear wheel off.

"Yeah, I've been watchin' him for a while," Rubin replied. "Looks like one man and one woman. We'd best cross a little farther over this way." He pointed toward a low bank east of the straw bridge the Doan family had built out of hay. In the summer, the river was usually down so low that there was a danger of quicksand, so they built the bridge for the cattle to cross. The charge was twenty-five cents per head, but after John's inspection of the river bottom, he decided it was unnecessary to drive their herd across the bridge. The two brothers were riding point on a cattle drive of three thousand cows that had left Lamar County, Texas, two weeks before. Having pushed the herd west far enough to reach the crossing at Doan's Store, they prepared to cross the Red River into Oklahoma and head north to Ogallala on the Western Trail. "Better signal Ollie to turn back this way."

"He's already thinkin' the same as we are," John said. Up ahead, Ollie Dinkler drove his chuckwagon on an angle to pass more to the east of the wagon on the Oklahoma side of the river. In about a quarter of an hour's time, the lead cattle entered the water. Soon the river was filled with Triple-G cattle, drinking the water, until being driven up the other bank. Following their customary drives, Ollie drove his chuckwagon across and unhitched his horses, preparing to spend the night there by the river.

Once the cattle were peacefully settled for the night, John and his younger brother, Perley, rode over the low ridge to see what the situation was with the broken-down wagon. As they approached the wagon, a man crawled out from beneath it and stood up, prepared to greet them. A woman holding a baby came from behind the wagon and stood beside the man, watching John and Perley. "Looks like you folks are havin' a little trouble," John offered in greeting when he and Perley pulled up beside the wagon.

"Reckon so," Possum said. "This wheel has been leanin' a little outta line ever since we crossed a stream earlier this mornin' and I think I musta bent the axle when I drove it up on a rock under the water. The wheel's been squeakin' ever since, so I pulled it off to put some grease on that axle. Sure 'nough, it looks a little bent to me."

"That's sorry news," John said. "How far do you have to go?" He glanced from the man to the woman standing beside him and assumed them to be father and daughter. There was obviously a sizable difference in age.

"Well, that's hard to say," Possum replied, "a-ways, maybe fifty or sixty miles, I expect." When both of their visitors responded to his answer with questioning looks, he tried to explain. "My name's Possum Smith. This here lady is Emma Slocum. Her husband met with an accident in Dodge City, up in Kansas territory, that took his life, so I'm tryin' to take her home."

"You've come all the way from Dodge City?" Perley asked, surprised.

"That's a fact," Possum answered.

"Where are you headin'?" John asked.

"You ever heard of a place called Butcher Bottom?"

"Can't say as I have," John replied and looked at Perley, who shook his head as well.

"Me neither," Possum said, "so I'm gonna have to look for it when we get down into Texas. That's where Emma's from, but she don't know how to tell me where it is. All I know is, it ain't too far from the Lazy-S cattle ranch, so I reckon I oughta be able to find it."

"Zachary Slocum," John said at once.

"That's right," Possum said. "You know him?"

"I know of him," John replied, "but I ain't ever met the man. He's got one of the biggest cattle operations in North Texas. We're from the Triple-G, east of here a couple hundred miles."

Perley looked at the forlorn-looking woman holding the baby. "If your name's Emma Slocum, then I reckon your husband was Zachary Slocum's son. Is that right?" Emma nodded. "Well, we're mighty sorry for your loss, ma'am. My name's Perley Gates and this is my brother John." While they had been talking, Perley had taken a quick glance in the back of the wagon. It didn't take more than that to see they looked awfully short of supplies. "You plannin' on campin' here tonight?"

"That's right," Possum answered. "I think our horses have had enough for today. I figured I was gonna have to try to fix a wagon wheel, but after I took a look at it, I think it'll hold up till I get Emma home."

"We're restin' the herd here tonight," Perley said. "If you folks don't mind eatin' some chuckwagon food, why don't you have supper with us? We've got a mighty fine cook."

Perley's invitation surprised his brother,

but from the obvious expression of delight in Emma's face, he concluded what Perley had already surmised. "That's a good idea," he said then. "Won't be anything fancy, but there'll be plenty of it."

"Why, thank you kindly," Possum said after glancing at Emma. "We'd be happy to take supper with you, wouldn't we, Emma?" There was no hesitation on her part to agree.

"Good," John said. "You'll hear Ollie when he bangs on his dinner bell. We'll look for you to come on over and join us." He glanced at Perley and said, "I expect we'd best get back to the herd." They climbed on their horses and headed back the way they had come.

When they were out of hearing distance, Perley pulled up even with John. "Did you take a look in that wagon?" When John said that he hadn't, Perley said, "It looked like it was filled up with clothes and furniture and such, but I didn't see anything that looked like food. You reckon they've run outta supplies?"

"Maybe," John replied. "I expect we'll find out when they come to supper."

Possum and Emma were treated like royalty when they walked over to join the crew of the Triple-G for supper. Ollie was more than pleased with the compliments he received for the meal he prepared, although they were not really needed. Judging by the enthusiasm with which his guests attacked his steak and biscuits, it was plain to see they appreciated his efforts. It also told Rubin and John that Perley had been right when he suspected they were desperately short of rations. It was so evident that the three brothers had a quick conference and decided it would go against their Christian upbringing to leave Possum and Emma in the dire straits in which they had found them. Before the evening was ended, they learned that Possum had no connection to Emma beyond the happenstance that he volunteered to ride in a posse with her husband. According to Possum, Emma's husband had been the unlucky victim of one of the bank robbers they had chased. Being the Christian man that he was, Possum could not turn his back on the grieving widow, so he had volunteered to take her home to Texas.

While they ate, Rubin brought up the subject of supplies. "You folks still have about fifty or sixty miles to go, you say?"

"Near as I can figure," Possum replied.

"How are you fixed for supplies?" Rubin

questioned. "Perley said it didn't look like you had much in the way of food."

Possum looked surprised. "Did he say that? Well, I reckon he's pretty much right about that. We ain't. We just had to do the best we could with the little bit we had, mostly livin' offa bacon till we could get to Doan's Store. There ain't many places to buy supplies between here and Dodge City. I was hopin' to run up on somethin' to hunt, but so far, I ain't had much luck." He paused to grin. "Maybe the deer are all waitin' down in Texas for us."

"I'll tell you what," Rubin said, "we'll make you a present of a cow, in case the deer ain't waitin' for you." He looked at John and Perley for their reaction and both his brothers nodded their approval. "We'll even help you skin and butcher it tonight, but we have to keep this herd movin', so it'll be up to you to take care of it in the mornin'."

The immediate display of gratitude on the faces of both Possum and Emma told him how much it meant to them. "That's mighty kind of you fellers," Possum said. "We'll surely appreciate the beef, but I can do the skinnin' and butcherin'. No need to have your men doin' that."

"All that beef needs some coffee and

beans to go with it," Perley suggested. "How are you fixed for that?"

Emma spoke up at once. "We're already out of coffee. I've been reusing the old grounds for the last two days."

Possum was quick to interrupt her. "We may look poorly, but we ain't flat broke. I was figurin' on buyin' some coffee and other stuff at Doan's Store when we crossed the Red. You folks have been more than generous, and I don't wanna take advantage of ya."

Rubin glanced at his two brothers. He could guess that their feelings were the same, he felt. Possum and Emma looked to be in a desperate situation and could use a little help in finding the settlement called Butcher Bottom. Then Rubin and John turned their glances to light on Perley, and he knew immediately what they were thinking. He frowned and shook his head slowly, hoping they would guess his reaction to their thoughts. Neither one made a comment, much to his relief, but there was a deep discussion to follow as soon as Emma and Possum expressed their thanks and returned to the wagon with their gift cow. Sonny Rice and Charlie Ramey volunteered to go with them to help with the butchering, even though Possum had insisted he

27

could handle it. Before the evening was over, Ollie Dinkler went over to supervise the smoking of most of the meat to keep it from spoiling.

"That poor woman looks like she's about to give up and die," John remarked after Emma returned to her wagon. "And the old fellow with her didn't look much better. You reckon he'll find that little place she says she's from?"

"I don't know," Rubin replied. "What bothers me is, she says he just happens to know her late husband. That old fellow looks plum wore out. He just might decide he's done enough for her and take off, leavin' her to try to find Butcher Bottom by herself — her and that little baby."

"I already know what both of you are thinkin'," Perley said, "and I ain't gonna do it."

With the first rays of the sun the next morning, Possum crawled out of his bedroll under the wagon. He had worked late the night before, saving as much beef as he could for the rest of their trip. He woke up only once during the night when he heard the sounds of the herd of cattle moving out of the river valley, so he figured they were out of sight by now. He listened for sounds that would tell him Emma and the baby were awake, satisfied when he heard none. He went at once to revive the fire, then when he was sure it was caught up, he turned toward the scrubby bushes on the riverbank to answer nature's demands. It was then that he first saw the horse and rider standing silhouetted against the early-morning light, no more than thirty yards from the wagon. "Hot damn!" Possum blurted in shocked surprise, thinking Jack Pitt had already found them.

"I didn't mean to startle you," Perley said. "I just figured I'd wait till you woke up before I went ridin' into your camp." Possum seemed unable to come up with a suitable reply, so Perley continued. "Good mornin'. You remember me? I'm Perley Gates."

"Good mornin'," Possum finally replied, relieved to find he wasn't about to be attacked. "Well, you sure as the dickens gave me a fright there for a minute. Whaddaya doin' here this mornin'? I heard the cattle when they started out earlier."

"I figured I'd give you a hand, help you and the lady find Butcher Bottom," Perley said.

"You stayed back to help me and Emma?" Possum asked, finding it hard to believe.

29

"Ain't you anxious to get your cattle to market?" While he would appreciate some help, it was natural to have suspicious thoughts about the young man willing to leave the herd to go with him and Emma. He had to tell himself there was no way Perley could know they were carrying a huge amount of cash money in that broken-down old wagon.

"Oh, I wanna see 'em get to the market," Perley replied, "but they don't need me to do it. My brothers will see to that. I'm not especially fond of working cattle in the first place. Besides, we figured I wouldn't be gone more than five or six days, if that place is about as far as you said. We were talkin' about it last night after you went back to your wagon. There's a lot of wild lawless men ridin' in northern Texas this time of year, so we figured it wouldn't hurt to have an extra pair of eyes and an extra gun with you. I brought a packhorse with me, so I've got my own supplies. 'Course, it's up to you. If you druther I didn't go along with you, just say the word, and I'll skedaddle outta here to catch up with the cattle."

Possum hesitated before answering. There was nothing threatening about the young man's appearance that would make him believe he was anything but honest in his offer to help. Before he could speak, however, he was interrupted by Emma, who called out from the wagon. "What is it, Possum? Is anything wrong?"

"No, ma'am," Possum answered and broke out a grin. "It's just Perley Gates, stayed back from the rest of 'em just to give us a hand in gettin' you safely home."

"Really?" Emma responded in surprise, pleased by the gesture on the part of the men of the Triple-G. "Well, we're mighty grateful, Perley. I know it'll take a little strain off of Possum, having somebody to help him."

"We're glad to do it, ma'am," Perley replied, resigned to the fact that he might be a week in catching up with the herd again. "I brought some coffee with me. Thought you might use a cup before we get started this mornin'."

CHAPTER 2

They crossed over the Red River after having their coffee, preferring to wait for breakfast until they stopped to rest the horses. Perley was right in his assumption that they were out of supplies, but was surprised when they restocked at Doan's Store. He had been convinced that Possum was just talking to save embarrassment when he had said they were not flat broke.

From Doan's Crossing, they followed a trail straight south that Emma thought she remembered. There was an odd-shaped knoll with one lone tree at the top and she was sure there could not have been another just like that one. To Possum, this was another indication that she and her husband had followed the cattle trail up through Texas. When Emma said they had crossed a river, then it was two whole days until they reached the Red River, Possum guessed she was referring to the North Wichita River. "I figure that to be about forty miles," he said, thinking her husband had likely driven his wagon twenty miles a day.

"I thought you said you were from Kansas," Perley said. "You know more about Texas than I do."

"I am from Kansas," Possum replied, "but it ain't the only place I'm from. I've rode a lot of trails before I crossed yours." He looked at Emma and grinned. "Yours, too," he said. "I know a little bit about some parts of Texas, but I ain't never heard of Butcher Bottom till I ran into Dan and Emma."

"That don't surprise me none," Emma offered. "Nobody in Butcher Bottom ever goes outside of it, if Raymond Butcher has his way — and he always does." She smiled a tired smile when she remembered the day when she thought she was going to escape the fate of most of the other women who had been unfortunate to land there. She couldn't help thinking now that she must be out of her mind to return to Butcher Bottom when she could choose to go elsewhere. Although leaving her a widow with a baby, Dan had left her with a comfortable sum of money. It bothered her not at all that it was money stolen from a bank. Like Possum, she thought of it as money stolen from a bank robber, that it was money the bank had already lost. Her problem was that she had no idea what she should, or could, do to provide for her and baby Daniel's life. Her thoughts were interrupted when Perley asked a question.

"Why do they call it Butcher Bottom?" he asked.

"It's not a very pretty name, is it?" she answered, then went on, "It was named for old man Simon Butcher. He was a preacher, so he said, and he convinced a small congregation in Mississippi to follow him to an unclaimed valley near the Brazos River. My parents were part of that congregation, and I wasn't much more than four years old when we went there. Accordin' to Reverend Butcher, they were gonna build their own country and provide for themselves, just like the Amish do, and live off the land."

"Your folks still live there?" Perley asked.

"No, they've both passed away," Emma replied. "Mama died three years ago. and Papa didn't last but about six months after she was gone."

"Maybe I ain't hearin' you right," Perley remarked, "but it sounds to me like you ain't too happy to get back. With your mama and papa gone, why do you want to?"

" 'Cause I've got a sister there and I don't know no place else to go," she said.

"Seems to me, about anyplace would be better than one you're sure you don't like," Perley said.

"That's what I told her," Possum said. "She won't admit it, but I think she's scared one of them men in that cult will be coming after her now that Dan's dead."

"No, I ain't," Emma responded at once. "I ain't even sure they'll let me come back after I married a cattleman. Raymond says cattlemen are the devil's seeds."

"Who's Raymond?" Perley asked.

"Raymond Butcher. He's Simon's son, and he took over when the old man died. He's a preacher, too. My sister, Rachael, said he liked to pitched a fit when I ran off with Dan, said his sermon was an hour long that Sunday."

"So you've got a sister there," Perley thought aloud. He looked at Possum, who was grinning at him behind Emma's back. "Well, that does beat all," Perley said, unable to respond with anything appropriate. He was rapidly coming to the opinion that Emma was going back to Butcher Bottom because she was penniless and had no way to survive otherwise. It didn't sound like much of a future for her and her baby, but there wasn't anything he could do to help her. Resigned to that fact, he decided he'd do what he could to see that she found Butcher Bottom and her sister. "Your sister," he thought to ask then, "is she married and got a family?"

"Yes, Rachael's married to Tom Parker," Emma said. "They've got two children, both girls. Raymond says that's a good sign because that means two more to bear children when they get old enough. But I think Tom wanted boys to help him farm. I haven't heard from her since right after I left Butcher Bottom."

"I reckon so," Perley said and decided that maybe it was best not to ask any more questions, and just concern himself with helping Possum take Emma home.

They hitched up the horses and continued on along the trail they had followed since crossing the Red River.

Approaching what looked to be a sizable creek, judging by the border of trees along its banks, Perley reined Buck back to let the wagon catch up with him. When he was even with Possum in the wagon seat, he said, "Looks like we've struck a creek just when we need one. I expect we'd best stop now, get some food, and rest the horses."

"I expect so," Possum agreed as he craned his neck to look toward the snake-like line

36

of trees stretching across the prairie before them. "Looks like this trail runs right through that biggest bunch of trees yonder," he said, pointing toward a point where the creek evidently took a sharp bend. "I would be surprised if that weren't a regular campin' place for most folks travelin' this trail." He turned and pointed downstream a good five hundred yards where there was a wide section with very few trees. "I expect that's where the cattle herds were pushed across."

A few minutes later, when they rode into the trees, they found an axle-deep creek, about twenty yards wide at that point. Seeing a small clearing in the trees on the other side that offered grass for the horses, they proceeded across. Perley and Buck crossed first to be certain of the depth and to make sure there were no hidden holes that might gobble up a wagon wheel. Once across, they discovered ample evidence that Possum had been right when he figured it to be a popular camping spot. There were several spots where campfires had burned. They unhitched the horses, and Perley pulled the saddle off Buck. Possum came up beside him as he let the big bay go back beside the creek to drink. "That's a right stout-lookin' bay you're ridin', Perley," Possum observed. "Why'd you name him Buck?"

" 'Cause he does," Perley said. When Possum looked confused by his answer, Perley went on to explain that Buck wouldn't permit anyone to ride him but him.

Possum's question caused Emma to ask one of her own, one she had wondered about from first meeting Perley. "Perley Gates," she asked, "Is that your given name, or just a nickname?"

"No, ma'am," he answered patiently, having had to deal with the question ever since he could remember. "It's my real name. I was named for my grandpa, who was named Perley. It sounds like those Pearly Gates, but it ain't spelled the same."

"It's an unusual name," she said.

"Yes, ma'am, it is that." He smiled, thinking she could never know the half of it. He went then to help Possum, who was already busy collecting some wood for a fire. It wasn't long before there was a hearty fire going and the coffeepot was working. After feeding the baby, Emma took over the cooking of the beans that had been soaking all morning and the frying of some sourdough pan biscuits to go with the smoked beef they had packed.

"Whaddaya think, Zeb?" Cal Hackett asked, his voice almost in a whisper. "They look kinda poorly."

"Maybe," Zeb answered. "Don't matter much. Poorly or not, they've got more'n we've got right now." He and his two brothers had been watching the three people busy making a camp near the creek. "A couple of them horses look pretty good, 'specially the bay that one feller was ridin'."

"Wonder what that woman is cookin' up?" Peewee muttered.

"I expect we'd best go down there and find out," Zeb said. "Let's walk up a little closer to get a better look. See if we got anythin' to worry about."

"I don't see no problem," Cal insisted. "I can see that from here. One of them fellers looks like somebody's grandpa, and the other'n's a young feller, but he don't look like no problem to me. Even if he gives us some trouble, there's the three of us against him."

"Maybe we oughta just pick 'em off with our rifles and be done with 'em," Peewee suggested. He was thinking about making their move before they had a chance to eat much of the food Emma was cooking.

"The last time we tried that was with them four drifters up on the Wichita," Zeb reminded him, "and that didn't turn out too good, did it? Killed that one feller, then the other three dug in that riverbank, and we had to call it off 'cause we was runnin' outta cartridges. And we're still short, so I don't wanna take a chance on it happenin' again." He paused to see if anyone was going to object, knowing they wouldn't question his judgment. "And if we ride on in to their camp, it's still just one young feller and one old man against the three of us. Right?" His brothers nodded in agreement. "All right," he said, "let's go down and pay 'em a friendly visit."

Emma, tending her biscuits, was the first to see the three men riding across the little clearing. She was at once alarmed, thinking of the small fortune they carried in the wagon. She called out to Possum, who was checking the left-rear wagon wheel again to see if it had gotten any worse. When he looked up and saw her pointing toward the trees, he immediately picked up his rifle and alerted Perley, who was taking a look at Buck's hooves. "Uh-oh," Perley muttered after spotting the visitors to their camp. He immediately walked up to the wagon to join Possum and Emma.

"This don't look too good," Possum commented to Perley when he joined them. "They got a look about 'em."

"Maybe just some drifters, lookin' for a meal," Perley said, even though he was prone to agree with Possum's assessment.

"Maybe so, maybe not," Possum said. "You might have to use that six-gun you're wearin' if they ain't comin' to welcome us to Texas." He was hoping at that moment that he could count on Perley, if their visitors didn't have peaceful intentions. Perley didn't have the look of anything beyond just a pleasant young man.

"Howdy," Zeb called out as they rode into the clearing, three abreast, and pulled up just before the fire. "We was passin' by on the other side of the river and smelled your coffee a-cookin', and we was wonderin' if you might could spare a cup or two. We've been out for a long time, food and coffee, and a cup of that would sure go good right now."

"Well, now," Possum said, "I reckon we could spare a cup or two. We're runnin' low on supplies ourselves, spent the last money we had to buy some beef from a trail herd we met at the crossin'."

"Where you folks headin'?" Zeb asked as he stepped down from his saddle. "Have you come far?"

"Headin' to a place called Butcher Bottom," Possum replied. "We started out from

Dodge City, up in Kansas."

"You've come a long ways," Zeb declared.
"Tell you the truth, I'm surprised you folks
took this trail. Most likely because you're
not from around here, so you didn't know
about the toll to use this trail." His two
brothers stepped down then, both wearing
poorly disguised grins.

"You're right, mister," Possum said. "I
ain't never heard of any tolls on any trails in
Texas, and that's a fact." He knew now what
he had hoped not to learn. The three of
them were low-down road agents, looking
to rob defenseless travelers. He figured his
only hope was to convince them that they
had no money. "I reckon we're just outta
luck 'cause we spent the last dime we had
to buy this food we're cookin'."

"I reckon you are out of luck," Cal spoke
up then as he and Peewee took a few steps
to either side of Zeb. "It's our job to collect
the toll from folks cuttin' across the county's
private land here."

"That's right," Zeb said. "Me and my
brothers work for the county. We'll just have
a look at what you're carryin' in that wagon
and see if you've got anything worth takin'
for the toll." Emma, already frightened,
almost gasped aloud in sudden distress at
the thought. Zeb picked up on her reaction.

"What's the matter, little lady, is there somethin' in that wagon you don't want nobody to see?"

Recovering her composure almost as fast as she had lost it, "It's my baby," she answered. "He's asleep in the wagon. I had a devil of a time gettin' him to sleep, and I don't want you to wake him."

"There ain't nothin' in the wagon but some furniture and beddin'," Possum said, "Ain't nothin' worth any money."

"We'll just take a look in there, anyway," Zeb said, his rude smile showing his confidence. "We'll be real quiet so we don't wake up your baby."

Up to this point, Perley stood to the side, a silent observer of Possum's handling of the situation. It was fairly obvious these three were no more than common thieves, looking to take advantage of some unlucky travelers. He figured it was time to step in. "You fellows say you work for the county?"

"That's right," Cal answered and took a longer look at him. "We're special agents for this county, and our job is to collect money from everybody usin' this trail."

Perley nodded, as if he understood. "That's an important job," he said. When Cal nodded in response, with a self-important grin in place, Perley asked another question. "What county is this, anyway?"

The smile on Cal's face froze, and he immediately looked to Zeb for help. Flustered as well as his brother, Zeb blurted, "It don't matter what damn county this is! It's just your bad luck you came this way. Now, I'm tired of foolin' with you people. Let's take a look in that wagon!" As if on cue, Cal and Peewee each took a few steps to either side of Zeb, ready for any resistance to their search of the wagon.

"I expect this has gone far enough," Perley announced calmly. "You fellows sure don't work for the county, and there ain't no toll roads in Texas, even if you called this game trail a road. So I expect you'd best get back on your horses and clear outta here before somebody gets hurt." He slowly reached over to take Emma's arm and gave her a gentle push toward the back of the wagon, never taking his eyes off the three facing him.

The shock of disbelief on the faces of the three would-be robbers was reflected on Possum's face as well. He couldn't believe Perley had chosen to challenge them. All three wore their guns in holsters hung low and tied to their legs, like many gunfighters he'd seen. If Perley didn't keep his mouth

44

shut, he was gonna get them all killed.

"Mister," Zeb pronounced, after a long moment's pause, "You can step aside, or we'll walk over your dead body. Either way, I'll have a look in that wagon." He was certain there was something valuable in the wagon, else they wouldn't have objected to the search that much.

"I don't want anybody to get hurt," Perley said, "so it's best if you do like I said and ride on outta here."

Possum looked nervously back and forth between Perley and Zeb Hackett. He figured he was looking death right in the face. A single thought suddenly flew across his brain, The Gates brothers had sent Perley to help them because he was crazy, and they figured it better to have him away from the herd. He was moments away from telling the bandits to go ahead and look in the wagon when Cal suddenly dropped his hand on the handle of his .44. The events that followed would remain a blur in Possum's mind amid the rapid reports of gunfire, so quick in succession they almost sounded as one shot, instead of three separate ones. He stared in disbelief at the sight of Zeb Hackett lying dead, a bullet hole near the center of his chest. To his right, Cal was sitting on the ground, his right sleeve already soaking with blood from the wound in his shoulder. To his left, Peewee was crawling on the ground, dragging his wounded leg as he tried to reach the pistol he had flung from his hand when he was hit. "You'd best pick up that pistol before he reaches it," Possum heard Perley calmly advise. Still in a fog, his own gun cold in his holster, he did as he was told and picked up Peewee's weapon.

"There wasn't any need for that," Perley told the two wounded men. "You shoulda gone and left us alone when I told you to. I'm sorry about your brother, but he didn't give me any choice. He was fast, and he meant business. It was either him or me, but there wasn't any sense in killin' all three of you, if I could help it. We'll get you on your horses, so you can ride outta here, but I'm gonna have to hold on to your weapons — pistols and your rifles, too — just in case you get any ideas about comin' back." He looked at Possum. "Come on and help me load 'em up."

Still at a loss for words, Possum dutifully helped Perley pick Zeb up, and they laid him across his saddle. Cal and Peewee sat stunned as they watched them do it. Then Perley helped the two wounded men into their saddles and handed Peewee the reins on Zeb's horse. "Reckon you'd best hold on to these, since your brother's got a bad shoulder. Anyplace near here where you can get some doctorin' on those wounds?"

Still in a shocked stupor, Peewee said, "Holden's," referring to a trading post about six miles farther up that creek.

"All right," Perley said. "You'd best get goin'. You're gonna need to stop that bleedin' pretty quick." Both brothers stared at him, still uncertain about what had just happened, feeling they had just been hit by a tornado. "Which way to Holden's?" Perley asked. Cal made no response, but Peewee pointed west. Perley took hold of the bridle and turned the horse in that direction. "Like I said, that's a terrible thing, your brother gettin' killed, but both of you are still alive. That's the way things happen sometimes. Best you bury him and forget about robbin' and killin' innocent folks." He gave the horse a slap on its rump and stood back to watch them leave. When they had disappeared through the oak trees past the far side of the clearing, he turned around to face his two aghast fellow travelers. "I expect we'd best eat that meal Emma fixed and then hitch up and find us another camp for the night."

"Reckon so" was all Possum replied, but he was still trying to wrap his mind around what had just happened. He glanced at Emma to be met with the same astonishment. After a few long moments, when Perley walked down by the creek to bring Buck back close to the camp, Possum finally turned to Emma. "I never saw that comin'," he muttered. "He ain't as tame as he looks."

"No, I reckon he ain't," Emma said. "And I guess we oughta be thankin' our lucky stars he ain't." She paused a few moments to watch Perley walking back from the creek, the big bay horse following along behind him. She turned to Possum then. "You reckon those two he wounded will be comin' back?"

"I don't know, but I wouldn't think so. It'd be my guess they'll wanna get to the doctor as soon as they can." He turned to watch Perley. "He's right, though, ain't no use takin' the chance. We'd best eat a little somethin' and get goin' again." Possum was struck by the chain-lightning reactions of the seemingly mild-mannered young man. He thought about the money in the canvas sacks, underneath a stack of quilts in the wagon, and couldn't help wondering if Perley had an evil side that matched his innocent bearing. Maybe he suspected that they were hiding something in the wagon. "Nah," he suddenly drawled, he'd decided from the first meeting with Perley that he was as honest as a silver dollar. When Emma gave him a questioning look, he said. "Let's eat that food you cooked up before them biscuits cool off."

They wasted little time eating, and soon they were all hitched up and on the move again. The horses did not get as long a rest as Perley would have liked, but under the circumstances, he and Possum judged it best to push them a little farther than normal. For that reason, he was glad to see the banks of the North Wichita River on the horizon a good bit sooner than expected. He estimated they had ridden no more than five miles. Still, that offered a small sense of a buffer between themselves and the two wounded outlaws, since they had headed in the opposite direction. "I don't think we'll see those two tonight," Perley speculated.

"Me neither," Possum spoke up. "They'd be crazy if they did show up here again." He glanced at Emma, then back at Perley. "I know I wouldn't come back for a second helpin' of that kind of lightnin'." He studied the self-effacing young man for a serious moment, thinking that Perley looked embarrassed by talk of how fast he was with a handgun. "You sure you were named for your grandpappy? Maybe you was really named that 'cause any man wantin' to draw down on you is headed for the Pearly Gates."

"No, sir," Perley replied. "I was named for my grandpa." He pointed to a group of trees on the other side of the river. "That looks like a good spot to camp for the night. Does that suit you?"

Possum laughed, amused by Perley's reluctance to talk about his speed with a handgun. "That looks like a good spot to me. How 'bout you, Emma?" She agreed, even though she wished they could have kept on going, but she knew it would be too hard on their horses. So they crossed over the river and pulled the wagon into the small clump of trees that Perley had pointed out. There was an open meadow about thirty-five yards wide between that stand of trees and the riverbank. Beyond the trees, there was nothing but open prairie for as far as you could see, so it looked to be a defensible campsite. While the men took care of the horses, Emma gathered some wood for a fire, thinking some coffee would be appreciated, even though they had eaten a hasty supper only about five miles back. Maybe this time they would have time to enjoy their coffee.

"Just based on what you and Dan have told me about that place we're lookin' for, I expect we oughta be gettin' pretty close," Possum said as they sat by the fire. "Any of this country look familiar to you?" he asked Emma.

"I don't know," she answered, hesitating to hazard a guess. "When Dan and I left, it was the first time I had been more'n two or three miles outta Butcher Bottom since I was a little girl. Anyway, you said this was the Wichita River. Butcher Bottom is on the Brazos."

"That's a fact," Possum said, "I think it's the North Wichita to be exact, but we oughta strike the place where it meets with the south fork of the river pretty soon, and that ain't very far from the Brazos."

The night passed peacefully enough, and they were on the move early the next morning on a course Possum figured would lead them closer to the confluence of the two forks of the Wichita, and consequently, closer to the Brazos. He guessed that river to be east of the Wichita, running north and south. His plan was to strike the Brazos and search up and down it until they found Butcher Bottom. When he told his traveling companions that, Emma apologized again for not knowing how to get home. "Ain't

51

your fault," Possum said. "We'll find it and get you there safely." He looked at Perley and winked, figuring Perley was as anxious to get this mission over with as he was.

"This country all looks the same to me," Emma said, "but this trail we've been following does look kinda familiar." She paused to remember, then said, "If we come to one place I remember, then I'll know it for sure, and it would lead us right to Butcher Bottom."

CHAPTER 3

"What can I do for you?" Joe Holden asked the sullen brute standing just inside the door of his store. Tall, heavyset, with a face as hard as granite, the stranger paused at the door only long enough to look the room over. His eyes lingered only a moment on the two men seated at a table, drinking whiskey, before he stepped over to the counter. There were no horses tied at the hitching rail, so he was mildly surprised to see there were customers.

"What are they drinkin'?" Jack Pitt asked. When told they were drinking pure corn whiskey, he said, "I'll take some of that." He didn't ask the price.

"You talkin' a shot, or you want a jar?" Holden asked.

"Gimme a jar. A pint'll take the chill off my throat." Holden reached under the counter and came up with a canning jar full of corn whiskey. He screwed the top off and pushed the jar over before the stranger, who took a long drink from it. Satisfied, he reached into a vest pocket and produced a roll of cash money and paid for his drink.

Impressed by the size of the roll of bills, Holden became immediately cordial. "Never seen you in the store before," he started. "I believe I'da remembered if you had. My name's Joe Holden. This here store is my place. I can fit you with most-bout anything you're wantin'. You just passin' through, or you lookin' to find work at the Lazy-S?"

Pitt didn't offer his name but answered Holden's question with one of his own. "You know where Butcher Bottom is?"

"Can't say as I do," Holden answered. "I've heard tell of it, but I don't know where it is. Ain't nobody from there ever come into my store that I know of."

Pitt scowled his disappointment. He had heard Dan Slocum telling Possum Smith that his wife was from a little settlement called Butcher Bottom. So when he went looking for Possum after he shot Dan, and found him gone, he searched every little road south of Dodge City, looking for the one Dan had been living on. He found a cabin and shed like the one Dan had described. It was empty, and there were wagon tracks leading out to the road. They had to be left by Dan's widow, and from the hoof-prints around the place, he had a pretty good idea that Possum had gone with her. It was a sizable gamble on his part, thinking Possum and the widow had headed to Texas, where the woman was from. But the payoff was more than twenty-two thousand dollars, if his hunch was right, so it was worth the gamble. He took another pull from the whiskey jar and asked, "You got anything to eat?"

"Sure do," Holden replied. "Mammy's just about done fixin' supper. That's what them boys over there are waitin' on. Set yourself down at the table and it ought'n be more'n a minute or two now."

Pitt paid him the twenty-five cents he asked for the supper, then went over to the table and sat down. The two men seated there stared openly at him, and he glared back in their direction. He had already noticed the bandaged shoulder and arm in a sling on one of the men — it was pretty obvious — but then he noticed the other one had a bound leg. "What the hell happened to you two?" Pitt asked bluntly, only mildly curious.

"We run into a gunslinger back down the creek a-ways," Cal Hackett answered. "Got the jump on us when we weren't expectin' it. He killed my brother, Zeb, and put a bullet in me and Peewee."

"Ha," Pitt snorted, "one man?"

"Yeah," Peewee spoke up. "It was one man done the shootin', but he had another man and a woman with him. Like Cal said, he got the jump on us."

"It's gonna be different next time," Cal declared. "I'm goin' after him, soon as this wound heals up a little."

Cal's boast never registered in Pitt's mind. His thoughts had been stopped when he heard there was a man and a woman with the gunslinger. He looked straight at Peewee. "The man and woman with him," he demanded, "was he an old gray-headed man? And did the woman have a baby?"

"That's right!" Peewee exclaimed. "Did you run into 'em, too?"

Pitt didn't answer his question. "They was in a wagon, right?" Peewee nodded, so Pitt asked, "Where did this happen? Where did you boys get shot?"

"Down Smoky Creek," Peewee answered.

"How far?"

"From here," Cal replied, "about six miles." Peewee nodded in agreement.

This news was quickening Pitt's anxiety by the second. He started to get up and leave right away, but Mammy came in with a tray holding three plates of food. The aroma of ham and beans served to remind him that he hadn't eaten anything since breakfast, so he decided to stay long enough to eat. As he destroyed the plate of food before him, he gave more thought to the existence of the gunman who had shot his two supper companions. "This feller that did the shootin'," he asked, "was he with the man and woman in the wagon?" He could picture someone with the same idea he had. Maybe he found out about the money Emma and Possum had between them and had the same thing in mind that he did.

"Well, he sure acted like it," Peewee answered, "and they sure jumped to do everythin' he told 'em to. The old feller helped him load our brother's body and get us on our horses."

The picture was clear in Pitt's mind now. Possum and Emma had made a deal with a hired gun to protect them. Either that, or maybe some gunslinger happened to find out they were carrying a fortune in stolen money, and he was thinking he was going to get it for himself. Whichever, there was little doubt that he had to move fast to catch up with them, or he was going to lose out altogether. With that thought to motivate him, he shoveled his supper in his mouth, the last spoonful when he was already on his feet. His only parting words were, "Upstream, or downstream?" At this point, he couldn't afford to go in the wrong direction.

Astonished by the strange man's reactions, Peewee replied, "Downstream." Pitt was already at the door when he heard it. Riding a blue roan that was already tired, he pushed the horse hard, afraid that some gunman was trying to move in on money that, in Pitt's twisted mind, rightfully belonged to him.

Behind him, the two Hackett brothers exchanged dumbfounded expressions. "What do you reckon was wrong with him?" Joe Holden asked, having come from the kitchen to see Pitt just as he rushed out the door. He looked at Peewee and Cal to see if they showed any signs of bolting for the door as well. It wouldn't be the first time Mammy's cooking had started a stampede for the outhouse, but they seemed serene enough, apparently as surprised as he was.

"I don't know," Peewee answered, "but he sure seemed in a hurry to find the spot where we got shot. Them folks are likely long gone by now."

"Maybe he's lookin' for that feller that

shot us, for some reason," Cal said. "Maybe that feller's got a reward out for him, or somethin'." He reached up and tenderly rubbed the bandage on his right shoulder. "I got a claim on that feller first and I aim to collect on it as soon as this wound heals up." He looked at Holden and shook his head. "I can't do nothin' with my left hand."

Holden stood there, considering the stranger's odd behavior for a few seconds before returning his attention to Cal and Peewee. "When you fellers finish your supper, I'd appreciate it if you'd move your horses before that body starts gettin' ripe." When they had first arrived to get Mammy to work on their wounds, they had tied their horses out front. Holden didn't notice the dead man lying across one of the saddles until after they had been in the store for a couple of hours. When he saw the corpse, he didn't think it looked good for business, so he had asked them to move their horses around behind the store.

"We'll move 'em," Cal said. "We're kinda handicapped with my shoulder shot up and Peewee's leg — hard to dig a decent grave — but we need to get our brother in the ground. Don't suppose you've got anybody that could give us some help with that?"

"Nope," Holden replied. "You could ask

Ned, down at the barn, but I doubt he would. He's by himself till his boy gets back from huntin'." When Peewee asked when that might be, Holden told him probably two or three days.

The Hackett brothers were faced with a problem. They had agreed to a deal to trade Zeb's horse and saddle for a couple of .44 pistols and ammunition to replace those lost in the confrontation with Perley Gates. Holden agreed to the deal, only if there was no corpse included. Cal looked at his brother and shook his head. "Ain't nothin' to say for it, we've gotta have the guns." When Peewee nodded solemnly, Cal looked at Holden again. "We'll take care of it right now, soon as we get through eatin', then we'll finish our deal."

"We'd best not wait too long," Peewee said. "It'll be dark before much longer." That caused him to think of something else. "I expect it'll be pretty close to dark by the time that feller finds that campin' spot where we got shot." They lingered at the table a little while longer until they had finished all the coffee Mammy was willing to bring them, then they went to tend to their brother's corpse.

With help from a crutch that Ned had made, Peewee hobbled out to his horse, and with Cal's help, he managed to climb up into the saddle. "I can't dig no grave standin' on one leg," he complained to Cal.

"Well, I sure as hell can't dig one with one hand," Cal said. "We ain't got much choice." He managed to pull himself up into his saddle. "Zeb's gonna have to feed the buzzards, I reckon, but we'll find him a spot away from here." He turned his horse and started back the way they had come. Peewee followed, holding the reins of Zeb's horse. They had ridden for no more than half a mile when Cal announced, "That looks like a good spot over yonder by that big oak tree. It's far enough up from the trail so anybody won't likely see him."

They rode up the bank of the creek to the big oak Cal had designated, then went through the cumbersome process of dismounting. Once that was done, they faced the problem of two cripples trying to lift a heavy body from a horse. It turned out to be simpler than they had anticipated, however, for Cal grabbed Zeb's boots with his good hand and yanked them up violently. Zeb's body, already in a high degree of rigor mortis, rolled easily off the saddle and landed on the ground. "He's already bent pretty much like he would be if he was settin' down," Peewee observed, "so why don't we just set him up against the tree? It'll be like he was settin' there watchin' folks ride by on the trail."

"I think you're right," Cal said. So they undertook the part of the plan that would prove to be more difficult than removing Zeb from his horse — handicapped as they were. Cursing the wounds that hampered them in their task, they managed by a foot or two at a time, to drag the stiff carcass up to the oak tree. Once they reached the tree, they found that Zeb was reluctant to sit upright against the trunk, preferring to keel over to land on his side on the ground. To contribute to the distasteful part of the farewell, Zeb began to impart a rather putrid odor, which encouraged a need for haste. Determined to leave their late brother with some degree of dignity, however, they didn't abandon him until they had fashioned a prop in the form of a short limb up under his armpit, wedged against a root of the oak. It held him upright, seeming to be sitting with his back against the tree. As quickly as that was accomplished, they backed a safe distance away from the putrefying corpse to say their final farewells, satisfied that Zeb would have done as much for them, had the roles been reversed. "Let's get back to Holden's and get our guns," Cal said.

■ ■ ■ ■

Six miles downstream from Holden's Store, Jack Pitt kicked the cold ashes of a campfire with the toe of his boot. "As cold as these ashes are, they didn't hang around long after that fellow did the shootin'," he mumbled. There was plenty of other evidence that confirmed their story. Tracks of a wagon were prominent, even in the fading light, as were hoofprints of several horses. How many, he couldn't tell, nor did he care. He was sure this was the party the Hackett brothers had described for him. He was also reasonably convinced that it was Possum Smith and Dan Slocum's widow. The only question mark in his mind was the gunman riding with them. Thinking of the two men he had met at Holden's Store, he was not convinced that they were much of a test, so he wasn't sure the gunman was as fast as they said. And he couldn't be much of a shooter, judging by the inaccuracy of his shots. Shooting at three men, at point-blank range, so they said, he killed only one of them. The other two were hit by what appeared to be wild shots, one in the shoulder, the other in the leg. Then he let them get away. *When I catch up with them,* he thought,

I'll take care of him first. The only uncertainty in his mind was how much farther was this place they're running to. It would be so much easier if he could catch up with them before they made it to Butcher Bottom. And depending how much farther it was, he could still catch them, since he could move so much faster than the wagon they were driving. He kicked violently at the cold ashes then, his frustration overcoming him. "It's gettin' too damn dark to follow their tracks. I'll have to wait till mornin'." Had he known the progress of those he pursued, he might have been more encouraged.

"I'm thinkin' we shoulda done come to this place by now," Possum thought aloud when they approached a small stream. They had already struck the south fork of the Wichita and should have reached the wagon road Emma said she might remember that would lead directly east to the Brazos River at the place she knew as Butcher Bottom. "Are you sure you can recognize that road?" Possum asked her.

"I know I can," she replied. She told him about her husband telling her she could say good-bye to Butcher Bottom forever when they drove past a certain tree on their way north. She was sure she would have remembered that road, for there was an old wagon wheel leaning against one lone pine tree marking the entrance to it.

"We musta passed it back yonder a-ways," Possum said. "There was two or three trails we struck between the North Wichita and the South Wichita. It mighta looked different comin' instead of goin'."

"But what about the pine tree and the wagon wheel?" Emma insisted.

"I don't know, Emma, but I'm pretty sure we've come too far south," Possum replied.

Perley listened to their discussion for a while before suggesting the obvious. "Accordin' to what you've said before, Butcher Bottom is actually on the Brazos, and the Brazos is to the east. And if you're sure we've come too far south, why don't we head east till we strike the Brazos, then follow it north till we reach Butcher Bottom?" He nodded toward the stream before them. "From the way that water's flowin', I expect it might drain into the Brazos."

Possum hesitated a moment, feeling a little foolish that he hadn't thought to do that sooner. His original plan had been to simply follow the Brazos River until he came to Butcher Bottom. But he had forgotten that when Emma started looking for her wagon wheel against the pine tree. "That's what I was fixin' to say," he lied. "So that's what I think we oughta do."

"That sounds like a good idea to me, too," Emma said, although still a little upset, thinking that she had not been able to lead them to Butcher Bottom when so close to it. Even perturbed by those thoughts, she could not help a feeling of depression to think that she was so close to her prior life. This might be a bigger mistake than she had first thought.

"Well, look what we got here," Ace Barnett said. "Wonder where they think they're goin'?"

"What is it?" Bob Rance asked when he pulled his horse up beside him. Ace pointed to the rider and wagon following the stream below the ridge, some fifty yards away. "We'd best see where they're goin'," he said and wheeled his horse on a line to cut them off.

When Perley spotted the two riders angling to cut them off, he turned and signaled Possum, who, in turn, signaled that he saw them, too. Then he reined Buck back to a walk to let Possum catch up. In a few minutes, the two riders intercepted them. "Where are you folks headin'?" Rance asked as he and Ace pulled up before the wagon.

Perley answered. "We're hopin' to get to Butcher Bottom."

"You're a little south of Butcher Bottom," Rance said. "This here is Lazy-S range, and you folks outta know you ain't welcome here."

"We ain't never been to Butcher Bottom," Possum said. "And we didn't know we were on anybody's range. We're just tryin' to get this lady and her baby home, so we'll get offa Lazy-S range as soon as we can."

"You do that," Rance said. "We'll let it go this time, since you sure as hell seemed lost, but I don't wanna see you folks on our range again."

"You're right," Perley said. "We're lost, so how about tellin' us how to find Butcher Bottom."

His suggestion caused Ace Barnett to chuckle, but Rance responded calmly. "Just keep goin' the way you're headed, follow this stream and you'll strike the Brazos in about three miles. Go north two miles and you'll be in Butcher Bottom."

Ace could hold his tongue no longer. "Better hurry up, though, 'cause Butcher Bottom might not be there much longer."

"Why do you say that?" Perley asked.

" 'Cause Mr. Slocum don't like that rat's

nest of Gypsies livin' down there," Ace replied.

"Does that include his daughter-in-law and his grandson?" Perley asked.

"Shut up, Ace," Rance ordered, then addressing Perley, he asked, "What did you mean by that? And just who are you, anyway?"

"My name's Perley Gates. My family owns the Triple-G over in Lamar County. The lady in the wagon is Emma Slocum, your boss' daughter-in-law."

This took Rance by surprise and he made no effort to disguise it. "Dan's wife?" He craned his neck then in an effort to get a better look at her. She in turn lowered her head as if trying to hide, not at all happy that Perley had volunteered her identity. "What in the world . . ." Rance started, then paused. "Where's Dan?"

"Dan's dead. Killed by a bank robber when he rode with the sheriff's posse," Perley answered, repeating the story he had been told by Possum and Emma. "I'm sure his widow is plannin' to carry that terrible news to his father." Had Perley been able to see the expressions on both Possum's and Emma's faces, he would have known at once that she had no intention of trying to contact Zachary Slocum. In fact, she had hoped he would never know she had returned to Butcher Bottom.

This shocking bit of news was enough to silence even Ace Barnett, sitting in the saddle with his mouth agape. Finally, Rance asked Perley, "What is your part in all this?"

"I'm just tryin' to help out," Perley replied. "I was on my way up to The Nations, takin' a herd up the Western Trail. We met Possum and Emma at Doan's Crossin', on their way to Texas. My brothers and I decided they could use an extra hand to help 'em get home safely. We ain't meanin' to trespass on your range, we're just tryin'to get the lady and her baby home."

Rance was not sure how this startling bit of news was going to strike Zachary Slocum, but, if he had to put some money on it, he'd bet his boss wasn't going to be very happy to hear it. However, he knew he had to tell him before Ace spread the news. "All right, mister. . . . What did you say your name was?"

"Perley Gates."

"Like the ones in the Bible?"

"Yes, sir, only it ain't spelled the same."

This brought another laugh from Ace, but Rance ignored it. "My name's Bob Rance, I'm the foreman of the Lazy-S. I'll tell Mr. Slocum that his daughter-in-law has come back to Butcher Bottom, and I'll let you get on your way now."

"Much obliged," Perley said and turned to Emma and Possum, puzzled to see the expressions of bewilderment on their faces. "Maybe you'll hear from your father-in-law now. Might be you'll decide to move out to the Lazy-S, if Butcher Bottom ain't to your likin'."

"Yeah, might be," Emma mumbled as Perley wheeled Buck around to continue on down the creek.

Behind them, Bob Rance turned to talk to Ace. "Boss is gonna be damned interested to hear about his daughter-in-law comin' back to Butcher Bottom, but it's liable to be bad news when I have to tell him Dan is dead. I'd just as soon you didn't pass this news around till Boss gets back from Fort Worth and I get a chance to break it to him. He oughta be gettin' back any day now. Can I count on you?"

"Why, sure, Bob," Ace assured him. "You know me, I don't run off at the mouth like some of the boys. It'll just be between me and you."

"Maybe we shoulda told him the whole story," Possum said to her. "He already figured out you don't particularly wanna go

70

back to Butcher Bottom. And I expect he just found out what Zachary Slocum thinks of Butcher Bottom, but ain't no need to tell him about the money."

"How are we gonna keep him from findin' out?" Emma replied. "We're gonna have to hide it somewhere before we get to Butcher Bottom. If Raymond Butcher finds out I've got that much money, he'll take it away from me." She looked at him and nodded her head to emphasize, "If he finds out you've got that money, he'll likely have his followers take it away from you, too."

"We might need to take him in as a partner," Possum said, referring to Perley. "It'd cost us a lot, but it'd be better'n losin' all of it to those crazy folks you told me about in Butcher Bottom."

"I don't know," Emma fretted. "He's so doggone honest, he might wanna take it back to the bank."

"There's that possibility," Possum said, "but we're gonna have to decide what we're gonna do, and we've got to do it now. If that feller was right, we ain't but about five miles from Butcher Bottom. We're gonna have to find a place to hide that money before we get there." They talked the problem over and over as they followed Perley down the stream. Then finally, he pulled

Buck to a stop and turned around to come back to them.

"Well, yonder's the Brazos," Perley sang out cheerfully. "Couple of miles and you'll be home, Emma."

Still uncertain, Possum made a decision. "That's good, Perley, but me and Emma decided we wanna make camp by the river and go into the settlement in the mornin'."

Astonished to hear that, Perley asked, "You wanna make camp now? It ain't even noon yet. We'll be there in about an hour, if it's where that fellow Rance said it is."

Thinking as quickly as he could, Possum said, "It's Emma, she's been away for a long time and she's needin' to fix up a little bit before she sees everybody again." He could see by Perley's expression that he thought that was pretty silly.

"That's right, Perley," Emma said, unable to think of anything better to offer. "It's been a while and I wanna look my best."

"Well, I reckon we can wait till tomorrow, if that's what you wanna do," Perley said. Although he found her attitude beyond surprising, he lectured himself to be patient with the still-grieving widow. He was eager to see Emma safe in her home and anxious to get started back north to overtake the Triple-G cattle drive. He received a second surprise when they reached the river and he suggested a camping spot that looked to be suitable.

"I don't know," Possum countered. "This stretch is kinda wide open. Might be better to look for a spot with a little more cover, maybe even that way," he said, pointing south.

"You remember that Rance fellow said Butcher Bottom is to the north, don't you?" Perley asked. When Possum responded with nothing more than a blank expression, Perley said, "Why don't you pick a spot that suits you?" Possum said he would, so Perley reined Buck back to walk beside the wagon when Possum turned the horses downstream. Possum continued to puzzle Perley as he drove the horses past several suitable camping spots, looking for one that pleased him.

"This'll do," Possum finally announced when they came to a point where the river took a sharp bend around a thick clump of trees, separated from another stand of trees by a grassy clearing. "We'll camp here."

"This suits you, does it?" Perley couldn't resist a little playful sarcasm. "For a while there, I thought you had a hankerin' to camp by the Gulf of Mexico." Possum made a weak effort to laugh at his remark as he exchanged worrisome glances with Emma. Their strange attitude did not escape his notice, but he was not concerned enough to question it. His mind was occupied with thoughts of delivering Emma to her sister's house and getting started back on his way to catch up with the Triple-G herd.

Possum drove the wagon into the midst of the clump of trees before stopping, causing Perley to wonder if he was fearful of an attack from some source. He pulled his saddle off the big bay while Possum unhitched the two horses from the wagon. As she did every night, Emma began to gather wood for a fire. When she found enough, she built the fire closer to the edge of the trees. A stray thought wandered through Perley's mind as he stood by the river's edge watching Buck drink. *She could have built her fire in the middle of the trees, a lot closer to the wagon,* he thought. *Maybe she thinks she needs some exercise, since she's been sitting on that wagon seat all morning.* He promptly dismissed the thought, since it was of no concern to him, and replaced it with another. He wondered, now that their journey was nearing an end, what Possum's plans were. From the beginning, he had the impression that Possum had no intention to remain in Butcher Bottom. Perley supposed he would find out tomorrow if Possum was planning to ride back north with him.

CHAPTER 4

As the afternoon wore on, Perley decided the time was well spent, for he took the time to give Buck a little attention. The big bay had not been worked especially hard, since his daily requirement had been mostly pacing that of the wagon and usually no more than twenty miles were asked of him each day. Since there was time and opportunity, he decided it was time he took a bath. There had been no real occasion to take one on the cattle drive across the northern part of Texas to Doan's Store. And while the nights were still on the chilly side, the late spring days were already warm. When he announced his intention to Possum, the old fellow thought that was a jim-dandy idea and encouraged him to do so. "I'd take one myself if I wasn't havin' one of my rheumatize spells," he said. Perley didn't push the matter, not particularly interested in having company, anyway. "Don't worry none,"

Possum said. "I'll take care of things here."

This was an opportunity he hadn't even expected, and Possum went at once to tell Emma. "Perley's gone over around the bend to take a bath. This is a good chance to bury that money while he's gone, so let's dig it outta the wagon."

"I thought we were thinkin' about tellin' him about the money," Emma said.

"I know," he replied, "and I reckon we will before it's over, but there ain't no use to put it on his mind till we have to." She shook her head, not really able to decide which was best.

There was more than plenty of privacy from the camp, since Emma had built the fire at the edge of the trees away from where Possum had parked the wagon. And since the river wrapped itself around the clump of trees, Perley found a grassy knoll near the edge of the water that just suited his purposes. He let Buck graze on the grass while he got ready for his bath. He stripped down to his long underwear and stopped there to decide how far he wanted to go. Summer was just approaching, but already he was finding the afternoon sun causing some sweating. He paused to make himself decide, time to come out of the winter underwear or not? Might as well, he decided, so he waded out into the water, still wearing his long-johns, thinking he'd wash them at the same time, then take them off to let them dry.

While Perley was enjoying his bath in the chilly water of the Brazos, Possum was working hard back in the clump of trees. Using a short-handled shovel, he was under the wagon, laboring to dig a sizable hole, one big enough to bury the heavy canvas bag containing two cotton bags holding both his and Emma's share of the stolen money. He wasn't sure what he was going to do, now that he had fulfilled his obligation to Dan Slocum's widow. But he knew he didn't want to roll into Butcher Bottom with that amount of money in the wagon. Like him, Emma wasn't sure what she should do with her share of the money, but she agreed that it wasn't a good idea to show up in that settlement with all that money. Trusting him, she told him to bury her share with his, and they would decide when to retrieve it after they saw what might have happened to the little community after she had been away for such a long time. All the way back, she had struggled with her decision to return to Butcher Bottom, thinking she might choose to change her mind. Finally, since she was here, she decided to try to persuade her sister and her husband to leave this place and try to find a place where they might survive on their own. Thinking about that now, she was certain that was what she wanted to do, especially since she had the money to start someplace else. Her thoughts were interrupted when she heard Possum call her name.

"I'm done," he said and motioned for her to come back in the trees to the wagon with him. "Take a good look around you, so you'll remember this place when the wagon ain't here." She tried to memorize the setting as best she could. "Now get down on your hands and knees," he said and dropped to his knees. Before crawling under the wagon, he asked, "Can you see where I buried it?"

She looked around on the ground, covered with dead, wet leaves. When she could see no place showing loose dirt or disturbed leaves, she asked, "Is it under the wagon?"

"Right under it," he answered, satisfied that she could not find it, "dead center. Here, lemme show you." He reached under the wagon and raked a handful of leaves back with his fingers, to expose some freshly disturbed dirt. "See this?" He placed a fingertip on a short piece of stick protruding straight up out of the ground. "That's

79

it, right under this stick." She reached out and touched the stick. "Now you know exactly where your money is, right?" She nodded and he raked the leaves back in place.

"How long will it be safe to leave it there?" she asked. "What if we have storms or floods?"

"It ain't gonna be buried here long," he said. "I'll sure be diggin' up my share right after I take you to Butcher Bottom. I didn't figure you'd leave yours buried very long, either, as soon as you figured it was safe to get it."

"Yes, of course," she quickly agreed. "I know I'll feel a whole lot better with that money out of the wagon. In Butcher Bottom, nothin' belongs to you. Everything belongs to everybody."

"Well, that don't make no sense to me," Possum said. "Let's get out from under here before Perley comes back and wants to crawl under here to see what we're lookin' at."

They went back to their campfire. Possum poured himself a cup of coffee from the pot sitting in the coals at the edge of the fire. Emma checked to make sure the baby was not fussing, then she poured a cup for herself and sat down to tell Possum what she had decided to do with her money. "Rachael's husband was a good farmer," she said. "I think we oughta be able to find a good piece of land and build our own place." She hesitated then before adding, "That is, if they would want to leave Butcher Bottom. I'm afraid they might be so caught up in Raymond's religious ranting they can't see right from wrong."

"You think he would try to stop 'em from leavin'?" Possum asked. She answered with a grimace that said *maybe.* "I reckon it's a good thing me and Perley are with you," he said, "else, he might try to stop you from leavin' again."

"Well, now, ain't this the prettiest sight for sore eyes? Ol' Possum and the widow woman havin' theirselves a friendly little cup of coffee." Startled, for the voice came from behind them, in the opposite direction Perley had taken to go to his bath, Possum froze, recognizing the voice. "You just set right still, so you don't give me no reason to shoot you," Jack Pitt warned when he walked around in front of them, his pistol aimed at them. "Howdy-do, Miz Slocum? It sure is a pleasure to meet you," he sneered. "I enjoyed doin' business with your husband. Too bad he ain't here for this reunion, ain't it?" Turning his attention back to

Possum then, he said, "I had a devil of a time trackin' you two down. You never told me you was fixin' to leave town." He paused to take another look right and left. "Where's your new partner you took in, the one that done all the shootin' back on Smoky Creek?"

"He took off," Possum replied, "cleaned me and Emma outta all our money and took off. Ain't that right, Emma?" Too frightened to answer, she made not a sound, to Possum's dismay because he had hoped she would have said something that might have distracted Pitt's attention from him. Even so, he put his cup down close to the rifle lying on the ground near him.

Pitt was not distracted. "Now, Possum, you'd be a damn fool to reach for that rifle," he said, his tone soft and deadly, as if he wished Possum would reach for it. "We're wastin' time here. Whaddaya say we go get that money? The sooner you two get me my money, the sooner I'll be gone and you and the lady won't have nothin' to worry about."

There was absolutely no doubt in Possum's mind that he and Emma would be killed as soon as Pitt had their money in hand. His only hope was to stall him as long as possible and hope that Perley would return in time to help. "We split that money up fair and square, so you got your share of it. Matter of fact, it was your idea. You was the one who said we'd split it three ways."

Getting impatient now, Pitt replied, "That's right, and now I'm sayin' my share is all of the money. I'm the one who shot that son of a bitch. You and Dan didn't kill him, I did. So all that money belongs to me. Now, let's get it up. I'm tired of foolin' with you."

Desperate now, Possum countered. "How do I know you ain't gonna shoot me and Emma as soon as we hand over the money?"

His question caused Pitt to grin. "You don't," he replied, "but you know for sure I'll kill you if you don't give me my money. So the only chance you and the little lady have is if you give me my money." He shifted his gaze directly on Emma and grinned. Thinking him distracted, Possum started to reach for his rifle again, but Pitt was too quick. He fired a shot into the ground between Possum's hand and the rifle. "I warned you, damn it!" Pitt roared. "Next time, it ain't gonna be in the ground, and me and Miz Slocum will go get that money without you."

"All right, all right," Possum exclaimed. "You win, Pitt. You're sure as hell holdin' all the cards. I'll get you the money, but we're gonna have to ride a-ways to get to the place we buried it." His only hope was to lead Pitt away from there and give Emma a chance to get to Perley.

The smirk on Pitt's face expanded to form a wide grin, testament to the pleasure he enjoyed at their expense. "You know somethin', Possum? I ain't knowed you very long, but it was long enough to know you ain't the best liar in the territory. I'll tell you what, why don't the three of us go have a look in that wagon back there in the trees? See if maybe you forgot you kept that money with you." He motioned with his pistol for them to get on their feet. "We'll just leave that rifle right where it is. You ain't gonna need it for nothin'." With no other choice, Possum and Emma got up. Trembling visibly, Emma struggled to her feet, taking a worried glance at her baby sleeping on a bundled-up quilt near the fire. Noticing her concern, Pitt said, "Don't worry about your young'un. If he starts cryin', I know a good way to shut him up." Horrified, she dutifully fell in step behind Possum as Pitt marched them to the wagon.

Feeling the chill of the soft breeze that swept over the river, Perley climbed out of the water, wondering if he had anticipated summer a little too soon. "I wish I had a towel," he muttered to himself, now thinking that it might take longer than he had thought for the sun to warm him and dry his wet underwear. With a whole afternoon to kill, he was in no particular hurry, so he picked a spot on the grassy bank that would be right to lie on his back and absorb the sunlight. It was then that he heard the gunshot. Just having settled back, he bolted upright. There was no mistaking it, the shot had come from the direction of their camp! "Oh, shit!" he muttered, thinking they had been attacked, and he had no time to spare. So he pulled his boots on and strapped his gun belt on as he ran toward the grove of oak trees and the wagon near the other side of it. Entering the thick stand of trees, he moved as quickly as he could manage, dodging small trees and the limbs of larger ones. As soon as he could get a glimpse of the wagon parked in the trees, he stopped running and moved more carefully, slowly getting closer until he stopped abruptly when he suddenly saw them near the rear of the wagon. He immediately dropped to one knee.

He was relieved to see Possum and Emma alive, and the gunshot he heard had not been for either of them. He had to wonder then if the shot had in no way been a threat to them. Maybe Possum shot at a snake or something. While he watched, Emma crawled up into the wagon and started pulling things out, passing them to Possum, who took them and put them on the ground. *What in the world . . . ?* he wondered, then realized what he was watching when Jack Pitt stepped around the end of the wagon, a six-gun in his hand, trained on them. *He's robbing them! Well, we'll see about that,* he thought and moved carefully through the trees until in a position behind the robber.

"You can drop that weapon on the ground!" Perley ordered. Pitt froze, but failed to drop his pistol. "I ain't gonna tell you again," Perley warned.

"All right," Pitt called out. "I'm droppin' it. Don't shoot." He bent forward, extending the .44 as if about to drop it on the ground, but instead, he suddenly spun around and sent a shot snapping through the leaves a foot or so beside Perley. In almost the same instant, he dropped to his knees when a slug from Perley's .44 slammed into his chest. Roaring out in rage, Pitt remained on his knees until he slowly crumpled to the ground.

"He didn't give me any choice!" Perley exclaimed, almost as if it was an apology, as he walked up to stand over the body.

"No, he didn't," Possum replied at once, "and I ain't never been so glad to see somebody in my whole life."

"I gave him a chance to surrender," Perley insisted.

"He didn't deserve a chance," Possum said. "Killin' is the best thing to happen to that varmint."

"You know him?" Perley asked.

"I know him," Possum declared. "Jack Pitt, the meanest gunslinger I ever saw. He's the low-down dirty dog that shot Emma's husband."

"I thought you said your husband was shot by a bank robber he was chasin' with a sheriff's posse," Perley said, looking at Emma, who had still not recovered from her fright.

"It was him" was all she could say.

Still confused, Perley looked to Possum for clarification. Before he could speak, they heard a cough from the body on the ground before them. "He ain't dead yet," Possum blurted and looked around for his rifle, forgetting that it was back by the fire.

"Just barely," Perley said and knelt beside the dying man.

Pitt was trying to say something. Perley could see that, but his throat was choked up with blood that made his words garbled and difficult to understand. In one last defiant effort, he managed to force a few words out before he surrendered to his fate. "Damn," Possum swore, relieved, "he's finally dead." He looked at Perley. "Could you make out anythin' he was babblin'?"

"Something about the bank's money was all I could make out," Perley said. "No tellin' what was goin' through his mind. A man like that probably has a head full of bad things that he did or were done to him." He paused for a few moments to try to sort it all out. "So you figure this fellow has been followin' you and Emma all the way from Kansas?"

"Looks that way, don't it?" Possum answered, realizing that it had been a big mistake when he said he knew Jack Pitt, and that he was the man who killed Emma's husband.

"But why was he comin' after you?" Perley still didn't understand. "Have you got something of his?"

"Don't know what it would be," Possum claimed. He glanced at Emma to see her cringing as the talk progressed. "I think everybody that knew Pitt would tell you he was sick in the head."

Perley shrugged, still puzzled by the dead

man's actions. "Well, I reckon he ain't the first man to catch a case of prairie fever. It was pure tough luck he forced me to shoot him. Maybe he's better off dead."

"I expect you're right," Possum said, his spirits lifted considerably. "But I tell you, I was mighty glad you came to the party. Next time, though, it ain't necessary to dress up for it."

It struck him then. In the excitement of the shooting, he had forgotten that he was still in nothing but his underwear. "Oh, hell," he blurted, totally embarrassed. "Pardon me, Emma, I didn't think about anything but gettin' here as fast as I could when I heard that gunshot. I beg your pardon. I'll just go and get my clothes on." He turned around and departed into the woods again, realizing how ridiculous he must look with nothing on but his boots and his gun belt. He could hear Possum laughing behind him.

"Next time don't forget your hat," Possum called after him. His spirits lifted considerably, he turned to find Emma visibly shaking, now that the danger was past. "What's the matter, honey? It's all over now, thanks to Perley. This ain't no time to be scared. You're safe now, we both are, and we've still got our money. We don't have to worry about that sidewinder no more. We oughta be celebratin' tonight."

"I know," she said. "I reckon you're right, but I'm still worried."

"About what?" Possum asked.

"Perley," she said. "Do you think he's as innocent as he acts? He's the only one of us that got close enough to Jack Pitt to hear what he said. He mighta told Perley about our money, and Perley just didn't let on that he did. Jack Pitt is just spiteful enough to tell on us, even when he's dyin'."

It worried Possum to hear her say that. He had a feeling about Perley, now that they had ridden together a few days. *Honest as the day is long* came to mind, and he truly believed that saying applied to Perley, even after hiding their money from him. "I don't know," he answered. "It's a possibility, I reckon. We'll sure find out in the next day or two." He took another look at Jack Pitt's body, positive now that there was no spark of life remaining. "Let's take a look at what Pitt's carryin' in his pockets," he said. "Then I'd best see if I can find his horse. He musta left it on the other side of the clearin', else we'da seen him come walkin' up behind us." A quick search of the body produced approximately five hundred dollars in his vest pocket. "Well, he ain't spent it all," Possum said. "I'll go look for his horse, see what he's got in his saddlebags."

Emma watched him until he walked into the trees on the far side of the clearing and disappeared from her view. She could not feel the same freedom that Possum obviously felt with the demise of Jack Pitt. The stolen bank money weighed heavily upon her, knowing that in spite of her feelings of guilt, she was not willing to give it up. A great deal would depend on Perley's actions, now that Pitt was dead. At almost the same instant she was thinking about him, Perley rode around the outside of the clump of trees between their camp and the river, just as Possum emerged from the trees on the opposite side of the clearing. He was leading two horses, one of them with a saddle.

"I see you found his horses," Perley said.

Possum pulled them up short of the fire and proceeded to make a show of searching Pitt's saddlebags and his packs on the packhorse. "Well, lookee-here," he sang out when he looked in the saddlebags, "Ol' Pitt weren't broke, not by a little." He held up a roll of banknotes for them to see. "Wonder how much is in this roll?" When he had heard Perley ride into the clearing, he made a hasty decision. Having already found the

91

roll of money, he thought it might serve to quell any suspicions Perley might have, especially if he proposed a three-way split with it. That might explain the dying words of Jack Pitt to Perley's satisfaction, like maybe that was the money he was babbling about. "I think I'll count it," he said and proceeded to do so, somewhat surprised that Perley showed more interest in the coffeepot sitting in the coals of the fire. He kept counting, however, and announced the total when he had finished. "I make it two thousand, seven hundred dollars. That's a helluva lot of money. We split it up and that's nine hundred dollars apiece. Ain't that somethin'?" Actually, Pitt had less than that amount in the saddlebags, Possum had added most of what he found in Pitt's pockets to make it easier to split three ways. "Whaddaya say, Perley? That's the only fair thing to do, ain't it? 'Course, I wouldn't really have no right to argue if you was to say it oughta all belong to you, since you're the one who did for ol' Pitt — and did the world a favor, I might add."

"I've got a better idea," Perley said. "Why don't you give the money to Emma? From what I've seen, she doesn't wanna go back to Butcher Bottom in the first place. With that money, she wouldn't have to. Twenty-seven hundred dollars ain't a big fortune, but it might be enough to get you and your sister's family a piece of ground of your own." He didn't tell them that he didn't want the money. He didn't like the idea of getting money for killing somebody. That was an occupation he had no desire for.

There was no immediate response to his suggestion from either Possum or Emma beyond an exchange of astonished glances between them. Finally, Emma spoke, knowing she had to say something. "That's mighty generous of you, Perley, but it ain't right for me to take all of Jack Pitt's money. I appreciate it that you'd like to help me go someplace else besides Butcher Bottom, but you've done your part just gettin' me here. I'll be fine, once I can talk to Rachael and Tom."

"Well, I reckon that's up to you," Perley said, "whatever you decide. But you and Possum can split the money. I don't need it." As far as he was concerned, the two of them could do what they pleased with the spoils of his killing. "Now, I expect it would be a little nicer around here if I drag this carcass off and bury it. Have you got a shovel on that wagon?"

"As a matter of fact, I do," Possum answered. "It's a short-handled shovel, but it'll dig a hole. You want me to help you?"

"Nope," Perley replied. "You can stay here and help Emma." He tied one end of a rope around Pitt's ankles and wrapped the other end around his saddle horn. Then he led Buck into the trees to find a spot to dig a grave. He hadn't walked far from the wagon when he came to a spot between two large oak trees that looked like it would do, so he stopped Buck there and untied his rope. He took a look at Pitt's huge body, then looked at the short-handled shovel. "On second thought, I think you'll serve the world better if you feed the buzzards," he decided and left the body there to rot.

CHAPTER 5

"You sure this is what you wanna do?" Possum asked one more time before starting the horses.

"All the family I've got is right here," Emma replied, her mind made up. She would return to her father's farm to see the condition of the old house. Once her things were placed there, she would then try to persuade her sister and her husband to join her in searching for a new place. They would look for a place where they could own the land and where their crop yield would not go to the general welfare. She remembered her late father saying that he never should have embraced Simon Butcher's religious philosophy, complaining that no matter how hard he worked, he would never get to enjoy the fruits of his labor. There were always members of the community who lacked the skill to work the land profitably, so those who could had to provide for those who couldn't. She and Dan had set out to escape the farm and ever-increasing conflicts between the community of Butcher Botton and the Lazy-S Ranch. She had refused to stay where she would ultimately end up as one of the wives of the Reverend Raymond Butcher. And Dan was not inclined to remain under the strict discipline of his father's cattle ranch. So now she was determined to save her sister, if she could persuade her to trust her, knowing she had the financial backing she needed, buried in a grove of oak trees by the river.

The trail narrowed just before they encountered the first indication they were approaching Butcher Bottom. It was a roughly painted sign that advised all strangers entering the private community that they should check in at Tuck's Store to state their business. They made their way slowly along the narrow wagon track that followed the east bank of the river and led them by the meetinghouse. Perley rode beside the wagon, leading his packhorse. Possum's horses and Jack Pitt's two horses were tied to the tailgate. Beyond the meetinghouse, they came to a small store and a blacksmith shop beside it. Those three structures comprised the settlement of Butcher Bottom. The town appeared to be deserted, save for two women standing outside the door of the meetinghouse, who paused in their cleaning of the steps to stare at the strangers who obviously elected to ignore the sign about checking in.

Past the store, the blacksmith, Edger Price, put his hammer down and stood there to stare at the three people passing his shop. Like the women at the meetinghouse, he said nothing to the visitors. When they had gone past, Price called to his son, who was working in the back of the shop. "Lemuel, go to the house and tell your mama Emma Wise just rode through town settin' on a wagon seat, holdin' a baby."

Emma cradled her baby and kept her eyes on the horses pulling her wagon, not wishing to make eye contact with anyone. "Friendly little place, ain't it?" Possum couldn't help commenting. "I wonder if I could get that blacksmith to straighten out your axle?"

"If there was a road around it, I woulda took it," Emma said, ignoring his question about the axle. "I was kinda hopin' nobody would recognize me. It won't be long before everybody knows I'm back." They were passing fields of young corn now with farms on both sides of the river, and a short distance later, she pointed to a house sitting back from the road, larger than the others they had seen. "That's Raymond's house," she said. "That's where I was supposed to be goin' on my sixteenth birthday."

"For a birthday party?" Possum asked.

"Yeah, a birthday party," Emma replied in disgust, "and after the party there was supposed to be a ceremony makin' me Raymond's wife."

Her remark surprised Possum. "I thought this feller, Raymond, already had a wife. What is he, a Mormon?"

"No, he ain't no Mormon. Mormon women most likely have a choice on whether they wanna marry a man or not. Raymond's religion don't give you no choice. If one of the menfolk wants a girl, he'll work a deal with her father. 'Course Raymond has to bless it. If Raymond wants you, there ain't no choice — for you or your father."

"I swear . . ." Possum drew out, appalled. He had not been aware of this before.

"That's the only reason I ran off with Dan Slocum," she confided. "I wasn't sure if I loved him or not, but I knew it would be better than being one of Raymond Butcher's wives." She paused, thinking back on their short marriage. Glancing down at the baby in her arms, she said, "He was a good man and I learned to care for him."

"I swear, Emma . . ." Possum tried to show compassion, but was at a loss for the proper thing to say. Instead, he asked, "What in hell did you wanna come back here for?"

"I told you, to save my sister and her two little girls. Rachael's got to know her daughters ain't much different from two calves. The men are just raisin' 'em till they're old enough to bear children."

"What about the feller your sister's married to?" Possum asked. "Does he think like Raymond does? He might not wanna leave Butcher Bottom. He might be thinkin' about takin' on another wife, himself."

"I don't know," Emma said. "I guess that's what I'm here to find out." They sat in silence then for about a quarter of a mile before she said, "Turn onto that trail on the right. That'll take you to my daddy's house." Possum called out to Perley to give him the signal.

They followed what appeared to be a well-used wagon track up from the river for a few hundred yards before reaching a simple frame house and a small barn, both of which appeared to be in a state of good repair. Expecting to find the place abandoned, Emma exclaimed, "It looks like somebody's livin' here." She looked at Possum as if seeking an explanation. "This is my daddy's house. This is where I lived."

Seeing Emma apparently upset, Perley pulled his horse up by the wagon. "What's the matter?" Possum told him that this was her father's house, and she was expecting to find it empty. The fact that it was not vacant did not seem surprising to Perley, just as he expected that someone in the community would take over the farm, instead of letting the land go fallow.

While they were deciding what to do, a man came out of the barn and started walking toward them. "Somethin' I can do for you folks?"

"Frank Lewis!" Emma exclaimed. "What are you doin' here?"

"Emma?" Frank responded when he got closer to the wagon, not sure it was her. He gave Perley and Possum an inquisitive look before shifting his gaze back to Emma. Judging by the differences in ages of the two strangers, he assumed the young man on the horse was the fellow she ran off with. "When did you come back?" Before she could answer, he asked, "Does Raymond know you're back?" Again, before she answered, he turned and yelled, "Barbara Ann! Come quick, it's Emma Wise!" Back to

Emma again, he thought to say, "Sorry," and nodded to Perley. "I reckon it ain't Emma Wise now."

"No, it's Emma Slocum," she said. "My husband was Dan Slocum, but he's dead now. These two gentlemen were kind enough to escort me back here."

"Slocum!" Frank repeated in surprise before she could go further. "Is that who you ran off with? I mean that's who you married?"

"Yes, that's who I married, and he's the father of my child, Daniel Seaton Slocum, Jr." She paused then when Barbara Ann ran out to meet them.

"Emma Wise!" Barbara Ann exclaimed. "Is that really you? I declare I never thought I'd see you again."

"It's Emma Slocum now," Frank told her, and the name had the same impact upon his wife as it had on him. As her husband had, she looked at once to Perley, sitting on his horse. "That ain't him," Frank said. "Her husband's dead." She looked back at Emma, properly shocked, but more eager to hear the circumstances that brought her back to Butcher Bottom. There followed an uncomfortable few moments of silence as the surprise visit became suddenly awkward. Barbara Ann thought to ask them to step down and come into the house, but she was not sure it was prudent to do so. What if Raymond found out? After all, Emma had been branded a nonbeliever and an instrument of the devil and ex-communicated from his church. When the silence became too uncomfortable, Emma finally asked, "What are you folks doin' in my daddy's house?"

"Well, you see," Frank sputtered, "it ain't really your daddy's house no more. It belongs to the church now, and we moved over here from that little cabin we had near the creek. Raymond says it's ours to keep as long as we keep the fields up and take care of the crops."

"How long was Daddy's body in the ground before you moved in?" Emma asked, unable to control a spark of temper.

"Ah, honey," Barbara Ann replied. "You've got no cause to be blaming Frank and me. Your mama and papa were gone and you ran off for good. There wasn't any reason for us not to take over the place. Your sister and her husband didn't want it, and we needed a better house than that leaky old cabin we were living in. So don't blame us. It was empty and Raymond charged us with the responsibility to keep the place up, and we've been doing that."

"I reckon you're right," Emma said, realizing she was wrong to blame them. "I was gonna stop here because I thought the house would be empty, but I'll go to Rachael's house instead. I don't mean to cause you any hardship."

"Emma," Frank warned, "you and your two friends best be careful. Things have changed around here since you've been gone. Raymond's got himself some men he calls his deacons. There's four of 'em and their main job is to make sure Raymond's rules are followed, especially on tithing and meetin' quotas. I'll be honest with you, Raymond ain't gonna like it one bit when he finds out you've come back. He's made it a sin to mention your name. I hope none of the deacons see you comin' from here. They'll be askin' me some questions."

"We'll go," Emma said. "We don't wanna cause you any trouble."

"You mind if we water our horses first?" Perley asked, nodding toward the water trough by the barn. They were the first words he had spoken since they had arrived.

"I can't deny a man's request to water his horses," Frank replied, even though he watched the road nervously until the horses were watered. "Good luck to ya," he called out when they left.

103

■ ■ ■ ■

"They sure was happy to see us leave," Possum said as he guided the horses back down the path to the main trail. Emma made no response to his comment, her mind still shaken by finding Frank and Barbara Ann in her old home. When she had still remained silent when they reached the road again, he asked, "Whaddaya aim to do now?"

Seeming to suddenly come back to the moment, she pointed and said, "That way, we'll go to my sister's house." Possum turned the horses back onto the wagon track they had followed since leaving town. He gave Perley a sideways glance without saying anything.

Riding beside the wagon, Perley understood Possum's concern. There was no telling what kind of trouble they might ultimately find themselves in from what started out as a simple journey to take a grieving widow home. He couldn't suppress a long sigh when he once again recalled what his brother John often repeated. *If there wasn't but one cow pie in the whole territory, Perley would likely step in it.* This little trip was beginning to look like another one of those adventures that he seemed to find himself in. This fellow, Raymond, sounded like a man with too much ambition, combined with a streak of "don't give a damn" for the rights of others. Emma said he was a preacher, but Perley wondered what kind of preacher needed four "deacons" to enforce his word? Raymond sounded more like a dictator to him. There was nothing to do but see it through until Emma was settled somewhere. Then maybe he could catch up with his brothers and the cattle.

A quarter of a mile farther brought them to another path leading to another homestead, this one the home of Tom and Rachael Parker. Perley didn't have to guess the anxiety Emma must be feeling. It was obvious in her face as the wagon followed a winding path to a modest dwelling with a barn and toolshed behind. Beyond the toolshed was a garden. There seemed to be no one about as they pulled up in the yard, but then a little girl came from the barn carrying a basket. She stopped when she saw the wagon and the man on horseback, then proceeded to approach them. "You must be Alice," Emma greeted her. The sight of the child seemed to make her forget the reason for her visit. "My, but you're quite the young lady now."

"I'm not Alice," the child said. "I'm Melva. Alice is in the house." She stared openly at Emma, possibly thinking the woman looked familiar, but she was not sure who she was.

"Melva!" Emma responded, surprised, then remembering it had been two years since she had seen the child, then only two years old. "I'm your Aunt Emma."

Melva still did not respond as a person would have expected. She seemed unaware of anyone named Aunt Emma. Perley speculated that her parents might have refrained from ever mentioning Emma's name, if they were strict followers of Reverend Raymond as he suspected. It crossed his mind that this could go little better than their visit to Emma's old home.

"Is your mama in the house?" Emma asked, and when Melva nodded, she said, "You run in and tell her Aunt Emma is here." The child turned and ran toward the kitchen door.

It was only a couple of minutes before the kitchen door opened again and Emma's sister and both her daughters came on the run. "My Lord, my Lord," Rachael muttered. "Emma, is that really you?" Emma climbed down from the wagon to meet her and the two sisters embraced.

Perley and Possum exchanged glances, thinking that maybe this was going to go better than expected. With that in mind, Perley dismounted and Possum climbed down from the wagon seat. "I swear," Possum saw fit to comment, "nobody woulda had to tell me you two were sisters. You look enough alike to be twins."

"Maybe," Rachael replied, "if you didn't stand close enough to see the wrinkles on one of us."

Standing with her arm around her sister, Emma smiled at Rachael's other daughter. "This is Alice. I thought Melva was you. I forgot how long it had been since I saw you. I'm your Aunt Emma. Do you remember me?"

"Yes, ma'am, I remember." She looked up at her mother before adding, "I don't think I'm supposed to, though. Reverend Raymond told Melva and me we're not supposed to think about you."

Her mother reacted with a deep frown of distress, but then immediately started to explain the child's comment. Emma stopped her quickly, saying an explanation was not necessary. "We stopped at our old house and Frank Lewis told us all about it." She went on then to tell Rachael about her husband's death and introduce her to Perley and Possum. After she had finished, Rachael had to ask a question. "Emma, honey, why did you come back here? Don't you know that Raymond has ordered the community to shun you? He won't allow you to stay here." Perley could only shake his head and wonder where this was all going to end up, after having heard the same warnings from Frank Lewis.

"I came back to save you and Tom," Emma answered Rachael's question. "To get you and your family away from that crazy man, so you can start a healthy life on land of your own, instead of working like slaves for Raymond Butcher."

Rachael was immediately distressed. "How in the world are you going to help us, if we pack up and sneak outta here like you did? We don't have any money to buy land. We're barely making it here, but at least we know we won't go hungry as long as Raymond takes care of us."

"Rachael," Emma implored. "You know why I ran away. I was supposed to move into that house Raymond has on the hill. Think of your daughters. Do you want Alice or Melva to have to move into that evil den when they reach sixteen? You've got Tom and he's a good man, but he might not be able to deny Raymond anything he wants."

Judging by the concerned frown on Rachael's face, Perley guessed she had thought about that possibility before. He was finding it hard to believe that such a community existed in the state of Texas. Looking down at Alice, Rachael could also see a look of concern in her daughter's face. She thought it best the child should not hear the discussion, so she sent her to get her father from the field he was working in. When the two girls ran to do her bidding, Rachael looked back at Emma. "We can't leave here. We don't have any money to buy land or build a new house."

"I've got the money to build a new place," Emma said softly, but not so softly that she was not overheard by Perley. He cocked his head around to see if Possum had heard her. He met Perley's gaze with a smile of embarrassment and a shrug, as if to say, *I was gonna tell ya.*

It occurred to Perley that there must be quite a bit of information that he was not privy to, and it was beginning to look like Emma was not going to be any more welcome here than she was at her old home. He wondered about the limits of his obligation to this unfortunate young woman. He had done all he had agreed to do when he saw her safely to Butcher Bottom, but he was reluctant to run out on her and Possum until she was safely settled someplace. His thoughts were interrupted then with the arrival of Rachael's husband and their two daughters.

"I declare," he said when he walked up to them, "it is you, Emma. I wasn't sure the girls knew what they were talkin' about when they said you'd come home. You comin' back to the church? Alice said your husband's dead."

"That's right," Emma said, "but I'm not comin' back. I just came to see you." Once again, she repeated the purpose of her visit to Butcher Bottom, and after hearing the whole story, Tom was not as receptive as Emma had hoped he would be.

"So Raymond didn't give you permission to come back," he said. "In fact, he doesn't even know you're here?" He paused to give that some thought. "I don't know, Emma. It'da been a whole lot better if you had gotten Raymond's blessin' before you came back. Things have changed some."

"Have they changed for the better?" Emma asked.

"No," Rachael answered for him. "They've changed for the worse."

110

"Well, maybe things are a little bit tighter now," Tom admitted. "I mean with the deacons and all. You won't get into any trouble, though, as long as you mind your farm and your business. Sure, I'd like to get away from this place and find a better spot to light, but it'd be hard to do." He started to say more, but suddenly stopped in mid-sentence to stare at the path Emma and her friends had arrived on. Perley turned to see four riders coming into the yard. He knew at once that he was looking at the deacons. Dressed alike, all in black, and all riding black horses, they rode in at a fast trot and stopped their horses in a half circle facing Emma's wagon.

Perley and Possum exchanged concerned glances, both getting the same impression of Reverend Raymond's deacons. Four rougher-looking men would be hard to find to carry out the Lord's business, if, in fact, Raymond Butcher recognized the Lord as his inspiration. Hard-looking men, all four were no doubt well experienced in wielding the weapons they wore.

Branch Cantrell, the leader of the deacons, reached up and touched his hat brim, "Miz Parker, Tom, I heard you had some company." He cast a critical eye on the three strangers before continuing. "I thought I'd best ride on over here to make sure these outsiders ain't come to make trouble for you."

"No, no trouble," Tom quickly replied. "Matter of fact, they just rolled up in the yard a few minutes before you rode up. Just stopped by to say hello on their way outta town." He cast a nervous eye toward his wife, hoping she wouldn't tell them that Emma was her sister. Cantrell and his thugs were not hired until after Emma had left the community, so Tom hoped they wouldn't know that Emma was supposed to be forbidden from ever coming back to Butcher Bottom. His hopes were in vain.

"Word I got says that woman right there is Emma Wise, a woman shunned by the congregation and forbidden to ever return," Cantrell said. "Now, Tom, you know you ain't supposed to go against the Reverend's orders. Raymond ain't gonna be too pleased with you for this. He might wanna have you stand up in front of the congregation Sunday to tell everybody why you sinned."

"We ain't done nothin' wrong," Tom implored. "I was workin' in the field when my daughters came to get me — said these folks came to the house, and for me to come see. I just got here about two minutes before you did."

"I reckon you can explain that to Raymond," Cantrell said.

Standing near the wagon, Perley remained silent for as long as he could manage. Astonished by what he was hearing, he found it hard to believe people like Tom and Rachael would live under rules made by some lunatic who called himself a preacher. "I think you're makin' a big mistake, mister. Tom, here, ain't broke any of your boss' rules," he finally said.

His interruption caused Cantrell to jerk his head back as if he'd been slapped in the face. The three men with him reacted as well, becoming instantly alerted from a state of boredom. "Just who the hell are you?" Cantrell demanded of Perley.

"My name's Perley Gates," he replied in much the same manner any gentleman would during a casual conversation with another one.

"Perley Gates?" Cantrell responded in the same way most bullies did upon hearing Perley's name. "You japin' me? I'll send you to see those Pearly Gates right now if you open your mouth again." Figuring that was enough to shut him up, he turned his attention back to Tom then, but Perley wasn't through.

"This lady you referred to as Emma Wise

is really Mrs. Emma Slocum and she ain't been shunned by anybody. Maybe you heard of her father-in-law, Zachary Slocum. Has a ranch and a full crew of hands to run it, and I don't expect he'll sit still for any disrespect to his daughter-in-law and his grandson. Best thing for you to do is to turn right around and lead your men outta here, and I won't say nothin' to the Governor of Texas about you insultin' his friend. We'll finish our little visit with these folks and take our leave when we're done. How's that? That okay with you?"

All four deacons sat stunned in their saddles, broadsided by the seemingly inane conversation coming from the glib young man. Accustomed to living off the fear of the meek, Cantrell found himself at a loss for words. After a long moment of silence, he felt he had to respond, but he was not sure how. Finally, he said, "Strangers passin' through Butcher Bottom are supposed to stop at Tuck's Store to state their business here. This is a private community."

"See, now, that's the thing," Perley replied. "We saw the sign, but it didn't look like there was anybody at the store when we got there. So, we figured we weren't doin' anything but takin' Mrs. Slocum to see her sister and that couldn't hurt anybody, and we came on in." He favored Cantrell with a friendly smile while the befuddled deacon tried to think what he should say. "But we won't take up any more of your time, sir," Perley continued. "We'll let you and your men get back to the important business of keepin' the citizens of Butcher Bottom safe. And I know Mr. and Mrs. Parker appreciate you checkin' on 'em to make sure they were safe, but they ain't gonna come to any harm from us."

It took a few minutes of awkward silence before Cantrell realized he had lost control of the confrontation with the stranger, and when he did, his anger flared to life. "Why, you slick-talkin' son of a bitch, I ain't shot nobody today, so I think I'll put a bullet in your head and stop your gums from flappin'. There ain't nothin' worse that a damn know-it-all. Now, Mr. Perley Gates, we've seen how good you can talk. Let's see if you can back it up. That looks like a Colt handgun, you any good with it?"

"Passable," Perley said, "but I don't see any need to start thinkin' about things like that. Like I said, we'll just be visitin' the Parkers for a little while, then we'll be on our way." He realized now that his attempt to fast-talk the stoic deacon was unsuccessful, and the net result had left him facing four violent men, apparently ready to shut his mouth for good. "It's not a good idea to be talkin' about gunfights in front of these young girls and their mother. How 'bout if we make an appointment to meet in the mornin' to settle this argument?" His plea caused a chuckle from the other three deacons. He knew he was in too deep to help himself now. "Well, why don't we make it a fair fight? It ain't even a contest, if I have to face four of you at the same time."

It was obvious by then that Cantrell really planned to kill Perley, and for his gang's entertainment, he decided to make a game of it. "You're right, we need to be fair about it, so you ain't gonna face but one of us. That's fair, ain't it?"

"Well, it sounds fair, but I think it would be best if we just call this a little misunderstanding and forget about it," Perley said. His plea for peace fell on deaf ears, and he was faced with four insolent grins, anxious for their fun to begin. "Which one do I go up against?" Perley asked.

"Let's stand in a line, boys," Cantrell told his men. They all dismounted and lined up, like he said. "Get a little more room between you. I don't want nobody to get hit with a wild shot, in case he gets one off." They put a couple of paces between themselves, all grinning in anticipation of the fun.

Perley centered himself in front of the line of gunmen. He took time to glance quickly at Possum, who met his glance with a helpless look. "Which one do I go up against?" Perley repeated.

"Well, I reckon you'll find that out when I count three," Cantrell replied. "We'll let Scofield do the job for us, boys." They all grunted in response, having played the game before, knowing Perley had no idea which one Scofield was. "You might be interested to know, Scofield's the fastest gun I've ever rode with," Cantrell added. "You ready, Scofield?" All four, including Cantrell, nodded. "All right, how about you, Perley? You ready?"

"All right," Perley replied, "you've had your fun, so it's gone far enough. You're attempting outright murder, if you're serious about this. I don't wanna do what I'm gonna have to do."

"I ain't never been more serious about anythin' in my whole life," Cantrell said. "When I say three, you damn sure better reach for that gun you're wearin,' 'cause if you run, you're gonna get four shots in that yellow streak down your back. Now get ready!" He paused for only a second. "One . . . Two . . . Three!" The sound of the word "three," was followed instantly by the report of two gunshots, so close together they sounded as one. The knees of the man standing beside Cantrell buckled, and Scofield slowly sank to the ground, his bullet having plowed harmlessly into the ground. All eyes were locked on Perley, who stood with his .44 cocked and ready for the next man to make a move. No one was inclined to test him again, still frozen, unable to believe what they had just witnessed.

They were further discouraged by the sound of the cocking of both barrels of Possum's shotgun behind them. "I reckon this little party is over," he announced.

"There wasn't any reason for this," Perley said. "A couple of you fellows pick him up and load him on his horse. Then you can ride on outta here and let peaceful folks go about their business without your boss stickin' his nose in it. And you tell him the straight of it. Tom Parker and his wife had nothin' to do with what happened here today. They didn't even know we were gonna show up at their door. I'm sorry you had to lose one of your men, but he pulled on me, so he didn't leave me no choice."

Without waiting for orders from Cantrell, Harley Justice and Pete Walker moved quickly to lift their partner's body and lay it across his saddle. Perley and Possum kept their weapons trained on the three stunned deacons, who were still in a state of shock. Something like this was not supposed to happen in Butcher Bottom. When they were back in their saddles, however, Cantrell was able to recover some of his bluster. "You got the jump on us this time, Mr. Perley Gates, but this ain't the end of it. You can't come in here and do whatever you want. I don't know what you've got on your mind, but you'd best be outta this bottom before the sun rises in the mornin'." He looked at Tom then. "And I expect the Reverend is gonna be wantin' to have a little talk with you."

"Get the hell outta here, before I unload this shotgun on your behind," Possum said, having heard enough out of Cantrell's mouth.

"You've been warned!" Cantrell spat as he kicked his heels into the blue roan's belly and loped away from the yard.

CHAPTER 6

For a long few minutes, no one said a word. They all stood watching until the deacons disappeared from view around the bend in the path that led to the road, half expecting them to appear again at a full charge toward them. The silence was broken by four-year-old Melva. "Mama, what are they gonna do? Are they gonna come back?"

"Thanks to Mr. Perley Gates, I expect they will," Rachael answered, more than a little perturbed over the incident that had just happened. Her mind could not hold the horror she had just witnessed, the killing of one of Raymond's deacons. She turned to her husband. "Tom, what are we gonna do? There's gonna be hell to pay for what just happened here. You know Raymond isn't gonna stand for this. There ain't no tellin' what he'll do." She swung around to glare at Emma. "We'll be like Emma, shunned, and forced to leave Butcher Bottom. Why did you come back, bringing this gunman with you?" Emma, as much disturbed as her sister, could find no words to answer.

"Now, calm down, honey," Tom said. "We'll just have to face whatever comes our way, but I'll take care of you and the girls, no matter what." His words were meant to calm his wife and daughters, but he couldn't hide all the concern he felt, himself. Raymond's word was law, and the deacons were brought in to enforce that law.

Also, at a loss for the proper words for his part in what had just happened, Perley was moved to apologize. He had not wished to kill a man, and the gunfight was not his idea, but he had not been able to resist protesting the liberty those deacons felt they could take. "Ma'am," he addressed Rachael. "I'm just as sorry as I can be for what I did. I mean, I ain't so sorry I did it. I'm sorry I *had* to do it. I was tryin' to talk to that fellow, but he plainly didn't wanna talk about it. When he decided to have that other one draw on me, I didn't have any choice but to shoot him before he shot me. I don't know how much trouble I've caused for you, but I'll surely stand by your husband to protect your family."

"I don't know what you and Tom can do

to. . . ." Rachael started before she was interrupted.

"And me," Possum volunteered before she went further.

She paused to give him a strained look before continuing. "I don't know what you can do against the whole community. We may be finished here, our land, our home, if Raymond orders us to be shunned. We've got no place to go."

At last able to speak again, Emma remembered her reason for coming to Butcher Bottom, and she was more determined than ever. "It doesn't matter if they shun you," she blurted, "or if they make you leave. That's why I came here, anyway, to persuade you and Tom to get out from under Raymond Butcher's thumb. I can help you find some land to own, yourself."

Not at all ready to be mollified by her sister, Rachael snapped at her. "Yeah, you look like you can help somebody. Come rollin' in here carryin' a baby, in an old wagon with one wheel that looks like it's fixin' to fall off. Travelin' with a gunslinger and a man old enough to be your father. And speaking of fathers, is that Slocum boy you ran off with really dead, or did he up and leave you with a baby?"

Emma took a step back, staggered by her

sister's fury, and now feeling her own temper rising. "Well, after hearin' what you think of my help, I ain't sure I wanna help you get off of this sorry piece of land that His Majesty, Raymond Butcher, lets you farm for him and his holy church of the devil. Maybe I'll use my money for something else!" Flabbergasted by the bitter argument between the two sisters, all three men stood mute, afraid to speak, lest they feel the heat from one or the other of the combatants.

"Your money," Rachael scoffed. "You talk like you've got money. You know what it costs to buy land and build a house and barn?"

"She's got the money." Everyone turned to look at Possum, including Perley. When no one said anything after his calm statement, but continued to stare at him, he said, "Emma's got enough cash to get a right smart homestead started."

As surprised as anyone, Perley had to ask, "Where does she have to go to get it?" He felt certain there was no money in the wagon, especially since Jack Pitt lost his life to find out.

"Back there where we camped last night," Possum said. "Me and Emma buried it while you was takin' a bath in the river. We

123

didn't think it was a good idea to come in here with that money in the wagon, in case somebody might get to snoopin' around in it."

"You mean we came all that way from the crossin' with a wagon full of money?" Perley asked. "And you didn't even tell me about it?"

"Well, you never asked me if we was totin' any money," Possum said, "and I didn't want you worryin' about protectin' it all the way down here."

Perley shook his head while he took all that into his brain. "So this fellow, Jack Pitt, the man I shot, he knew you had some money, and that's why he tracked you down? Where'd the money come from?" He paused and held up his hand. "No, wait a minute, I don't wanna know." He had a definite feeling that they had not come by it honestly.

"We didn't steal it, if that's what's worryin' ya," Possum was quick to respond. "It's some money me and her husband came by, and there ain't nobody else knows about it." He paused, trying to think of every reassurance he could. "And ain't nobody else gonna come lookin' for it. Pitt was the only other person who knew we had it."

After Possum's lengthy guarantee, Perley was more convinced than ever that whatever money they had come by had to have a smelly side to it somewhere, so he simply said, "Well, that's good. It's your and Emma's business, and I don't need to know nothin' more about it."

When Perley saw the way Tom and Rachael were looking at each other, it was apparent they were thinking how great it would be to pack up and leave Butcher Bottom to raise their daughters somewhere else. A few minutes later, Rachael approached Emma and put her arms around her. "I'm sorry I flew into a fit, honey," she said. "I was just so upset and afraid after Branch Cantrell came here lookin' for you. I didn't know what was gonna happen to my family. I should have known you were my angel lookin' after me and my girls."

Ain't nothing better to patch up a fight between two women than to spread a little money between them, Perley thought as he watched the sisters make up again. "I reckon we'd best be thinkin' about what we're gonna do if those deacons are gonna pay us another visit," he said. "I don't think that one fellow, the one who does all the talkin', was very happy with the way things went."

"His name's Branch Cantrell," Tom said. "He's the boss of those gunmen Raymond calls his deacons. The one you shot was Scofield — never heard his first name — the other two were Harley Justice and Pete Walker. And any one of them is just as liable to shoot you in the back as any dry-gulchin' murderer out there. They ain't been deacons but about a year now. Nobody here knows where they came from, but Raymond made a trip over to Fort Worth and came back with the four of 'em. Everybody calls 'em deacons 'cause that's what Raymond said they were, but ain't none of the four ever showed up in the meetin'house on Sunday."

"Strictly enforcers," Possum commented.

"I reckon you're right," Perley said, then back to Tom, he asked, "Other than the three gunmen he's got left, has he got anybody else?" He wanted to get an idea of how many might be coming to punish Tom and Rachael for their sins, and of course, him and Possum as well. "What about the rest of his flock? Will the other members of his congregation step up to come against us?"

"I swear, I don't know," Tom replied. "There ain't but a few men my age or younger in the community that might grab their shotguns and come after us. Maybe he'll just say we broke his laws, so we'll have to get out, and we'll just be shunned like Emma was."

"Looks to me like you've got to make a decision, and move on it right away," Perley said. "I'm sorry I pushed you to make that decision right now, but as young as your family is, the sooner you find a place that's better for your daughters to grow up in, the better it'll be for all of you."

"What about Bison Gap?" Rachael suddenly suggested, finally calming down to the point where she could give some consideration to what Perley had just said. "Remember that mule skinner that brought those sacks of coffee beans to Tuck's Store?" She and Tom had been there when the driver and Jeremy Tuck unloaded the coffee and he was tellin' Jeremy about settlers startin' to claim land around Bison Gap. "Remember he said there was a lot of good land still available for farmin' or cattle?"

"I remember," Tom said. "Maybe we shoulda settled there. He said they had a post office there now."

"Then, if Emma's tellin' the truth about wantin' to buy us a place," she turned to look directly into her sister's eyes, "why don't we pack up and go now?"

"Suits me," Tom answered.

"Now you're talkin'," Emma piped up.

The decision to leave was made that simply, with little more discussion on the feasibility or the quickness of it. They would go on the reliability of the mule skinner's word, encouraged to do so by the certainty they all felt that they would be driven out of Butcher Bottom by Raymond and his congregation. The question to be answered next was whether they would be able to pack up all their belongings and leave safely. There was sure to be retaliation from the deacons, even if the others chose not to drive them out. Then, if they were successful in pulling out of Butcher Bottom unharmed, there was the matter of driving their wagons and their cow to Bison Gap, a distance of close to one hundred miles, according to the mule skinner. Nevertheless, there was a certain spark of spirit generated by the thought of a new life in a new place where there would be no Raymond Butcher controlling their lives.

The job now was to pack up everything they could fit into the two wagons and onto the horses. It was obvious they were going to be unable to take everything they had managed to accumulate since building their house, but Possum fashioned packsaddles for Jack Pitt's two horses, plus loaded down Perley's and his packhorses. Since Rachael insisted that Emma should live with them, there were items of furniture that Emma had left behind, creating more room in her wagon. When they had filled every square inch of space, they rounded up Tom's extra horse and the cow, and the two-wagon train rolled out of the yard to take the road south out of Butcher Bottom. It was the same road Perley, Emma, and Possum had ridden in on. Riding ahead of the wagons, Perley rested his rifle across his thighs, ready in the event their exodus was challenged. They passed the meetinghouse with no sign of anyone outside. Tuck's Store was the first place they met anyone.

Jeremy Tuck saw the two wagons approaching his store, so he stood on the porch to see who they were. When he recognized Tom and Rachael sitting in the first wagon, he called out to them. "Hey-yo, Tom! Where you folks headin'?"

"Away from Butcher Bottom!" Tom called back and encouraged his horses with a little slap of the reins.

"Are you comin' back?"

"Ain't plannin' on it."

Astonished to see them heading out of town, Tuck could only think to say, "Good luck!" He wondered if Raymond was aware of their leaving.

After they passed the sign that greeted all strangers who chose to visit Butcher Bottom, Perley reined Buck back to wait for Possum to catch up to him. When he did, Perley rode along beside him. "We got a late start on the day," Perley said. "How far are you plannin' on driving these horses? They're sure as hell loaded down."

"I figure we'd best stop at that little place on the river where we camped before," Possum said, which surprised Perley. "I know that ain't but about four miles," Possum continued, "but if we don't stop there, ain't no use headin' to Bison Gap."

"Oh, that's right," Perley said, "that's where you buried the money." He had been thinking about the extra time it was going to take to reach Bison Gap. Five days at best, and by the time he returned, there would be no telling how far behind the Triple-G cattle drive he would find himself. He had only agreed to go with Possum and Emma to Butcher Bottom, and he should be able to return to the herd in good conscience now. But he couldn't bring himself to desert them now when he had been the major reason they might be in danger. *I should have kept my mouth shut,* he told himself.

"I just hope like hell nobody's dug it up while we was havin' that little visit with the deacons," Possum said.

"Where did you bury it?"

"Under the wagon," Possum said and grinned.

"What does he want?" Raymond Butcher asked when Jenny Bloodworth rapped loudly on the door of his study and announced that Branch Cantrell wanted to talk to him.

"He didn't say," Jenny answered, "but I reckon it's got somethin' to do with the feller he's got layin' across his saddle, dead as that chicken I cooked this mornin'."

That was enough to capture Raymond's attention at once. "Who was it?" He got up from his chair and started for the door. "Where is he?"

The crusty old woman was his housekeeper and cook, having held the same position for his father before he died and left Raymond to build on his religious cult. As such, she enjoyed a certain immunity from the spiritual messages that Raymond received, supposedly directly from God. Her place in Raymond's house was never threatened by any of the young girls who were brought into the house for Raymond's personal guidance and training, training that had very little to do with the kitchen. In her usual tone of indifference, she answered his questions. "He's out at the front porch, and the dead man is one of your deacons, the one called Scofield."

"Damnation!" Raymond muttered as he went past her in the doorway, obviously annoyed at having been interrupted while teaching his latest live-in student.

"Amen," Jenny responded sarcastically. "Ain't it a shame?" After he went out the front door, she looked back at the young girl. "Come on, Blossom, you can go with me and help me in the kitchen. Maybe you'll learn how to do somethin' useful you can use after Raymond finishes with your spiritual trainin'."

Raymond walked out on the front porch to find his deacons sitting their horses, awaiting him. "I suppose you've got some explanation for this," he said to Cantrell.

"Ain't no explanation to it," Cantrell replied. "We went over to Parker's place, and the blacksmith was right. It was that girl, Emma Wise, that run off. She was in a wagon with some old man and she had a hired gun ridin' with 'em. He's the one who shot Scofield. Scofield was fast, but that feller cut him down before Scofield cleared leather."

"So he's dead, I reckon," Raymond said.

Cantrell seemed puzzled by the question. He shrugged and glanced toward the body laying across the saddle. "Oh, he's dead, all right, there ain't no doubt about that."

"Not him, you idiot," Raymond reacted angrily. "The hired gun, you killed him, I assume."

"Oh . . . well, no, we didn't kill him. We never had the chance. We was all kinda took by surprise when he beat Scofield, and that old feller with him had us covered with a double-barrel shotgun, and they had Parker with 'em, too." He didn't admit that Tom Parker wasn't armed, but he thought it would sound more acceptable to make the odds even.

Raymond was visibly not pleased by his report. "So you just rode away with your dead man?"

"Well, like I said, they had us covered, front and behind. Me and Pete and Harley didn't even have our guns out of the holster. If one of us had drawed, they coulda cut down all three of us. I know this ain't the way you'd like to hear it, but we didn't have no choice."

"I hired you and your men to take care of

things like this," an irritated Raymond Butcher advised him. "Good money that comes from the toil of these people in my congregation. Now you're telling me I wasted my money?"

"No, sir," Cantrell quickly responded. "I told that feller that this ain't the end of it. And we're fixin' to go back to see that hired gun, only this time we know what's what. We won't have no surprises this time. Right, boys?" Harley and Pete nodded casually. "Outta respect for Scofield, we thought we oughta bring his body back to bury him." He paused then, but upon seeing the irritation still registering on Raymond's face, he added, "Right after we reported to you, so you'd know what was goin' on."

Raymond was clearly not satisfied with Cantrell's accounting of the incident at Tom Parker's home. He was especially unhappy to find that a shooting had occurred at one of the homesteads. And to make it worse, one of his fearsome deacons was the victim. He felt it was important for the people in Butcher Bottom to know that it was costly for anyone who dared break any of his rules. "Here's what I want you to do," he finally instructed. "You go back out to Parker's house. You either kill that gunman, or run him outta town, I don't care which. Then you escort that woman, Emma Wise, and the old man with her out of my town and tell them you have orders to shoot to kill, if they ever come back."

"Right," Cantrell replied. "And what about Parker?"

"You can tell him that Sunday he and his wife will be asked to explain to their neighbors why they went against the rules of the church and welcomed a woman shunned by the church." He started to turn to go back into the house but paused for one additional order. "And haul that corpse off somewhere and bury it." He paused again. "Not in the church cemetery, somewhere else. He didn't do the job he was hired to do, and I don't want him in there with the faithful."

"Yes, sir, Reverend," Cantrell dutifully replied. "Don't you worry, we'll take care of everything you said." They backed their horses away from the porch and wheeled them toward the path. "You snake in the grass," he mumbled as soon as he was out of earshot.

"We goin' back out to Parker's now?" Harley asked when they got back to the road.

"What are we gonna do about Scofield, Branch?" Pete asked.

Cantrell was anxious to settle with Perley

135

for turning the tables on them, but he didn't want to be hampered in any way by Scofield's corpse. "We'd best take care of him first. We'll take him back to the cabin and bury him, then go after that fast gun."

"What are we gonna do about his belongin's?" Harley wondered aloud.

"We'll worry about that after we take care of the bastard that shot him," Cantrell replied. That was the end of the discussion of Scofield's possessions until they rode back to the small cabin Raymond let them use. A shallow grave was dug in no time at all, during which the discussion of Scofield's possibles was renewed. It resulted in the dividing of their late partner's wealth before they were in the saddle and on their way to Tom and Rachael Parker's farm.

This time, when approaching the house, they dismounted and left their horses tied just before the curve in the path that would expose them to anyone watching from the house. With rifles ready, they waited until the light started to fade away behind the trees that lined the river a quarter mile away. When Cantrell thought it was dark enough, he said, "All right, let's go hunt us up a gunslinger. Spread out some. I don't wanna make it too easy on him if he does see us." After they advanced a couple dozen yards closer to the house, Pete commented, "It's awful dark in that house. There ain't a lamp lit nowhere." His observation caused his two partners to study their target more closely.

"It don't look like there's any smoke comin' outta that chimney," Harley said.

A moment later, Cantrell realized there were no horses in the corral and Parker's wagon and the one the strangers arrived in were missing. He stood up straight from the crouch he had been in while they approached, to announce, "I swear, they're not here, they've took off." To prove it, he stepped out onto the path again and walked up to the house.

Inside, they saw the evidence of the hasty departure, in the form of discarded items of furniture and the disarray of a family choosing what was important and what was not. They poked around, looking at what items were deemed unnecessary until Pete asked, "Now what?"

"Whaddaya mean, now what?" Harley answered him. "They've just saved us the trouble of runnin' 'em outta here. Ol' Raymond oughta be happy, they're gone, so he don't have to worry about 'em no more."

"That may be so," Cantrell said. "But I aim to settle that little deal with that gunslinger. My guess is they're headin' out to some town, and there ain't one within fifty miles of here. They can't be gone from here long, and they'll have to stop pretty soon if they're gonna cook any supper and rest their horses. There ain't but two ways outta here, and if they went south, the way they came in, they had to pass by the store. And Tuck mighta seen 'em." When both of his partners showed no interest in going after them to shoot some hired gun who might shoot one of them instead, Cantrell went on. "He's the one I'm goin' after, but there's other things worth goin' after, too. There's two wagons full of no tellin' what, and won't nobody give a damn what happened to them folks. They just pulled outta here and nobody's gonna hear about 'em again."

His comments caused Harley and Pete to exchange a quick glance. That opportunity was something that had not occurred to them. There was no telling what the two wagons might be carrying, maybe even money. If the woman named Emma could afford to hire a gunman, she might have a good amount of money. That alone was worth the trouble to find out. Another thought occurred to Harley, though. "There's women and children to think about. Killin' the men ain't no problem with me, but I ain't wantin' to shoot them little girls and their mothers. Hell, that one woman's got a little baby."

Cantrell thought about that issue for a few moments before responding. "I feel the same way you do, Harley. I ain't wantin' to shoot no women either — unless they're shootin' at me. And I don't wanna shoot any children. After we take care of the three men and take what we want, we can leave the women with a wagon and a team of horses. They oughta make out all right. Hell, we might even leave 'em a couple of guns and some ammunition."

That served to satisfy both of his partners' consciences but led to a question from Pete. "What if they was to turn around and come back to Butcher Bottom?"

"I hope they do," Cantrell replied emphatically, thinking about his job with Raymond. " 'Cause I'm thinkin' I've had about as much of the Reverend as I want. Summer's comin' on and I think it's about time to get back to what we know best. We oughta find enough in those two wagons to give us a good start. How 'bout you boys, you had enough of the salvation business?" They were unanimous in agreement. "Good," he said, "let's go see Jeremy Tuck and see if they passed the store this evenin'."

CHAPTER 7

The growing darkness made it a little more difficult, but both Perley and Possum were pretty sure they could find the very spot where the wagon was parked on the night before. They proved to be right, and Possum found the exact spot when he found the impressions left by the four wheels where the wagon had sat all night. They were only a few miles outside the boundaries of Butcher Bottom, but after the three men talked it over, they decided it best to camp there that night. It wouldn't take much time to dig up the money Possum had buried there, but it was well past the time to be cooking supper. Rachael raised her concern about the possibility of being visited again by the deacons. That had also been of concern among the three men, but they decided they might be better able to defend themselves in the darkness with the wagons and the trees to protect them. While Rachael and the girls searched for wood, Perley talked with Tom and Possum about the possibility of an attack that night. Tom was understandably the most concerned. "I just know that damn Cantrell ain't gonna let us get away from there clean, after you shot Scofield," he said, then quickly added, "I ain't sayin' you had any choice, but we'd best get ready for him pretty quick."

"You might be right," Possum said. "That's why I think it's best to pull your wagon up here beside mine and we'll build our fire between the wagons. Then we can tie the horses up on either end, build ourselves a little fort, just like the wagon trains did when the Injuns were runnin' wild around here."

"That sounds like a good idea," Perley said, "but I'd like to do a little something different. In the first place, I think we've got time to get supper, because I would expect Cantrell and his men will wait till they think we're all asleep. Next, I don't think it's best for us to sleep between the wagons, so I think you and Tom need to take the women and children on the other side of this clump of trees to sleep. You know, Possum, where I took a bath, around the bend of the river. There's pretty good cover on that riverbank and you could protect 'em there."

"What are you gonna do?" Possum asked, not convinced that it was the best defense.

"I figure Cantrell doesn't care that much if you folks leave," Perley answered. "It's me he wants. I'm the one who shot his man, so I oughta be the one waitin' at the wagons for him. And another thing, let's tie the horses on a rope line, off to the side over there." He pointed to a small opening in the trees. "I don't wanna take a chance on losin' the horses, mine especially. Buck would never forgive me. If these jaspers found our horses in the way between the wagons they might start shootin' 'em down to try to get a clear shot at us."

"I don't know, Perley," Possum allowed. "It don't seem right to leave you to take on the three of 'em all by yourself."

"He's right, Perley," Tom said. "Raymond calls them deacons, like they were members of his church, but everybody knows they're nothin' but hired guns he pays to be his policemen."

"I'll try to be careful not to get myself in a position I can't get out of," Perley insisted. The words "cow pie" came to his mind, but he continued. "If they start shootin' up those wagons, it ain't gonna be any place for the women and children to be. The main thing here is to keep them safe." There was really no logic to argue that point, so the three agreed on Perley's defense plan.

Tom got a fire started, so the women could cook some of the ham they had brought to go with the cornbread Rachael had baked the day before, and Possum got ready to go to work under the wagon with the shovel Perley returned to him. Although he had done a first-rate job of disguising the hole, he found the stick he had driven down in the middle of it with no trouble at all. "Looks like nobody ain't bothered it," he said, looking up to give Emma a reassuring grin. He hesitated, however, when Emma wondered if it wouldn't be best to leave the money buried until they were ready to leave in the morning.

"If you dig it up tonight, you'll put it in the wagon," she said. "What if they somehow manage to run off with the wagon, or set it on fire?"

"That wouldn't be too good," Possum said, scratching his chin whiskers. "Maybe we'd best leave it in the ground. Won't take no time a-tall to dig it up."

When Perley took a coil of rope and walked to the opening in the trees to rig up a line between two trees to tie the horses to, Tom couldn't help asking Possum a question. "Are you uncomfortable with his plan at all?" When Possum answered with a questioning expression, Tom said, "We're gonna be around the bend, all of us, and leave Perley here, by himself, where the money is. Ain't you worried a little bit that he might just dig up the money and run? And he'll have all the horses, too."

"Now, that is somethin' to think about, ain't it," Possum replied with a smile. "Lemme put it this way, half that money buried here belongs to me, and I ain't worried about him takin' off with it."

Tom studied the confident face of Possum Smith for a moment. "Well, I reckon if you ain't worried, then neither am I, so let's help him tie up the horses." They walked over to the opening where Perley was stretching his rope out between two trees to make sure he had enough.

"Ain't you gonna pull your saddle offa your horse?" Possum asked, noticing Buck standing nearby still saddled, which seemed unusual since it was always Perley's habit to see to his horse's comfort before doing anything else. He couldn't help grinning when he glanced at Tom and saw the sudden look of concern on the young man's face. He was no doubt thinking about the discussion he just had with him.

"No," Perley answered. "I think I might

take a little ride back the way we came, while the women are cookin' supper. I just wanna take a look in case I'm wrong about Cantrell and his boys and they come after us sooner than I think."

Possum was in favor of that idea, so he and Tom took over the care of the horses while Perley stepped up into the saddle and guided Buck back toward the road. When he reached it, he turned the big bay horse toward Butcher Bottom, holding him to a gentle lope while he peered ahead as far as he could see on the dark river road. He was counting on being able to spot the deacons before they spotted him. He rode what he figured to be about halfway back to Butcher Bottom with no sign of anyone coming toward him. Reluctant to ride any closer to Tuck's Store, he decided to pull off the road when he came to a small knoll that looked like it might be a good spot for a lookout. There were a couple of runty trees on top, and he could sit there in the dark without being easily seen from the road.

It was a pleasant night, perfect for just about anything except what he was doing. *John and Rubin are probably wondering what the hell I'm doing,* he thought. *Well, I stepped in another one, John.* He brought his mind back to concentrate on the road. Over his shoulder, he caught sight of a full moon, just visible over the hills on the far horizon. *That's going to be a beauty,* he thought. He wasn't sure how long he sat there, but when the moon had clearly risen free of the hills, he figured Cantrell was not coming until late, as he suspected. That meant the folks back at the wagons should have plenty of time to finish up supper and walk back around the bend of the river. He had to admit that he was enjoying his perch atop the knoll, so he was reluctant to mount up and head back. But he was hungry, so he climbed back into the saddle and guided Buck down to the road again. As he rode, he again wondered if he was totally wrong. Cantrell and his men might not have any notions to come after them. He shook his head and told himself he was right, Cantrell would come late tonight.

"I was startin' to wonder if you were comin' back," Emma greeted him when he returned to the wagons. "You must be hungry. I saved you a couple of pieces of cornbread and some ham."

"Much obliged," Perley replied. "I could sure use some." He stepped down and led Buck to the river after pulling his saddle off.

Possum walked with him, cradling his rifle

on one arm. "Good thing you hollered before you came ridin' in," he said. "You was gone longer'n I expected and I was fixin' to shoot the first rider that showed up. Looks like those boys are comin' later tonight, right?"

"I still think that, but it's just my opinion, for whatever that's worth," Perley replied. "I don't think Cantrell is gonna let me off with killin' one of his men. And unfortunately for you folks, this is where he expects to find me."

"I still ain't so sure it's a good idea for you to stay here and wait for those jaspers by yourself," Possum said, sounding genuinely worried. "If they get on both sides of this camp, they might make it so hot, you won't be able to stick your head up, much less shoot back."

"I ain't gonna hole up here," Perley said. "I'm plannin' to keep out of sight out there in the dark and wait for them to come in to catch us all asleep. I'm gonna build that fire up a little, so I can get a good look at 'em when they do."

"That's an old trick, settin' your camp up to make somebody think you're in there sleepin'. You reckon they're dumb enough to take the bait?"

"I don't know," Perley answered, "but I

think since we ain't gonna lay any dummy bedrolls around the fire, he might think we're all sleepin' in the wagons, or under them."

Possum scratched his beard thoughtfully. "I still think you need help."

"I could surely use some, but we can't take the chance to leave those women and kids unprotected," Perley responded, "and they'll have a lot better chance with two of you to protect 'em. 'Course, that's if Cantrell and his men get by me and come lookin' for you. But I'll guarantee you, all three ain't gonna get by me."

Possum paused to take a hard look at the young man who had volunteered to leave a cattle drive to help Emma and him get to Texas. And now, he was willingly risking his life for them once more. Maybe his name should be spelled like the Pearly Gates in the Good Book. "All right, partner, we'll take care of 'em. You just be sure you don't get yourself in a corner you can't get out of."

When everybody was ready to go, each person carried the blankets they were going to sleep in. Perley stood by the corner of Tom's wagon and watched them follow Possum, who was holding a lantern. Possum confessed that, without the lantern, he would be unable to find his way through the bushes on the path Perley had taken in his underwear. To Perley, standing by the wagon, they resembled a giant reptile, snaking its way through the bushes and trees. When he could no longer follow the light, he announced. "Well, it's time to see what we can do to get ready for Cantrell's visit."

The first thing he did was to make sure he carried enough ammunition for his Colt .44 and his Winchester 73. Then he dragged a piece of a large log over and left it up against the wheel of the wagon, hoping it would look like it was placed there for cover. After he put more wood on the fire to make sure it would burn for a long while, he went to look for the help he had told Possum he could surely use. It couldn't hurt to have another lookout to watch one end of the camp while he watched the other. Even in the darkness of the trees, he went right to the spot, thanks to the trail Buck had blazed the day before. The moon was now high enough to afford little shafts of light through the branches of the trees, which also helped him see his way.

"Well, good evenin' to ya," he greeted him. "I'm mighty glad to see you're still hangin' around." He paused for a moment to look closely at the body of Jack Pitt. "You don't seem to be much worse off than yesterday. I was afraid the buzzards mighta found you before now." Pitt had been dead long enough for full rigor mortis to set in, rendering him stiff as a board and not very cooperative. Perley hoped that the body might have begun to relax again after this much time had passed, but it was still in the same position he had left it. He took a deep breath and resigned himself to the task facing him.

The only way to find out if the stiffness had left the body was to grab the legs and arms and see if they were easily moved. He found that they were not, but he wasn't inclined to give up, so he kept bending and pulling until, to his surprise, Pitt's limbs gradually became more bendable, at least enough to satisfy his purposes. When he found that he could now pose him, he looked around for the best place to position him. He decided on a large stump from a tree that had evidently grown taller than his brothers and was consequently struck by lightning. By propping Pitt against the stump, he would have a patch of moonlight to highlight him. So he took hold of Pitt's feet and started dragging him toward the stump. "Damn," he grunted, "you're a big man. You didn't look that hard to move when Buck dragged you over here." He wanted him in a sitting position, so when he got him to the stump, he turned him around and started working on bending him in the hips. That seemed to work, so he got behind the stump and pulled him until his back was against it. That accomplished, he sought to keep the corpse in that sitting position. He found that he could do this by spreading Pitt's legs wide, stabilizing him like a tripod. Satisfied with his sentry, he said, "You got a chance to do something for the decent folks for a change, so do a good job." He started back toward the other side of their camp where he would now find the best spot he could to await whatever came. As he left the stump behind him, he muttered, "I hope to hell I don't ever have to do that again for the rest of my life."

"Wake up, Harley!" Branch Cantrell kicked the bottom of Harley's boot. "It's time to take a little ride." He turned to knock the hat off Pete Walker's head. "Get up, Pete, we're wastin' time!"

"What time is it?" Harley asked. "I just got to sleepin' good."

"You been snorin' like a rootin' hog for over two hours," Cantrell said. "After this night's over, you can lay in bed a month if you want to. Come on, we gotta ride."

Knowing the wagons they were going after could not have gotten very far from Butcher Bottom, their plan was simple. Ride until they struck their camp, and when they did, jump them before they knew what hit them. Cantrell figured they would come upon their camp sometime between now, midnight, and two o'clock in the morning. He based his estimate on the time that Jeremy Tuck had seen the two wagons and the gunman pass by his store. He and his men had spent much of the early evening getting their packhorses ready with all the meager possessions they kept in the small cabin they shared. Their intention was to never return to Raymond Butcher's community, convinced as they were that there were two wagonloads of valuables within their reach, plus horses and tack to go with them. It was a chance to make a score that would set them up for a while.

With Cantrell's constant badgering, the packhorses were loaded and their personal horses saddled, and as a final farewell gesture to Raymond Butcher, Cantrell kicked the small iron stove over. He paused to watch the burning coals scatter on the floor before going out the door and climbing on his horse. There was no one awake at Jeremy Tuck's store to see the three dark riders pass by, leading three packhorses, on the road south along the Brazos.

As Cantrell had figured, it didn't take them long to catch up to the wagons. Pete was the first to spot the camp. "There!" he exclaimed and pointed to a faint glow of firelight in the trees. "Yonder it is, right where the river starts to take that sharp bend!"

"You were right, Branch," Harley said. "They didn't get far. We coulda rode after 'em just as soon as we found out they was gone."

"That's right, dummy," Cantrell mocked. "Then they coulda seen us comin' and we'da got a chance to see if he's as good with a rifle as he is with a handgun."

"Oh . . ." Harley exhaled slowly. "I didn't think about that." He favored Cantrell with a wide smile. "I reckon that's why you're the boss and I ain't."

"One of the reasons," Cantrell came back sarcastically. "Now I wanna take a good look at that camp before we pull a trigger. Come on." He led them about seventy-five yards south of the glow in the trees before cutting back toward the riverbank. They had not gone far when they heard a horse whinny. Cantrell signaled them to halt and dismount. Standing in the darkness of the trees, it was hard to tell at first where the sound had come from, but it was apparent that it was between them and the fire glow they were cautiously approaching. Once again, Pete's sharp eyes located the source of the whinny.

"I see 'em," he whispered. "It's their horses, all of 'em, it looks like, in a little openin' ahead."

"You sure?" Cantrell asked, and when Pete said he was, Cantrell told them to tie their horses there and continue on foot. Harley, decidedly the best at handling horses, crept ahead of Cantrell and Pete to calm the horses. Upon reaching the horses, Cantrell felt impelled to remark. "Mighty nice of 'em, weren't it, leavin' all their horses tied up here, waitin' for us?" He was already thinking about how much they could sell the horses for. His mind was brought back to the job at hand when he heard Harley's forced whisper.

"Yonder they are!" He said and pointed to the two wagons parked side by side and the fire they had been homing on between them. He looked back and grinned when his partners joined him. "Peaceful as can be."

Cantrell stared at the camp between the wagons for a long moment. "Yeah, it's peaceful, all right, but I don't see no bedrolls around that fire."

They all stared hard at the wagons for a while then until Pete spoke. "Most likely they're all sleepin' under the wagons." His eye was caught then by the short piece of log by one of the wagons. "Reckon what they got that log up against that one wheel for?"

"Most likely for protection for somebody to shoot from behind," Cantrell said. "I bet you're right, they're sleepin' under the wagons. Maybe the women and children are sleepin' in the wagons."

His comment triggered the return of a discussion they had before starting out that night. Harley, being the most uneasy about the matter, brought it up again. "You still ain't plannin' on killin 'em all, right? You'll leave the women and the children?"

Impatient with the simpleton's weak streak when it came to the two little girls, Cantrell growled, "Damn it, Harley, we've got to be smart about this. If we don't leave nobody alive, we don't leave nobody to tell. It ain't no different shootin' women and children than it is shootin' men, and you don't have no problem with that. But you better be damn sure you're with us on this deal. Me and Pete are gonna make sure every livin' soul in that camp is dead when we leave here. So you make up your mind before we start shootin', else it's just gonna be a two-way split between me and Pete."

Pete spoke up then. "Harley, it ain't no different from knockin' newborn puppies in the head when you don't wanna raise all of 'em. Come to think of it, it'll just be mercy killin's, 'cause after we kill all their menfolk, them young'uns would be better off dead."

Harley hesitated a moment to think about it. "When you put it that way, I reckon you're right."

That settled, Cantrell gave them instructions for the assault upon the wagons. He decided it best if he worked in a little closer from this end of the camp, and the two of them should circle around to come up and take positions on the other end — Harley, since he could hoot like an owl, and Pete to make sure Harley didn't go soft on the little girls. He told Harley to hoot when they got in position and were ready to shoot. "I want everybody to cut down on them at the same time, so when I hear your signal, I'll know you're ready to shoot. Then you wait for my shot, and when you hear it, we'll open up on those two wagons and wipe out anybody under 'em. That's plain enough, ain't it?" When they both nodded, he said, "Let's get goin' then."

It was a good twenty minutes before Pete and Harley completed a wide circle around the camp, planning to creep in a little closer to the wagons. Suddenly, Pete grabbed Harley's arm and pulled him down on one knee beside him. "There's a lookout! We damn near walked right out in front of him."

"Did he see us?" Harley rasped.

"If he did, he ain't actin' like it. He ain't moved a hair, just settin' there against that stump." They remained on a knee, watching the lookout for a few minutes, undecided what to do. Ideally, they needed to advance a little closer to the camp to be able to pour the storm of lead under the wagons that Cantrell wanted. "I don't think he's seen us," Pete said. "If he had, he wouldn't just set there like that. He'd be gettin' his ass around on the other side of that stump."

"You're right," Harley said. "He don't even know we're here."

"Let's circle around and come up from behind him," Pete suggested. "We'll keep an eye on him to make sure he don't move before we get a little closer to those wagons.

The dumb horse's ass don't even know we can see him settin' right there in the moonlight." Harley nodded his agreement. "When we hear Branch's shot, we'll put a bullet into the lookout first thing. Then we can pour it on the rest of 'em."

"You reckon that's that hired gun that shot Scofield?" Harley whispered as they moved cautiously from one tree to the next.

"I can't tell," Pete replied and squinted his eyes in an effort to sharpen his vision. "He almost looks bigger settin' there in the moonlight, but I hope it's him, 'cause he's gonna get the first bullet when Branch starts the show."

"He's gonna get the first two bullets," Harley whispered, his eyes locked on the man sitting next to the stump. His gaze captured, he didn't notice that he was about to step on a small dead branch lying across a small gulley formed by rain runoff. Both men jumped when the branch snapped, sounding as loud as a gunshot in the still trees of the riverbank. It happened that Pitt's body, still coming out of the full stage of rigor mortis, relaxed to the point where it keeled over sideways at almost the same moment. "He's tryin' to crawl behind the stump!" Harley exclaimed, giving no thought to the unhurried slide of the body as it yielded to gravity. Both men opened up with their rifles, both finding the target.

"He ain't crawlin' no more," Pete announced confidently. "Let's get to work on them wagons." Wasting no more time, they hurried to move in closer. When they reached a gully no more than forty yards from the two wagons, they scrambled into it and began to fire in earnest at the deserted campsite.

Their barrage of rifle fire stunned two other men hiding out in the thick growth of trees along the riverbank. "What the hell?" Cantrell blurted. "They started before I signaled!" Left with no choice, he moved up to a point already decided upon, which was closer to the wagons. As soon as he reached the log he had already selected, he started to throw shot after shot into the camp.

Closer to the north end of the camp and barely forty yards from Harley and Pete, Perley spotted the muzzle blasts coming from a gully to his right. He quickly moved through the trees until he reached a spot where he could look straight down the gully and see both shooters, side by side. He hesitated only a moment to decide the right or wrong of it, then pulled the trigger. Harley yelled and jumped straight up when the bullet struck him, then collapsed. Startled, Pete turned to see what had happened, in time to be met with Perley's second shot in the center of his chest. He collapsed on top of Harley. When he was certain both rifles were silenced, Perley began to make his way back through the trees toward the southern end of the camp.

As quickly as he emptied the magazine on his rifle, Cantrell reloaded and continued to crank shot after shot into the unresponsive camp until he realized that he was doing all the shooting. There were no more shots coming from the other end of the camp, and there were no sounds of any kind coming from the wagons, no return shots, no cries of pain or fear, nothing. Only then did it occur to him that he was firing into a deserted camp. Panic quickly replaced his heartless desire to kill. If there was no one in the camp, where were they? Behind him? It was plain to him that Harley and Pete were dead, and he was in mortal danger himself. There were no thoughts of standing to fight. He couldn't even see where they might be coming from in the darkness of the riverbank. He could feel his throat tightening, as if he was choking on his fear. And he knew then he had to get to the horses before they found them. To run was the only thought on his mind, so he scrambled up from the log he had used for cover and ran, crashing recklessly through the bushes and brush, expecting to hear the snap of a bullet at any second.

When he reached the spot where the horses were left, he found them gone. Already panting for breath, he turned around and around, thinking to see his blue roan gelding standing somewhere close by, but there was no sign of a horse. Thinking he must have gotten lost in the darkness, he looked frantically from side to side. "You lookin' for horses?" The voice came from behind him. Terrified, he spun around, drawing his .44 as he turned, and put a bullet into the ground at his feet before he sank to his knees. When he tried to raise his arm again, Perley's second shot slammed into his chest.

Perley stood over the body for a few moments to make sure Cantrell was dead, and when he was sure, he took the reins of the horses he had found. By nature, it never set well on his mind whenever he was faced with an occasion to kill a man, even one as evil as Branch Cantrell. But he had learned to live with it, since it seemed that no matter where he went, or what he was doing, his path seemed to somehow cross someone's path that needed killing. "From now on, Lord, would you mind sending these fellows somewhere else?" He shook his head slowly and started walking back to the camp, leading the horses. When he got to the horses on the rope, he pulled the saddles and packs off before tying the new horses to the rope.

CHAPTER 8

Both Possum and Tom had stayed awake all evening and well into the morning, so they were already awake when they heard the shooting around the bend of the river. It was only a matter of minutes before everyone else was awake as well, with the exception of Emma's baby and four-year-old Melva. Immediately frightened, both women were inclined to take their children and run down the river to hide. "I think we'd best stay right here," Possum advised. "Perley's right. This is a good place to take cover. You women take the children and stay down behind that bluff. Me and Tom will stay right here where we can see anybody coming outta the trees, and they're gonna have to come across about sixty feet of open ground to get to this bank. That all right with you, Tom?" Tom said that it was, so Emma and Rachael took the girls and baby Daniel, and huddled them all up under the

163

bluff Possum had indicated. They all went eagerly with the exception of Melva, who fussed and complained that she wanted to stay there in her blanket and sleep.

"It sounds like there's a damn war goin' on over on the other side of the bend," Tom said when the women had gone. "I hope Perley can come outta there alive."

"I reckon I do, too," Possum allowed. "Perley Gates is the most unusual young man I believe I've ever run into. I'd bet my life against a chaw of tobacco that Perley's the fastest gun hand between here and the moon." He looked at Tom and shook his head slowly. "And he don't even know it. He was just born with them reflexes like a cat. Perley will come outta there all right. I guarantee it." As Possum had promised, they were startled thirty minutes later by a yell from the trees in the bend.

"Possum! Don't shoot. It's me, Perley."

Possum looked at Tom and grinned, then he yelled back. "Come on in, Perley!"

There were a few things to take care of during the morning before the party could get started again, but no one was anxious about leaving. The threat of being chased had been eliminated. It was just a question now of a trip of about one hundred miles, five days if

164

they ran into no problems along the way. The men searched the three bodies for anything of value but found very little. The spoils from the one-man massacre was in the form of horseflesh and tack, which could always be worth something in trade. This comprised the contribution of the deacons, but also created a problem. To keep all that had come to them on that ill wind, they were facing a task of driving two wagons, plus driving a herd of extra horses and a cow. That was no problem — if there was a spare man to act as the wrangler and drive those horses. When Perley looked around, the only available man he could see was himself. The women cooked breakfast while the men considered the problem.

"It's gonna be hard on Emma to drive that wagon while she's got a tiny baby to tend to," Possum said. "I reckon she'd just have to do it if I drive that herd of extra horses. She ain't never drove a wagon before." He paused and added, "And I ain't much of a wrangler."

"Rachael ain't no better at drivin' a wagon," Tom commented. "She's scared to death of a horse." He exchanged a quick glance with Possum, then they both looked at Perley for his reaction.

Now that the imminent danger had been

avoided, Perley had figured they could find Bison Gap without his help. And he was so far behind his brothers and the Triple-G herd, he was going to have to push Buck hard, day and night, to hope to catch up before they got through Kansas. "I expect I've been gone from the herd a heck of a lot longer than my brothers thought I'd be. They mighta wrote me off for dead by now." His statement only seemed to cause Tom and Possum to look up at him like dogs begging for bones.

"I understand you gotta do what you gotta do," Possum said. "And I wanna tell you that we, all of us, appreciate what you've done for us. Without you, I don't know what woulda happened to any of us. Whatever it woulda been, it most likely wouldn'ta ended up like this, with all of us still alive. From here on to Bison Gap, we'll just get on the best we can."

Finally Perley cracked. "All right, you can just cut out the horseshit, Possum. You and Tom can get down to Bison Gap without my help. But I'll go with you and damned if I know why."

Both Tom and Possum whooped their delight, since neither one had any idea what might await them between there and Bison Gap, about a hundred miles of wild, unsettled Texas plains. There might be any number of occasions when they would need the guns of a man as skilled as Perley. "I can't wait to tell Emma you're gonna go with us," Possum said. He looked at Perley and winked. "She told me to talk you into goin'."

"I swear," Perley said, "I oughta change my mind. I ain't got no business in Bison Gap, wherever that is."

"Before this is over, you'll be glad you decided to come to Bison Gap with us," Possum said. "It's been quite a spell since I've been down in that part of Texas, and there weren't no sign of any settlement of any size back then. There was a few souls gathered on Oak Creek where buffalo had a waterin' hole. It was mostly buffalo hunters that found that hole. That might be what folks are callin' Bison Gap."

"If you've been there before, whaddaya need me for?" Perley thought to ask.

" 'Cause, like I said, it's been a while since I rode through that country," Possum replied. "I ain't as young as I used to be, and my memory ain't that good. Besides, you already said you'd go with us." He gave Perley a wide grin.

Cow pie, Perley thought. "Yeah, I reckon I did." It was plain to see that he wasn't going to back out of his commitment, so he resigned himself to make the trip. "While the women are cookin' breakfast, I'm gonna take another look at my lookout."

"I'll go with you," Possum said, leaving Tom to inform the women that Perley had decided to go with them.

Perley led him out the north end of their camp to the stump where he had left Jack Pitt. They found the corpse where Harley and Pete had left it, the only difference being Pitt was lying on his side beside the stump. "He was sittin' up against the stump when I left him," Perley said.

"Is that a fact?" Possum replied. "It looks like he was tryin' to take cover behind it when they shot him." It was obvious that two of the bullet holes happened long after Pitt was dead.

"I reckon we oughta be thankin' him for doin' his job," Perley allowed. "Because of him, I was able to spot those two in the gully before they saw me." He studied the corpse for a long moment, trying to decide. Finally, he said, "I reckon I'll just leave him where he is, instead of draggin' him over to the gully and throwin' him in with the two that shot him."

"I know ol' Pitt would appreciate it," Possum said. He was not particularly interested in helping to drag his big body anywhere, especially since Pitt had developed an eye-watering putrid smell. "It'll give him a little longer to enjoy the evenin' air. Besides, he might not like the idea of travelin' to hell in the same stagecoach with them that shot him." The two of them had carried Branch Cantrell's body over to join his two partners in the gully, just to make sure the women or the little girls didn't stumble upon it. He didn't mind that as much, since Cantrell had not as yet developed that distinctive odor. "Let's get on back," he suggested. "The women oughta have breakfast ready by now. Ain't nothin' makes me hungry like the smell of a really ripe corpse," he said facetiously.

Emma and Rachael greeted Perley with big smiles when he and Possum walked back between the two wagons. He answered with a shy smile of embarrassment, knowing that Tom had assured them that he was going to accompany them to Bison Gap. He knew they saw him as their protector, and he was not especially comfortable in that role. He wanted to tell them that things just happen the way they happen and sometimes he was lucky, but sometimes he wasn't. At least, it was a good thing to see everybody's spirits uplifted again, now that they knew no one was chasing them. It made for a lighthearted breakfast and an eagerness to get started in search of the place they planned to settle in.

When everything was packed up, with Emma's and Possum's money stowed away under every thing else, the horses were saddled and hitched up, Possum started out in the lead, with one wheel leaning to the left as before. At Tom's advice, they would follow the river south until reaching a point where the Brazos took a turn leading off more to the southwest. He remembered, when talking to the mule skinner at Tuck's Store, he had said Bison Gap was straight south from there. Since none in their party had any more information than that, they set out along the river. They figured to avoid trouble with the Lazy-S Ranch by traveling on the east side of the river. According to Tom, the Lazy-S range was supposed to end at the western side of the Brazos, so they would not be crossing the Lazy-S range at any point this way. With Perley pushing their little herd of horses behind them, the wagons set the pace. And as Perley suspected, they had a tendency to follow the wagons with a minimum of herding by him. There was some concern about Emma's wagon and the bent axle, but they had no way to straighten it, so Possum said he would drive it until the wheel broke down, and so far it was still doing the job.

"Lookee yonder, Ace!" Billy Watts said when he pulled his horse up beside him.

"What is it? Where?" Ace Barnett asked.

"Over yonder," Billy said and pointed, "on the other side of the river."

Ace reined his horse to a stop and studied the two wagons for a few seconds. "The other day when Rance was over here with me, we run up on these folks in a wagon with another feller on a horse. They was part of that bunch of Gypsies squattin' on that bottomland. Me and Rance stopped 'em and they said they was tryin' to find their way to Butcher Bottom. Rance let 'em pass on through, even told 'em how to get there. I swear, that wagon in front looks like the wagon we stopped. Looks like they picked up another one."

"Lookee yonder," Billy exclaimed again when they saw the little herd of horses coming up behind the wagons. "Looks like they're drivin' about half a dozen horses."

"That jasper drivin' those horses looks like the one me and Rance talked to. He's ridin' that same bay. Looks like he's picked up another wagon and a few extra horses

171

somewhere. We might better ride over there and see where they're headin' with 'em." He wheeled his horse around and gave it his heels, heading at an angle to cut the wagons off.

Perley was at once concerned when he looked up ahead and saw the two riders crossing the river to cut the wagons off. Possum pulled his wagon to a stop when the two riders approached, their rifles drawn and resting across their thighs. "You're the feller I saw the other day when you cut across Lazy-S range," Ace said as he and Billy pulled up on either side of the wagon.

"That's a fact," Possum replied. "What can I do for you fellers?"

"Looks like you picked up some more Gypsies and some horses since you been here."

"Well, you're half right," Possum replied. "We picked up some horses, all right, but we didn't pick up no Gypsies." By this time, the extra horses began to catch up and gather around them, and Perley rode up to the wagon.

Ace gave Perley a hard looking-over before returning to Possum. "I reckon we're gonna have to take a closer look at those horses you're drivin'."

"Why is that?" Possum asked.

"To make sure they ain't Lazy-S horses," Ace came back sharply. "We run up on horse thieves from time to time."

"How come some of them horses have got saddles on 'em?" Billy suddenly interrupted.

" 'Cause it's easier to carry 'em that way," Possum answered.

"Makes me wonder what happened to the fannies that was settin' in 'em. Like I said," Ace continued, "we'll take a look at them horses.

"Reckon not," Possum said. "This ain't Lazy-S range on this side of the Brazos, so it ain't really no concern of yours where we got our horses. But it was a pleasure seein' you again, and now we'll be on our way. If you still think you've gotta look at our horses, why, go right ahead. You can admire 'em while Perley drives 'em by you."

"Take it easy, Billy," Ace told him when he started to lift his rifle off his thighs, noticing that Perley had his Winchester out of the saddle sling. "All right, mister, I reckon you're right, we ain't on Lazy-S range. We're just doin' our job. Come on, Billy." He pulled his horse back and watched the wagons start out again.

"Damn, Ace . . ." was all Billy could say, being accustomed to Ace's usual brash and bullying behavior.

173

Without waiting for Billy to ask questions, Ace said, "That feller's name drivin' the horses is Perley Gates. Ain't that a helluva name?"

"Perley Gates?" Billy exclaimed, even more amazed that Ace didn't jump on the opportunity to give the fellow a little hell, just for the fun of it.

"Did you look at the woman settin' there in the first wagon, holdin' the baby?" Ace continued. Billy nodded. "Well, that little woman is Dan Slocum's wife, and that's his little boy."

"What the hell are you talkin' about, Ace?" Billy responded. "Where's Dan?"

"Dead is what they told us, and now we'd best get on back to the ranch and tell Rance about it and that they're on the move again." He gave Billy a wide grin. "Boss is gonna spit fire when Rance tells him."

Margaret Cross answered the knock at the kitchen door to find Bob Rance standing on the steps. "I heard Mr. Slocum got back this mornin'," Rance said. "I was out on the east section, but I came in as soon as I heard Boss was back. I've got something he needs to know."

"Come on in, Bob," Margaret said. "I'll go see if he's up and about yet. He got in this mornin', but he'd rode half the night, he was so anxious to get home. I made him go to bed after I fixed him somethin' to eat." Rance didn't doubt her word. The tall, somber woman, of uncertain age, ever neat and clean, even in the midst of cooking or cleaning, was always polite and soft-spoken. She had served in the Slocum household several years before Zachary Slocum's wife passed away, some nine years before this day. There was always speculation floating around the bunkhouse regarding the range of services Margaret performed for the boss, but none was ever verified. As for Rance, he had always found her to be quietly cordial. "There's still some coffee on the stove, if you'd like a cup," she said. When he politely declined, she said, "Very well, I'll go check on Mr. Slocum."

In a few minutes time, she returned to tell Rance to go into the study, and that Slocum would be in after he pulled a shirt on. She stepped aside to let Rance pass into the hallway, knowing he needed no directions. When Slocum entered the room, he seemed to be in a good mood. Rance figured it was because he was home where he wanted to be. He feared that the news he was bringing might destroy that mood. "Rance," Slocum greeted him — he never called Rance by his first name. "Glad you came in. I was gonna check with you this afternoon to see how things were going while I was in Fort Worth. You want some coffee or something?"

"No, thank you, sir," Rance replied respectfully. "Margaret offered me some already. I wouldn't have bothered you after you just got back from a long trip, but I figured you'd wanna know about this as soon as possible." He paused, hesitating to go on with the news he had brought.

"What is it, Rance?" Slocum pressed, sensing his foreman's reluctance.

"Well, sir, I hate to be the one to bring you the sad news that your son, Dan, is dead."

Slocum's reaction was what Rance had feared it would be. Stunned, the old man was speechless for a long minute before he uttered, "My son, dead?" He paused again, as if trying to digest the fact. "How did he die?"

"Sir, I'm told he was shot by a bank robber he was helpin' a marshal capture in Dodge City, Kansas."

"So that's where he ended up," Slocum said, hanging his head sadly, but only for a few seconds before his anger arose. "What the hell was he doin' in Dodge City?"

"I don't really know, sir, but he died

helpin' the town marshal go after a bank robber," Rance repeated, hoping to give the shaken man some pride in his son, even though they had parted with bad feelings. Slocum had never forgiven his youngest son for taking up with what the old man called a Gypsy bitch. The trouble between them caused Dan to run off with the girl and marry her. Tempted to leave it at that, Rance hesitated, but decided he'd best get it all out, because it was bound to come out sooner or later. "That ain't all, sir. The girl, Emma Wise, has a baby, a boy, named Daniel Seaton Slocum, Jr."

It was as if he had been hit with a club. Slocum rocked backward and gasped when he heard the name. It hit him especially hard, since his other son, Brent, and his wife, Raye, had been unable to produce a son, giving birth to three daughters instead. Slocum had been hoping that Dan might be the one to provide him with a grandson, someone to carry on the Slocum name, a tradition that Zachary Slocum held dear and important. Lost in the tragedy of the news for a long few minutes, he suddenly asked, "How do you know this?"

"Well, sir," Rance started reluctantly. "Just the other day, I intercepted a wagon cuttin' across our range. The woman, who calls herself Mrs. Daniel Slocum, and her baby were in that wagon. She was travelin' with one older man and a young man named Perley Gates. They were headin' back to Butcher Bottom."

Slocum hung his head and slowly shook it, overwhelmed by the news. "So the bitch took my grandson back to that hellhole she came from."

"That's not all, sir," Rance continued. "She's done left there. Ace Barnett and Billy Watts saw them on the other side of the Brazos this mornin'. They were headin' south." He went on to repeat the report he had gotten from Ace, that the party now consisted of two wagons and they were driving a small herd of horses.

By the time Slocum heard the whole story, he had worked himself up into a livid rage. The woman, Emma, who was by law his daughter-in-law now, was of no consequence to him. She was no more than a broodmare who had given birth to his grandson. His son, Dan, was the sire of that birthing. That baby had Slocum blood in his veins and no business growing up with the likes of Emma Wise to raise him. Maybe he could save his son by virtue of saving his grandson. After an extended period of eerie silence, Slocum spoke again. "That baby boy has to be brought back to this house. Here's what I want you to do. Get some of the men ready to ride this afternoon. We'll catch that ragtag bunch of Gypsies and take my grandson."

"Are you ridin' with us?" Rance asked.

"You're damn right I'm ridin' with you!" Slocum roared. "Get Ace and Billy, and we'll take Tate Lester. He's a good tracker. That's all we'll need, if you say there ain't anybody ridin' alongside the wagons, just the two families. That'll leave the rest of the men to continue gettin' the cattle ready to drive to market. They can handle it till we get back. It shouldn't take long before we're back here to help."

"Ace said there wasn't anybody else with 'em," Rance replied. "The one fellow on a horse is a wrangler that said his family owned the Triple-G over in East Texas. I talked to him the first day when I saw 'em cuttin' across our range. His name's Perley Gates. I reckon he just came along to drive those horses to wherever they're headed. I don't think he'll give us any trouble."

"Gates, you say?" Slocum asked. "The Triple-G is owned by the Gates family." He paused momentarily to decide if that made any difference in what he planned to do. "No matter," he decided. "I expect we'll

179

just have to tell him he's fell in with a sorry crowd of Gypsies. You go ahead and get some fresh horses saddled and better take enough chuck for a day or two, just in case. We oughta catch those wagons by nightfall, if we can get away from here right away." He walked Rance out to the kitchen door. "And Rance, find Brent and tell him I wanna see him. He'll be in charge here till we get back."

"Yes, sir, I expect he's in the barn," Rance said and went out the door.

CHAPTER 9

Brent Slocum, Zachary's eldest son, was still in the barn, where Rance had seen him last. Rance had to go over the complete report he had just given Boss and received the same reaction of shock, as he had from his father, with one exception. Brent had not felt the bitterness his father had over the issue of Dan falling in love with the girl in Butcher Bottom. He had never told his father, but he had met the girl once when Dan had arranged for Emma to meet him at the river. Dan wanted him to meet her, so he could see she was a good person. Brent had agreed that she was a nice young woman. But he had also tried to convince Dan that their father would never allow him to marry a girl from Butcher Bottom. So, he had not really been surprised when Dan picked up the girl and took the trail north to Kansas Territory after their father had forbidden him to see Emma Wise. He knew nothing about the girl beyond what Dan had told him, but his attitude had always been that, if Dan thought she was the woman he wanted to live with, then maybe he would make it work. "So Papa said we're goin' after 'em?" Brent asked.

"Yup," Rance replied. "Only, he said you were gonna stay here to keep the rest of the men workin' up the herd. We're already later than we had planned to start the drive and I think Boss is gettin' kinda anxious to get started."

Brent smiled. "He's got it in his bones, I reckon, but we've got plenty of time. It's still early summer." He paused, then said, "So Papa's finally got a grandson. I'm tickled to hear it, since he's been hard on me for shootin' blanks three times in a row."

Rance grinned, but made no comment, well aware that Brent's father was blaming him for that. "Well, anyway, Boss said to tell you he wants to see you, and I expect I'd better get ready to go after those two wagons."

After breaking away from the Brazos, Possum turned his horses to a more southerly direction, and upon coming to a small creek approximately five miles farther, decided it to be the best place to rest the horses. Perley guided his little herd of horses downstream while the women prepared some coffee and bacon with Alice and Melva helping. "I declare," Rachael commented, "if you'da told me two days ago that I was gonna be wearin' my fanny out on a wagon seat, I'da told you, like hell I was." She looked at her sister, feeding her baby. "I was just prayin' for a miracle to get my family outta that little farm in Butcher Bottom, till I just gave up on it. And then one came along." Emma smiled back at her, feeling more and more confident that she was doing the right thing with her money. "We'll rustle up something a little bit better when we stop for supper tonight," Rachael said to Possum when he came back from the creek. "I've got a couple of jars of beans soakin', and we'll make some pan biscuits to go with it."

"Coffee and bacon suits me just fine," Possum said. He was more concerned about finding his way to Bison Gap. He was banking heavily on his guess that the little settlement he had once visited on Oak Creek was the same one that had grown into Bison Gap. He seemed to be the only one of the party with concerns of any kind. Since the tensions that rose with the earlier meeting with two men from the Lazy-S were resolved with no real trouble, their spirits were high.

As a result, the simple fare of coffee and bacon seemed like a picnic, especially to Rachael's daughters. They both took the plates their mother handed them and sat down next to Perley, one on each side.

"Is that your real name?" Alice asked, unable to hold her curiosity any longer. "Pearly Gates, that's in the Bible, ain't it?"

Rachael started to correct her, but Perley interrupted her. "That's a fact," he said, "I was named for my grandpa. His name was Perley Gates, but it ain't spelled like the Pearly Gates in the Bible."

"Why is it spelled different?" Melva asked, equally as curious as her older sister.

" 'Cause my great grandpa couldn't spell too good," Perley said.

"Well, I think it's a good name," Alice declared, "and I wanna know how to spell it right." Perley took a stick and spelled his name out on the smooth sand of the creek bank, and Alice sounded out each letter as he wrote it.

"Girls, let the man eat in peace," Rachael finally told them.

"It's all right, ma'am," Perley assured her. "It ain't the first time I've had to explain my name to somebody." *Most of the time it's somebody who's fixing to whip my ass,* he thought. It was nice that this was not one of

184

those occasions. The rest stop remained just that, restful, which was sorely needed by the women especially. The time since leaving Butcher Bottom had been one of seemingly constant threats. But now, it appeared they were past the time when they had to be constantly worried, and the two sisters began to look forward to what might await them in Bison Gap.

After the horses were rested, they moved on, their navigation based mostly on the lay of the land, for they found no roads to guide them. The two wagons rumbled on across the lonely prairie, one of them leaving an odd-looking trail on one side, due to the crooked wheel. Relying on Possum's sense of direction, the rest of the party figured they'd end up in the right place. As the light began to fade away with the setting of the sun, it looked as if they were going to have to make a dry camp for the night. Off to the side, the horse herd plodded along in the growing darkness at the pace set by the slow-moving wagons. Then, when Possum was about to give up and signal Perley, the horses started to increase their pace to a fast trot. Buck increased his pace as well, and Perley knew the horses sensed water ahead. He let them go and guided Buck over next to Emma's wagon. "Drive on a little farther, Possum, there's water up ahead, not too far."

Sure enough, they drove across a low rise in the prairie less than a quarter of a mile ahead and found the horses drinking in the middle of a wide stream. If it had not gotten dark when it did, they would have seen the scruffy trees and bushes outlining the stream from a distance. They pulled the wagons up to sit side by side, as they had done the night before, with space for bedrolls and a fire between them. On this night, however, they planned to sleep there, having no reason to go elsewhere to hide. Perley and Tom managed to find enough firewood to start the fire, although it was scarce among the runty trees. The women began preparing the supper of beans, bacon, and pan biscuits, to be washed down with the usual coffee.

After the horses were taken care of, Perley said, "That ain't gonna be enough wood for that fire. I'm gonna walk downstream a-ways." He pointed to some dark forms against the sky. "Looks like there're some bigger trees down there."

"I'll help!" Alice immediately volunteered.

"Me, too!" Melva sang out.

"Perley don't wanna bother with you two young'uns," their mother said. "You can stay right here and help me and your Aunt Emma." She glanced at her husband and said, "Besides, he might have some other business to attend to." Tom nodded his agreement.

"They won't be any bother," Perley assured her. "I could use the help — two big strong girls like that. I might be able to bring enough wood to build us a cabin."

Rachael shook her head as if doubting his sincerity. "If you're sure you don't mind, but you'd best get at it because we're gonna be eatin' pretty quick now."

"Come on," Perley said, "if you're comin' with me, you'd better be ready to work." He started off downstream, the two little girls skipping along behind him.

"I swear," Rachael commented as she watched them fade into the darkness. "They took to him like ticks take to a dog." She tried to see them a few moments longer. "I didn't think I'd have ever let my two little girls wander off in the darkness with a man I ain't known any longer than I have Perley Gates."

"Well, you don't need to give it a thought," Emma spoke up. "Your girls are in the safest place they can be when they're with Perley. And I ain't known him a helluva long time, myself."

"Somebody's comin'," Billy Watts announced. The others turned, expecting it to be Tate Lester, and watched until his horse approached.

"They made camp up ahead, Boss, about half a mile," Tate reported.

"Well, it's about time we caught up with 'em," Zachary Slocum replied, his patience having long departed. "Is there water there?" Their horses were in need as well.

"Yes, sir, there's water. I got close enough to see a stream. They got the wagons lined up side by side, got a fire built between 'em. They look just as peaceful as you please, don't seem to be worried about anybody botherin' 'em."

"That's good," Slocum said, "now we'll ride down there and pay 'em a little visit." They all climbed on their horses and followed Tate back the way he had come, five men bound to kidnap a mother and her child. Zachary Slocum was interested in taking the baby only, but Margaret had warned him that separating the child from his mother might cause him much more trouble than he wanted. If the baby was as young as they thought, it might still be on

188

his mother's breast, so they were leading one extra horse for Emma.

Back at the camp beside the stream, the women were in the process of serving supper. Tom took his plate and coffee over and sat down beside Possum to eat. Rachael peered into the darkness, looking for Perley and the girls. "I told him to be quick, told him supper was almost ready," she complained.

"Alice and Melva are liable to be drivin' him crazy," Tom commented.

"Don't nobody move, and nobody'll get shot!" The deep, thunderous command came from behind them, causing both Tom and Possum to drop their plates and start to scramble to their feet. "Hold it right there," the voice commanded, "or, by God, I'll cut you down where you stand." Shocked motionless, the four of them stood helpless, awaiting their fate. In a few minutes, they emerged from the dark night, five mounted men, riding abreast, their horses slowly approaching them.

"There ain't nothin' here worth stealin'!" Possum exclaimed. "Go along and let us be!"

"You'd best keep your mouth shut," the rider in the middle of the five roared. "I'm short of patience for all of you Butcher Bottom scum. Just give me what I came for, and I'll leave you be."

"And just what might that be?" Possum asked. His first thought had to be that somehow someone had found out about the large sum of money they carried.

"Which one of you women is Emma Wise?" Slocum demanded.

Emma stepped forward. "I *was* Emma Wise," she volunteered bravely, "but my name is Emma Slocum now."

"The hell it is!" Slocum came back angrily, then sought to control his temper. "I'm Zachary Slocum, and I've come to take my grandson back to the Lazy-S where he belongs."

"My baby belongs with me!" Emma responded defiantly.

"If you insist," Slocum said, his tone a shade calmer than before, remembering what Margaret had told him. "I brought an extra horse for you, if you want to come with us. But make no mistake, the baby comes with me, with or without you."

"You made it very plain to Dan what you think of me," Emma replied, finally with an opportunity to speak her mind to Dan's father. "You disowned him because of me, so I'm not goin' anywhere with you!"

"I reckon you heard the lady," Tom spoke

up for the first time. "Now, turn around and ride outta here the same way you came in."

"Mister, you're talkin' mighty big, considerin' the spot you're in," Ace Barnett could hold his tongue no longer. "You figure you'll take on all five of us all by your lonesome?"

"Shut up, Ace," Bob Rance said. "Boss'll do the talkin'."

"Is that what we come here for, to do some talkin'?" Ace sneered. "What these folks need is a little dose of hot lead, and I'd be tickled to start the party. Hell, there's five of us, you wanna make your move?" His hand on the handle of his .44, he was looking directly at Tom.

"No, he ain't as dumb as you. Take your hand off the gun." All five of the riders looked stunned when the calm voice came from the darkness behind them. Only one moved. With his hand already resting on the handle of his Colt .44, Ace drew the weapon and tried to turn around far enough to fire. The fact that he was sitting on a horse restricted his turn, and when he could see behind him, he found himself peering into the darkness, unable to find a target. Standing at an angle to the line of horses, beside a laurel bush, Perley gave him another chance. "Drop the gun," he ordered, but Ace was already too far committed to back

191

down. With no target visible, he fired wildly in the direction the voice came from. Two shots ripped through the leaves of the laurel, prompting Perley to stop him before he got lucky. When Ace saw the muzzle flash from Perley's gun, it was almost at the same instant the bullet went into the shoulder of his gun hand. The pistol dropped to the ground and Ace howled in pain. The other Lazy-S riders tried to turn to face Perley, but their horses were too close together to turn without bumping into each other. They ended up in a tangle with half of them still facing the camp and half facing in the opposite direction. By the time they got them under control again, Possum and Tom had their guns in hand and Rachael had Tom's shotgun aimed and ready.

"Everybody hold it!" Bob Rance yelled. Other than Perley, he was the only one calm enough to realize the situation was about to blow sky-high. "Let's talk about this before somebody else gets shot!"

Furious after Ace had caused a complete turnaround of their advantage, Slocum was about to draw his handgun when he encountered the sharp gaze of Possum Smith, his pistol aimed at him, as if inviting him to pull the weapon. Slocum thought better of it, realizing that the possibility of his getting shot was very likely under the circumstances. He had no choice but to try a more civil approach. "Rance is right, we need to put the guns away. I only came here to give Miss Wise the opportunity to come to the Lazy-S with my grandson, so he could be raised like a real Slocum." He paused, then added, "Where she'd be a lot better off than ridin' all over the prairie in a broken-down wagon."

"Well, now that sounds a little different from the first way you said it," Possum said, his handgun still in hand. "That sounds like a nice, polite invitation, don't it?" He glanced over at Emma, still standing fiercely defiant. "Whaddaya say to that, Mrs. Slocum?" He grinned when he saw Slocum cringe at the use of the name.

"I say he can go to . . ." she started, then mindful of Possum's polite approach, she started over. "I say thank you, sir, for your kind invitation, but my family and my friends have other plans."

"Well, I reckon that about sums up this little meetin'," Perley said. "Sorry you rode all the way out here for nothin'. We'd invite you to stay for supper, but most of that ended up on the ground when you showed up unannounced."

Slocum was burning inside, but he knew

he had lost all the advantage he had ridden in with. When he looked at Ace, holding his arm painfully against his side, he was tempted to put another bullet in him for triggering the mess. "All right," he finally managed to say. "We'll go. The woman's makin' a mistake. That boy coulda been raised as a Slocum, but we'll go, no need for any more gunplay." He started to turn his horse around but paused again. "Where are you folks headin', anyway."

Quick to answer before someone might say, Possum said, "Mexico, we've got us a nice little ranch south of the Rio Grande." He ignored the puzzled look on Emma's face, hoping none of the Lazy-S men had noticed it. "We've been tryin' to brush up on our Spanish as we go along."

"You best get that wagon wheel fixed or you ain't gonna make it to the Rio Grande," Tate Lester mumbled, as they backed their horses away from the camp. Following Slocum's lead, they went to the creek to water their horses before starting back the way they had come. Rance pulled up beside Slocum and asked, "Whaddaya wanna do now, Boss?"

"I think it's obvious they won that deal," Slocum answered, surprising Rance with his calmness. "We didn't handle that worth a damn. We should have made sure we knew where everybody was, before we let that bastard get in behind us." Thinking about the situation again, he continued. "Then that damn hothead fool, Ace, blew the lid off with that fool move he made, or we mighta still been in control. But not only did he get himself shot, he gave the rest of 'em time to get their guns out." He didn't say anything more for a few minutes, his mind occupied with the time he could afford to spend at this particular time. Reluctantly, he decided. "We need to get the men back to the ranch. We're in the middle of gettin' the cattle ready to drive to market, and I don't want to delay that any more than we already have. Comin' here tonight has already delayed us two more days." He turned to look squarely at his foreman. "This thing with my grandson ain't finished yet, not by a helluva lot, but we'll take care of business first. I don't plan to be the last herd to Dodge City."

"Yes, sir," Rance said, pleased to hear Slocum wasn't going to risk more men and waste more time on his pursuit of the baby. "We've only got the woman's word that it really is Dan's baby."

"There's that possibility," Slocum allowed, "but it won't take long for me to tell if there's Slocum blood in his veins or not. And I aim to find out when you and the men get back from Dodge."

"We goin' down to Mexico to look for 'em?" Rance asked.

"Hell, no," Slocum came back quickly. "They ain't on their way to Mexico. That was just that old man tryin' to throw us off the scent. They'll likely light somewhere between here and the Colorado River, but if they're in Texas, I'll find 'em."

"Whatever you say, Boss. We'll find 'em. That baby will still be too young to know where he belongs, anyway. By then, that woman might be ready to accept the chance to live a better life on the Lazy-S." Satisfied that his boss was doing the sensible thing now, he said, "I reckon I'd better see if Ace is doin' all right with his shoulder."

"That's somethin' else I'm thinkin' about," Slocum said. "We can take care of him back there where we waited for Tate to find their camp." When Rance seemed surprised, he said, "No sense in us ridin' half the night to get back to the ranch. We brought supplies with us. We might as well bed down there and ride home in the mornin'. Then I'll decide whether or not I'm gonna fire that hothead when we get back to the ranch — goin' off half-cocked like that."

Back at the stream, there was great concern for their safety and hasty preparations were being made to defend against an attack surely to come. As soon as Perley walked back to the wagons, he was met by Rachael and Tom. "Where are my girls?" Rachael asked, approaching a panic.

"They're all right," Perley assured them. "We were on our way back when your visitors showed up, so I found a little gully next to the stream and told 'em to wait there till I came back. I'm fixin' to go after 'em right now."

Possum stopped him on his way back. "I'm thinkin' we'd best get set up for another visit tonight. Whaddaya think?" When Perley said that he agreed, Possum asked, "You think we oughta grab our blankets and get away from the wagons, like we did when Cantrell and his boys came after us?"

"That might be a good idea," Perley allowed. "As soon as I get Alice and Melva, I think I'll saddle Buck and go see if I can trail ol' Slocum and his men, maybe get an idea what he intends to do. He didn't sound to me like the kind to give up that easy. So I'll go get the girls, and it wouldn't be a bad idea for everybody to find some cover, in case they do come right back at us."

"I wish to hell they'da waited till after we'd et," Possum said.

"Me, too," Perley said as he started back down the stream. "My belly was already thinkin' about those biscuits."

He hurried along in the dark, dodging bushes and low-hanging tree limbs, hoping he remembered where that little gully was. When he found what he was sure was the right one, it was empty. A moment of panic threatened him when it occurred to him that if Slocum somehow knew the girls were hiding here, what would be better than to take them and force a trade — the two little girls in exchange for the baby? "Are the bad men gone?" Alice asked from behind him, causing him to jump in reaction.

"You like to gave me a heart attack!" Perley exclaimed. "Yes, the bad men have gone for now, but I don't know for how long. I need to get you back somewhere safe till I find out if they are or not. I was thinkin' there was two pesky little girls when I came down here. I reckon I remembered wrong."

Alice laughed. "Melva came with us, she went to hide by that pile of wood you were carryin' back to the fire."

"Why didn't you wait in the gully?" Perley asked.

"Melva had to pee, so I made her get out," she answered.

"Makes sense. Come on, let's get Melva and the wood and get back to camp."

Out of the heavy shadows of the tree-lined stream, he steered Buck back along the same track the two wagons had taken across the open prairie. He figured it most likely to be the same way Slocum had gone. He held the bay gelding to a steady lope over a tree-less expanse of buffalo grass, under a starry moonless sky, while keeping a sharp eye for any riders up ahead of him. After a ride of close to an hour, he came upon what he was looking for, the small glow of a fire lighting the branches of the trees up ahead of him. They had gone into camp, but still to be determined was if it was to rest their horses before returning to attack the wagons. Or had they given up on the idea of taking Emma and her baby?

He rode closer to the glow of the fire before turning Buck to intercept a line of trees. Then he dismounted, tied the horse in the trees, and made his way toward the camp. After a walk of about forty yards, he came to a wide place where the bushes were about waist high. He stopped because he could see the camp from there and knelt down with just part of his head above the bush. He could see they were cooking something on the fire, their horses were unsaddled, which looked as if they had stopped for the night. That didn't make sense because he had been sure they would make another attempt before morning. Unless, he thought, they could overtake the wagons again with no trouble, so they might think it to their advantage to attack them in daylight when they could see that no one could slip in behind them again. That had to be it! So he decided he'd best get back to the others and get them on the way tonight to get as much lead as they could.

"Is that you, Tate?"

Caught in a crouch as he was just starting to get on his feet, he froze in that position, his hand dropping to rest on the handle of his .44. Realizing he had been discovered, he carefully eased the Colt out of his holster and answered with a low grunt, "Uh," not yet sure where the voice had come from.

"Well, you almost got shit on," the voice responded. "I'll go on the other side and find me a bush with them wide leaves. I don't know about you, but I'm glad Boss decided to go on back to the ranch instead of tryin' to take that damn baby."

"Uh," Perley grunted again, then heard the branches of the bush he was hiding in as they were brushed aside when the voice passed behind him. *Cow pie,* Perley thought as he eased away from the bush, and as quietly as he could manage, backed toward the trees where he had left his horse. Just to be sure, he led Buck a couple of dozen yards farther before climbing up into the saddle.

Behind him some twenty minutes later, Billy Watts walked into the light of the fire, still buckling his belt. Seeing Tate Lester sitting by the fire drinking a cup of coffee, he was moved to comment. "Danged if you ain't a fast dumper, Tate."

"What the hell are you talkin' about, Billy?" Tate replied, but Billy only laughed in response.

CHAPTER 10

When Perley returned to the wagons, he called out to identify himself before riding in and was satisfied to find that everyone was very much on alert, ready to defend themselves if necessary. They were relieved to hear him say they didn't have to worry about another visit that night, and maybe not ever. Possum wondered how Perley could feel sure about that, so he asked him why he thought so. Perley said he heard it from one of Slocum's men. Possum kept pressing to find out how that could have been possible without him being caught.

"How did you get close enough to hear what they was sayin?" Possum asked. He couldn't help chuckling when Perley finally related his conversation in the bushes.

"It wasn't that funny at the time," Perley said. After they all enjoyed a chuckle of relief at his expense, he saw fit to warn them. "It doesn't mean that old man won't change his mind and turn around again. So I suggest we keep a watch tonight, and get an early start in the mornin'."

"Amen to that," Possum said. "We was dang lucky tonight. It coulda gone the wrong way right quick."

"I reckon I owe everybody an apology," Emma spoke up, "puttin' everybody in danger because of me and my baby."

Quick to defend her, Possum replied, "No such a thing. It ain't none of your fault that your father-in-law is half crazy."

Rachael and Tom quickly joined in her defense. "Possum's right," Rachael said. "We'll find this little town of Bison Gap and build us a house and farm and dare anyone to attack our family." It was with that spirit that the little two-wagon wagon train set out the next morning, after the three men had taken turns standing watch all night.

It was an uneventful day of travel as the little party held a steady course to the south with Perley taking frequent pauses to keep an eye on their back-trail. His herd of horses soon adapted to the pace of the wagons, and more often than not, plodded along on both sides of the wagons. Before the day was over, Perley occasionally stopped to wait on a hilltop, to watch for a while, knowing he didn't have to keep the horses moving. He finally concluded that Slocum meant it when he said he was not coming after them. That was a relief, but it left him with a stronger feeling of urgency to be done with this endeavor and return to his life. Even though he knew the Triple-G cattle would not average the daily mileage of the slow-moving wagons, he was afraid he would not overtake the herd before they made the Kansas border. He and the herd had been going in opposite directions for too many days, and there were still days ahead of him before he could turn around. *What the hell?* He thought. *They can sure get on without me, and I ain't any too fond of driving cattle, anyway.*

The next three days were much like the first one since leaving the confrontation with Zachary Slocum and his men. The little party followed Possum's sense of direction over land that didn't look prime for farming. It was mostly mile after mile with low rolling hills thick with scrub and small trees. "That mule skinner musta been drunk when he told you that folks was claimin' land down here to farm," Possum said to Tom when he poured himself a cup of coffee. He sat down beside him by the campfire. "We ain't seen any land that looks like it's waitin' for the plow."

"I reckon I can't argue with that," Tom allowed, unable to mask his discouragement. He was about to say more but was interrupted by a call from the darkness near the edge of the trees.

"Hello the camp! Mind if I come in?" Caught by surprise, everybody scrambled for cover behind a wagon. The voice called out again. "Ain't no use for alarm. I'm peaceful and there ain't nobody with me."

"Well, if you're peaceful, come on in," Possum yelled back. "I reckon if you ain't, you'd be shootin' 'stead of hollerin'." To prove he trusted his word, Possum went back by the fire to await their guest. A touch more cautious, Tom and Perley walked back around the other end of the wagon beyond the reach of the light from the fire. With guns ready to use, they watched a solitary little man walk into the camp, leading a severely hobbled saddle horse, with a pack-horse plodding along behind. Perley slipped off into the darkness to see if he really was alone.

"Evenin', folks, my name's Rooster Crabb, and I surely appreciate you invitin' me in." He was plainly in need of help from someone.

Possum sized him up pretty quickly. "I

205

don't suppose you'd say no to a cup of coffee and a biscuit."

"No, sir, I surely wouldn't, and I'd thank you kindly for the offer," Rooster said.

Perley walked back into the firelight. "He's right, there ain't no one but him."

"You do well to check, young feller," Rooster said. "It don't never hurt to give everybody a good lookin'-over around here. I took a good look at your camp before I hollered. I was glad to see women and children."

Possum turned to see Emma come out from behind the wagon with a coffee cup and go to the pot to fill it. When she handed it to their guest, she said, "You're lucky there's a biscuit or two left."

"Thank you kindly, ma'am," the odd little man said and immediately took a gulp of the hot liquid.

"You look like you had a little bad luck," Perley said, looking at the crippled horse.

"That's a fact," Rooster said. "My poor ol' horse went lame about ten miles back, near as I can figure. I had to get off and walk, else I'da had to put her down. She stepped in a hole or somethin', I couldn't see that good, but I heard the bone crack when she did it. I come off over her head and landed on my back."

Perley gently lifted the horse's crippled leg. "She's got a clean break," he said. "the bone's stickin' out. She's in some real pain. You thinkin' about puttin' her down?"

"I thought about it, but I couldn't bring myself to do it," he said. "I've had that horse a long time. I got my pistol out and held it to her head and she looked me in the eye. She knowed what I was fixin' to do, and I just couldn't pull the trigger, so I started walkin'. I hope she'll make it on three legs, then I'd keep her like one of my hounds."

Possum exchanged glances with Perley, both thinking the same thing. Possum expressed the thought. "Ain't none of my business, it's your horse, but if she was mine, I'd put that horse outta her misery." He glanced at Tom then and Tom nodded his agreement. Rooster didn't say anything. He took the biscuit Emma handed him and looked up at her, his sorrowful eyes searching for understanding.

"I think that horse wants you to put it outta its misery," she spoke softly.

"You think so, ma'am?"

"I do."

"Then I reckon I ain't really doin' her no good, makin' her hobble like that on three legs," he gave in. "I just hate to do it." He seemed to be explaining himself to the two little girls who were quietly watching him.

"You want one of us to do it?" Possum asked.

"I'd appreciate it, but I don't wanna see you do it," the simple man replied.

"All right," Possum assured him. "It'll be quick and painless, and she'll be a whole lot better off." Tom pulled Rooster's ragged saddle off the horse and led it away from the camp. A few minutes passed before they heard the shot. Rooster flinched when he heard it. Possum tried to get his mind off his loss right away. "Where are you headin' in the middle of the night, Rooster?"

"Bison Gap," Rooster answered. "I've got a little cabin on Oak Creek, right outside of town." That got everybody's attention right away.

"How far is that from here?" Perley was the first to ask.

" 'Bout five miles," Rooster said and held his cup up when Rachael approached with the coffeepot.

"That's where we're goin'," Emma exclaimed. "We were hopin' we'd get there tomorrow."

"Well, I reckon you made it then," Rooster said, "but it'll be a lot easier on them wagons if you don't cross the creek right here. The road into Bison Gap ain't but about two miles from here," he pointed toward the west, "and there's a bridge across it there."

"Right," Possum spoke up. "I was plannin' on cuttin' over that way to catch that road in the mornin'." He shrugged innocently when Emma cast an accusing eye in his direction. Returning his attention to Rooster, he said, "I reckon this was your lucky day when you ran into us. You lost your ridin' horse, but we're drivin' a herd of horses and five fine saddles you can pick from."

Rooster shook his head sadly. "Ah, mister, I ain't got no money to buy a horse. When I get back to my cabin, I reckon I'll just have to unload my packhorse and throw my saddle on him."

"Is that so?" Possum replied. "I never said nothin' about sellin' you a horse and saddle. Are you too proud to accept a gift from your new friends?" It was after the fact, but he looked at Perley then to see his reaction. Perley might consider the horses his property, since it was he who was responsible for attaining them. It seemed natural to Possum to assume the horses were simply the property of the whole party, thinking they were all in this endeavor together. Perley set his mind at ease when he acknowledged Possum's unspoken question with a positive nod.

Rooster, having been silenced by the unexpected offer, finally recovered his voice. Looking totally confused, he glanced from one stranger's face to the next, halfway anticipating them to bust out laughing at his gullibility. All he saw were smiling faces. "Why, no," he finally spoke. "I shore ain't too proud." Still a little suspicious of the offer, he asked, "Whadda I have to do to get the horse?"

"Well, that's the hard part," Possum replied. "I'll show you which horses you can pick from. Then you're gonna have to look 'em over and decide which one you want."

"Which one I want?" Rooster echoed, now beginning to suspect he was being japed for sure.

Seeing the little man's befuddlement, and thinking Possum was enjoying his confusion a little too much, Perley stepped in. "You don't have to do anything, Rooster. We happened to come by a bunch of extra horses and you happen to need one at the same time. So it doesn't cost us to let you throw a saddle on one of them, so you don't have to walk home."

"Right," Rooster said, thinking he finally understood. "Then I give the horse back to you when we get to Bison Gap."

"No," Perley said. "The horse is yours."

"The horse is mine." Rooster repeated, still suspicious. His eyes darting from one face to the next, waiting for the catch.

Finally weary of the odd little man's suspicions, Rachael blurted out. "For goodness' sakes, Rooster, we're givin' you a horse. Just say thank you and take the darn horse."

At last convinced, the worried look on his face melted to form one of absolute gratitude as he exclaimed, "Thank you, ma'am!"

His exuberance caused her to laugh. "If you really think you should do something in return, why don't you camp here with us tonight? Then you can lead us in to Bison Gap in the mornin', keep us from followin' Possum all the way to the Rio Grande, lookin' for it. You can have a little breakfast with us and you'll be able to see a little better what kinda horse you're pickin' out."

It seemed almost too much for Rooster to handle, such a kind act in a brutal territory. He had to ask, "Who are you folks? You ain't a bunch of angels, are you?"

"Ha!" Emma responded loudly. "Some angels! We ain't even told you our names." She then introduced him to each one by name, ending with, "And this young man's

211

name is Perley Gates."

"I knowed it!" Rooster exclaimed. "I knowed there was an angel in here somewhere." His remark prompted Perley to once again go through the origin of his name. When he had finished, Rooster responded with a simple, "If you say so," still not convinced.

The gift of a horse turned out to be well worth the information they gained about the situation in Bison Gap. Rooster had been there since the first store was built by a man named Ralph Wheeler, whose father, Randolph Wheeler, had a trading post there back when the buffalo were still running through the natural pass between the hilly ranges. Rooster said Oak Creek was a favorite buffalo watering hole back then. "The buffalo were long gone when I built my place," he said. "But Ralph Wheeler built his store right next to the ashes of his papa's tradin' post. The Injuns had burnt it down. Now, there ain't no buffalo here. There ain't no Injuns, neither, but there's a lot more that is there. They've divided up the town in lots, and the land outside town in sections after the railroad ran a line through there. We've got a post office and a sheriff, a saloon, a blacksmith, and Wheeler, he's the mayor, is tryin' to get somebody to build a hotel."

He had the rapt attention of everyone, especially Emma and Possum, who had over twenty-two thousand dollars between them, and were looking for the best use for it. They talked late into the night, the women too excited to see the place they had chosen for their futures to think about sleep. Perley was the only member of the party who was not too excited to sleep, so they lost him to his blanket long before midnight. When the first light of morning crept through the leaves of the trees by the creek, he woke up to feel something warm pressing against his back. It turned out to be four-year-old Melva, so he climbed out of his blanket very carefully and folded it back to cover the sleeping child. He found that he was the only one up, and he was in the process of reviving the fire when Possum staggered out from under the wagon. "You ain't lookin' too bright-eyed and bushy-tailed this mornin'," Perley greeted him.

"I'll be all right as soon as we get some coffee goin'," Possum responded. "That little feller sure seems to know everythin' about Bison Gap you'd wanna know, and a few things you don't."

As if having heard his name, Rooster

Crabb came out from behind the other end of the wagon where he had spread his bedroll. "Mornin," he greeted them cheerfully. "How are you fellers this mornin'?"

The look on his face made Perley think their guest was wondering if the gracious promises of the night just passed might have faded away with the birth of the new day. To set his mind at ease, he said, "Mornin'. We'll get us a pot of coffee workin', and after we've had a cup or two, whaddaya say we go take a look at those horses?" As he suspected, Rooster perked up right away.

While they waited for the women to fix breakfast, Possum and Perley watched Rooster trying out several different horses. They offered to help put all five of their extra saddles on the horses, but Rooster wanted to do that himself. "I wanna make sure the one I pick don't have nothin' against me. I ain't wantin' to fight him every time I try to saddle him."

That was fine by Perley and Possum, so they watched while he hopped about like a kid in a candy store. While they watched, they talked about the evening just past. "Did Rooster say there was any decent land for farmin' near that town?" Perley asked.

"Yep, he said there was," Possum replied, "but there was more talk about the town than any farmland near town." When Perley said he thought Tom and the women wanted a place to farm, Possum said, "So did I, but I swear, they asked more questions about the hotel this feller, Wheeler, wants somebody to build. Especially Emma, she's the one with the cash, but she got Rachael to thinkin' about maybe the two of 'em runnin' a hotel. I told 'em they was crazy, two women tryin' to run a hotel in this wild country. Emma said it wouldn't hurt to talk to Wheeler and see why he's so interested in havin' one. I swear, Perley, I think they're seriously thinkin' about it."

Perley shrugged, amused by Possum's obvious concern about it. "Are they tryin' to get you interested in it, too?"

"Well, they was kinda actin' like it, but hell, I don't know nothin' about runnin' a hotel."

Perley laughed. "I reckon nobody knows much about doin' anything until they try their hand at it. You might be just what that town needs."

"I'll be damned," Possum snorted, causing Perley to chuckle again.

Perley quit joking for a moment and asked, "Has Emma got enough money to do something like that?"

Possum nodded and said, "She's got

enough to get somethin' built. What she's workin' on, I think, is to get Tom and Rachael to help her run it." He paused to reflect on the prospect. "If I was to throw in with her, we could build a damn nice place."

"I swear," Perley blurted. "What did you two do, rob a bank?"

"No, we didn't rob no bank," Possum came back right away. "We didn't do nothin', we was just lucky." Perley stopped him right there, in case he was going to confess how they came by their money. As he told them before, he didn't want to know. The conversation ended then when Rachael called for them to come to breakfast.

Having heard the call to breakfast, too, Rooster rode up on one of the black horses that one of Raymond Butcher's deacons had ridden. "I like this'un best," he said. "All right if I keep him?"

"Yeah, you look good on him," Possum said. "Let's go eat, so we can go see this town of yours."

"Just wait till I ride back and tie this handsome devil at the hitchin' rail in front of The Buffalo Hump," Rooster almost giggled with delight. When Perley asked what The Buffalo Hump was, Rooster said, "It's the saloon. They used to make fun of my old horse, just because she was old." One thing

Perley was sure of about this whole ill-fated journey, it had made one little fellow extremely happy.

"Well, you picked out a good one there," Perley said. "They'll have a hard time findin' something wrong with him."

Although most every member of the party was looking forward to seeing the town of Bison Gap, no one was in a particular hurry on this morning. With Rooster to show them the way and only five or six miles to go, it seemed a relief not to be in a hurry to get rolling. Since they knew they were near a store where they could replace their supplies, the women didn't try to ration the bacon and grits. While they were eating, Emma thought to ask Perley a question. "Looks like you saw us through this journey all the way to Bison Gap. It seems like a month ago when me and Possum met you and your brothers at the crossing on the Red River. You think you might wanna stick around a while now? We've been through a lot together. There might be somethin' in Bison Gap that would catch your interest." She didn't say everything she was thinking, and it had only entered her mind since the constant danger of being overtaken had ended. But of late, she could not help thinking that Perley would make a good husband

217

for some lucky woman.

With no notion of anything like that on her mind, Perley shrugged and replied. "No, I reckon not," he said. "I thought about just leavin' you folks this mornin' and startin' back to where I'm supposed to be. But I think, since it's so close, I'll ride on in to Bison Gap with you just so, if anybody asks me, I can tell 'em I've been there. Come to think of it, I forgot I have to drive the horses in for you, then decide what we're gonna do with 'em. I guess I'd kinda like to see that you find you a spot to get settled in, too. I wanna make sure you've got lumber to build a good strong cage to keep Alice and Melva in." He pretended to try to protect himself when both girls made a big show of trying to hit him.

When all was packed up, hitched up, and saddled, the two-wagon wagon train started out to strike the road into Bison Gap. Riding proudly beside Emma's wagon, Rooster rode his new horse and led his packhorse. The dark roan showed a tendency to break away to return to the small herd Perley was driving behind them, but Rooster had a strong hand and soon settled him down. He wasn't even aware of the circle of buzzards over the creek they had left behind, his only thought being the mental picture of himself riding through town on his new black gelding.

CHAPTER 11

The busy little settlement of Bison Gap was growing up on both sides of Oak Creek with the town's main street running along beside the healthy creek. The first structure when approaching the town from the north was Wheeler's Merchandise, owned by Ralph Wheeler. At an angle across from Wheeler's, on the other side of the creek, a small building housed the sheriff's office and jail. About thirty yards south of the jail was The Buffalo Hump Saloon. These two were the only businesses on the east side of the creek. Everything else was on the west side where the road was built, running right along beside the railroad tracks. Taking Rooster Crabb's advice, Perley drove the horses behind the line of buildings beyond Wheeler's, past the stable at the end of town where there was space to let them graze close to water.

Possum and Tom pulled their wagons

around to the side of Wheeler's stores and they all followed Rooster inside. Ralph Wheeler looked up in surprise when he saw Rooster walk in. "Rooster," Wheeler greeted him cheerfully, "is that gang of people chasing you?"

"These here folks are friends of mine," Rooster replied proudly. "They're thinkin' 'bout lookin' Bison Gap over. Thinkin' maybe they might wanna settle here. I told 'em you're the man they need to talk to."

"Is that a fact?" Wheeler replied. He turned to address Possum and Tom. "Well, Rooster is right, I can certainly tell you what's available. You're looking for land to farm, I suppose."

"I reckon you might say that," Possum said and Tom nodded his agreement.

"Well, you're in luck, there is a lot of acreage that isn't spoken for, depends on what you're looking to raise. I noticed somebody just drove some horses behind the store. Was that some of yours?"

Before Possum could answer, Emma interrupted. "Tell us about that hotel Rooster said you wanted to build. Do you think you've got a need for a hotel here?"

Wheeler paused to give her a condescending smile. "Yes, ma'am, there's no doubt about that. We're gonna need a hotel." He

221

started to get back to the farm acreage, but she interrupted again.

"If you find somebody with the money to build it, I suppose the town would give 'em the land. Is that right?"

He hesitated before answering, not sure now that her questions were trivial. "I suppose the town would, ma'am. Do you know someone with the money to invest?"

"I might at that, dependin' on whether I can believe a hotel would make it here."

Completely confused now, Wheeler looked from Possum to Tom, but saw no inclination on either face to stop the woman's questions. "You're serious, aren't you?" he asked.

"I am," she answered.

"Cora! Come up front and meet these people," he sang out. In a minute or two a small gray-haired woman came from a room in the back, and Wheeler said, "This is my wife, Cora. Cora, say howdy to Mrs. Slocum and Mrs. Parker. They're thinking about joining our community here."

When Perley felt he could leave the horses temporarily without worrying about them, he rode back up the street to Wheeler's, where his party of pilgrims had pulled their wagons around to the side of the store. When he pulled Buck up to the hitching

222

rail in front, he found the whole party inside, including Rooster. They were already in a lively conversation with Ralph Wheeler, who glanced up when Perley walked in. "He's with us," Emma said just as Wheeler was about to apologize for not remembering everybody's name to this point. He turned toward Tom and Possum, but hesitated, not certain.

"I'm Tom Parker," he quickly reminded him. "I'm Rachael's husband and this is Possum Smith — he's a friend of Mrs. Slocum's."

Wheeler nodded, thinking that explained who the young man was who just walked in. "So this is Mr. Slocum?"

"No, sir," Perley said, "Mrs. Slocum is a widow. My name's Perley Gates." He released a tired sigh when he saw the expressions on their faces, expressions he felt he had seen a thousand times before. He hoped he would be spared the necessity to explain.

"I'm sorry, I didn't catch that," Wheeler said.

"Perley Gates," he repeated his name slowly. Wheeler nodded politely, as did his wife, but he did not pursue the novelty of it.

Returning his attention to Possum and Emma, he said, "I've got some plat maps on some property available for homestead-ing I can show you, but I'd like to talk to you some more about the town property set aside for the hotel."

The talk went on for quite some time, until Perley began to get impatient and reminded them that they were going to have to set up camp for the night. "You've got two wagons and a bunch of extra horses that have to be taken care of. And since the hotel ain't been built yet, I reckon we'd best find some other place to situate you folks."

"You can take 'em out to my place," Rooster suggested. "My cabin's kinda small, so there ain't enough room in it for all of ya, but there's plenty of land around it and it's right on Oak Creek. It'd be a good place to set up your camp in my pasture till you decide what you're gonna do."

"That sounds like a good idea to me," Wheeler said. "Rooster is sitting on one of the best parcels of land in this little valley, forty acres, only one mile from town." He glanced at him and raised an eyebrow. "Folks here wonder if he's ever gonna start making it pay off."

"I'll set a plow to it when I'm ready," Rooster replied. "There's just some other things I gotta take care of before I'm ready to try my hand at farmin' again."

"Somebody's gonna come along and buy that whole section one day and put the squeeze on you for that one parcel you're sitting on," Wheeler said.

"They ain't gonna find it easy to do," Rooster responded. "I built my cabin on that land before the post office was built and there weren't no surveyors in this county then."

"But doggone it, Rooster, you shoulda filed claim with the county then, instead of just squatting on it. What you need is for somebody to buy that section who might let you stay in your little cabin," Wheeler suggested, thinking he might give Rooster's new friends something to consider. "That's six hundred acres, not counting that forty acres you're sitting on. Two families, or even one big one, could do a lot on that amount of land." He turned his attention back to the newcomers then. "As mayor of Bison Gap, let me welcome you folks to the best little town in Texas. I'd be glad to show you land available close in to town. That is, depending on what your plans are."

Possum spoke for all of them. "Our plans are to settle these two families down in Bison Gap if we see somethin' that suits 'em. We'll take a good look around, then we'll most likely talk to you again." He

225

turned to Emma. "Is that about right, Emma?"

"I reckon," she answered. "I'd like to hear some more about that hotel, too."

"Good, good," Wheeler said. "Be glad to talk any time you want."

"We'd best get out to Rooster's place and set up our camp now while we've still got plenty of daylight left," Possum said, and stood aside to let the ladies and the children pass out the door.

Wheeler and his wife stood by the door as they walked out, and when Possum followed behind them, Wheeler put his hand on his elbow to cause him to pause. "I mean no disrespect to the Widow Slocum, but is she serious about wanting to know more about the hotel?"

"She is," Possum said.

Rooster Crabb's cabin was just as he had described it, neat and clean, unless a person considered the use of horse dung to decorate his little front porch a bit unattractive. There was also the use of what appeared to be hog excrement smeared on the two windows. Upon seeing the decorations, Rooster was immediately embarrassed and was quick to apologize for the affront to the two ladies. "I'm awful sorry about this, ladies. I reckon I shoulda come out here ahead of you folks to clean this mess up. It's got to where it's happenin' every time I have to leave the place for a couple of days. You folks pick you a spot anywhere you want to park them wagons, and I'll have this cleaned up in a jiffy, if my mop and bucket ain't gone."

Astonished, his new friends could only gape at the obvious mess on his cabin until Possum asked, "So this wasn't the way you left it?"

"Gracious, no," Rooster replied. "This is the doin's of Coy Dawkins and his no-good friends."

"Who's that?" Tom asked.

"Coy rides for Cal Colbert, punchin' cows. Leastways he did till Colbert found out him and two friends of his was cuttin' out a few head of cattle every week or so to sell down in San Angelo. The three of 'em have been hangin' around Bison Gap ever since they was fired last fall."

"What are they devilin' you for?" Perley asked.

Rooster shrugged. "I reckon it's because I was the one that told Cal Colbert they was stealin' from him. So what I think they're up to is, they're tryin' to run me out so they can take over my place, here."

227

"Have you told the sheriff about it?" Tom asked.

"I did, but Sheriff Pylant said ain't nobody seen 'em around here, so there ain't nothin' he could do about it. He said he asked Coy about it and Coy said he didn't know nothin' about it. 'Course, I've seen 'em, but the sheriff says it's my word against Coy's and them other two Coy runs with swear he's tellin' the truth." He shrugged again. "Ben Pylant ain't too anxious to mix it up with the three of 'em, anyway. So I reckon I just have to put up with their shenanigans till maybe they decide to move on." He offered up a helpless expression and said, "I'd best go see if they let my pigs out again. Last time they was here, I had to hunt for 'em — found 'em rootin' down at the creek."

They followed him around behind the cabin to a small shed and a fenced-in hog lot. "Yep," Rooster announced when they rounded the corner of the cabin, "the gate's wide open." He hurried toward it, only to stop suddenly when he reached it. "Oh, Lordy," he sighed and shook his head. Perley stepped up beside him and saw the cause. There lying in the muck of the pigpen was Rooster's sow, a bullet hole in her head. "My sow," Rooster mourned softly. "They shot my sow. She was gettin' ready to have pigs, too."

The act had gone far beyond mere hazing. Rooster's food supply was affected by such an act of cruelty. With the killing of his sow, there could be no more pigs until he bought another one. It was too much for Perley to ignore. "If you were lookin' for Coy and his friends, where do you think you might find 'em?"

"Oh, I know where to find 'em," Rooster replied. "They'll be settin' around in The Buffalo Hump, raisin' hell and drivin' Jimmy McGee crazy."

"Is that a fact?" Perley replied. "I expect they wouldn't get too wild since the sheriff's office is within hollerin' distance from the saloon."

"Ben locks up his office pretty early and don't want nobody botherin' him after dark. So Jimmy just puts up with it till Coy and his friends get tired, or too drunk, to keep at it."

"Seems to me this Coy fellow owes you the price of a new sow," Perley said. "How much does a sow like that cost?"

"I bought Sally there from Luther Boston. I gave him thirty dollars for her. I don't know if that's a good price for one that small or not, but Luther's a fair man."

"I don't know, either," Perley said, "but that fellow oughta pay you for killin' your pig."

Rooster shook his head. "There ain't much sense in takin' this up with Coy, 'cause he ain't likely to give me a penny for his mischief." He shook his head again as he thought about the likely outcome of his demand for payment. "I reckon I'll just have to be grateful him and Whit Berry and Shorty Thompson didn't decide to burn my cabin down 'stead of just smearin' poop all over it. I reckon they still think they'll get the cabin when they run me off."

Perley couldn't help his feeling of sympathy for the simple man, but he reminded himself that he had already lost enough time. He should have been back with his brothers long ago, and it seemed that each new day had caused him to get farther and farther away. He had planned to start back north in the morning, come hell or high water. And now, Rooster presents this cow pie to step in. *This ain't none of my business,* he thought. *I've got business of my own to tend to.* He looked at Sally, the dead hog, then back at Rooster, who just kept slowly shaking his head. It was hard to decide which one looked more pitiful. "All right," he finally decided, "it ain't but a mile back to town. Grab hold of her back legs and help me throw this hog up on your pack-horse. A man buys a sow, he deserves to get the damn sow." Confused by the young stranger's actions, Rooster stood undecided until Perley told him again to grab Sally's hind legs.

They picked up the dead sow and laid it across the horse's back. Perley gave it a firm nudge and judged it heavy enough not to fall off on the short ride to town. "Perley, what the hell are you doin'?" Possum asked when Perley stepped up into the saddle.

"Rooster and I have to make a delivery of a hog he just sold," Perley said. "Give us something to do while you folks are settin' up your camp." He looked back at Rooster and said, "Come on, Rooster." Rooster duti-fully climbed on his new black horse, although he clearly showed little enthusiasm for it.

"Howdy, Fred," Jimmy McGee looked up to see Fred Brooks walk into the saloon. "I was wonderin' if you'd forgot today's Satur-day." He reached down and picked up a clean glass, then poured a shot of whiskey in it. Fred was a hardworking young man. He worked with his father, Horace, who owned the stable. "Where's your pap? He ain't drinkin' today?" It had become sort of a ritual. Father and son usually walked over to The Buffalo Hump every Saturday afternoon for a drink of whiskey before going to the house for supper.

"Papa's messed around and caught himself a little case of the bellyache," Fred replied, "said he better not put any of your whiskey on top of it."

"Hell, a shot of my good corn whiskey woulda most likely cured his bellyache," Jimmy joked.

"That's what I told him," Fred laughed. "He said it was Mama's cookin', but I told him I'm eatin' her cookin' and I ain't got no bellyache." They both laughed at that.

It was enough to catch the attention of the three men sitting at a table against the wall. "Ain't that somethin'?" Coy Dawkins remarked. "Feller came to the saloon without his papa to hold his hand. Whaddaya think about that, Shorty?" Feeling ornery, which was his usual state, he made sure his comments were loud enough to be heard at the bar. Most of the usual crowd had already gone, even though it was early for a Saturday. Jimmy knew the reason was because of the three drifters.

"I don't think a little boy that has to have his daddy hold his hand is man enough to come in a place where men are drinkin' is what I think," Shorty said.

"Maybe you oughta ask him to leave," Coy said. "But do it politely, so you don't hurt his feelin's. He might go get his daddy."

Amused by his two partners' japing, Whit Berry joined in the fun. "You'd best watch what you say, Shorty. He's wearin' a gun."

"Damned if he ain't," Shorty responded and pretended to shake with fear. His performance brought a big laugh from the other two.

Since it was impossible to pretend not to hear, Jimmy moved to the far end of the bar and motioned for Fred to go with him. "Don't pay no attention to those bastards," he said softly. "The one called Shorty is supposed to be a fast gun, so don't pay any mind to what they're sayin'. Matter of fact, it might be the best thing to just walk on outta here."

"Hell, I'm not gonna slink outta here because of some loudmouth drunks," Fred insisted. "I'll stay till I finish my drink, and maybe I'll have another one."

"Fred," Jimmy started, "I just think it's best to . . ."

"Don't worry, Jimmy," Fred interrupted. "I ain't about to face any of 'em in a gunfight. Let 'em talk, I ain't gonna rise to the bait. I've got better sense than that."

Jimmy gave him a shake of his head. "These boys are bad news. Don't give 'em any trouble." He caught a movement at the table out of the corner of his eye and already knew it was too late. "Well, all right, Fred, I know you gotta go. Hope your pa gets better." He said it loud and fast, hoping to push Fred toward the door.

"That's right, Fred," Shorty slurred, "you'd best get your girly ass outta here. I'm sick of lookin' at you." He waited for his response but when there was none, and Fred did not move, he said, "You're wearin' a gun, maybe you're thinkin' about usin' it."

"No, I'm not," Fred stated flatly. "So, I'll finish this drink and then I'll leave." He tossed the whiskey back and put the glass down on the bar. When he turned to leave, he caught the round from Shorty's .44 in the middle of his chest. With one feeble attempt to grasp the bar, he slid to the floor, shot through the heart.

"You see that, Coy?" Shorty blurted. "That old trick, bang the glass on the counter and go for his gun. You saw it! It didn't work this time, by Ned. I caught him. I've seen that move too many times to get took by it."

"I saw it," Coy said, "You were a step ahead of him. Hell, anybody could see what he was up to. You were just too fast for him." He turned to Jimmy. "That's what you saw, too, weren't it?"

"If you say so," Jimmy said, afraid to say otherwise. "Somebody oughta go down to the stable to tell Horace."

"I'll do it," one of the two men who were sitting at another table volunteered as they hurried toward the door. "We're leavin', anyway."

"Drag him outta here!" Coy demanded, pointing a finger at the two men. They immediately turned back and collected Fred's body, then carried it out the door.

Whit stood at the door, watching the two men hurrying across the creek to the stable after leaving the corpse in front of the saloon. He remained there for only a few minutes before he looked back at the table. "Here he comes." He returned to the table to join his friends, where all three were ready to receive their victim's father.

In an effort to prevent more bloodshed, Jimmy went to the door to intercept him. "Horace, don't come in here, you're liable to get shot, too. I'm sorry as I can be. I tried to get Fred to leave. I don't want you to get killed."

Horace pushed on by, far enough to get inside the door. "You damn murderers!" He yelled at the three leering faces.

"You're lookin' to get the same as he got," Coy replied. "And I'll sure be glad to accommodate you. It ain't none of our fault that fool son of yours tried to outdraw Shorty Thompson. He was lookin' for trouble and he got it."

"You lyin' son of a bitch!" Horace blurted, bringing Coy to his feet. "Fred ain't never started no trouble!"

Jimmy grabbed Horace's elbow and dragged him out the door. "Get your boy and get outta here! There ain't no use in you gettin' yourself killed, too. Go on!" He ordered. "Give him a hand, Zeke," he said to one of the two who had taken the news to the stable. To the other one, he said, "Go get the sheriff." A moment later, he was shoved aside when Coy came out the door, his gun in hand. Seeing the two men carrying the body away, he raised the pistol and took aim. Then realizing it would be hard to convince anyone that it was anything other than outright murder, he reconsidered and holstered the weapon.

In a matter of minutes, Sheriff Ben Pylant walked cautiously in the door. Before he said a word, he was greeted by Coy Dawkins. "Come on in, Sheriff! 'Preciate you comin' over to check on things. Don't know what that young feller was thinkin' when he drew on Shorty. He shoulda knowed better, but we was lucky, didn't nobody get hit but him."

"You say Fred pulled on Shorty first?" Pylant asked.

"That's what I say," Coy answered, then cut his eyes over at the bartender. "Jimmy there'll tell you the same. So would anybody else."

Although Jimmy remained silent, Pylant said, "So it was a case of self-defense, was it?"

"Pure and simple," Whit answered him.

Desperately seeking to avoid any confrontation with the dangerous three, Pylant said, "Well, I reckon that's that." Then aware of a look of contempt in the eyes of Jimmy McGee, he said, "I'm surprised to hear Fred Brooks would have done something like that, though."

Whit smiled. "You know how it is, Sheriff, whiskey makes some fellers do crazy things, things they wouldn't do most of the time. He mighta heard Shorty had a reputation and he wanted to be the one who took it from him."

"Well, I just wanted to get it all straight,

so I guess that's all I can do," Pylant said and retreated toward the door.

"Yep," Coy said, "you got it all straight." Pylant went out the door, hearing the chorus of raucous laughter behind him.

CHAPTER 12

Holding Buck to a slow walk, so as not to inspire the pig to slide off Rooster's pack-horse, Perley led them down the street and crossed the little bridge built over Oak Creek in front of The Buffalo Hump Saloon. There were three horses tied at the hitching post in front of the saloon that Rooster recognized as those belonging to the three men they sought. "I ain't so sure this is a smart thing to do," Rooster said. "Maybe I'd best go get the sheriff."

"He'll most likely tell you the same thing you said he always does, that nobody saw these fellows at your hog lot." He stepped down from the saddle. "Do you know which one's Coy's?" he asked, nodding toward the horses.

"That gray on the end," Rooster answered nervously.

"Gimme a hand," Perley said and took hold of the dead hog's front feet. With Per-

239

ley's direction, they laid the pig across Coy's saddle. When he was sure it would stay put, Perley stepped back and commented, "It's pretty near the same color as the horse, ain't it?"

"I reckon," Rooster answered quickly. "Let's get outta here before somebody sees us."

"Whoa!" Perley stopped him. "We've just delivered the pig. We ain't collected payment for it yet."

"You tryin' to get me kilt?" Rooster exclaimed. "Coy's gonna raise enough hell when he finds that pig on his saddle. We'd best get the hell away from here before he comes out and sees it!"

"Maybe not," Perley said, trying to calm him. "He might not realize how much trouble he's causing you by shootin' that pig. This'll give him the chance to do the right thing by you — might make him feel better when he thinks about it." Rooster couldn't think of anything to reply to that, so he reluctantly followed Perley inside.

Perley paused just inside the door of the expansive barroom, unnoticed by the three men standing at the bar, who were absorbed in a contest involving a dartboard on the wall. Instead of throwing darts, however, they were competing with their skinning knives. One of the three, Shorty Thompson, turned to look toward the door when Rooster walked in behind Perley. He grinned and nudged Coy Dawkins, who turned to see what he wanted. "Well, I'll be . . ." Coy started. "Rooster Crabb, I ain't seen you in a couple of days. I thought you'd crawled back in that hole in the ground you came out of." Jimmy McGee, on his knees, his back to the door, scrubbing up a puddle of blood recently left by Fred Brooks, could only groan in dismay upon hearing the remarks.

Taking an easy guess, Perley said, "I reckon you'd be Coy Dawkins." He could see why Rooster was intimidated by the burly dark-featured brute who was standing with his feet spread apart and a wide grin beneath a heavy mustache.

"That's right," Dawkins sneered. "Who the hell are you?"

"My name's Perley Gates. I'm a friend of Rooster's."

"Perley Gates!" Whit Berry exclaimed. "Did he say his name's Perley Gates?"

"That's what it sounded like to me," Coy said. "Perley Gates," he repeated. "You musta been lookin' for the church, Perley. This is the saloon. You'd better get the hell outta here, this is where the devil hangs out." His two partners laughed to show their appreciation for his humor. Encouraged by their chuckles, he continued. "And the devil's kinda particular about who hangs out with him."

Perley said nothing, waiting patiently for the coarse humor to run its course. When the laughter was finally replaced with three puzzled faces staring at him as if wondering why he was still standing there, he spoke again. "Like I said, I'm a friend of Rooster's, and I'm just helpin' him deliver a pig you bought from him."

"What the hell are you talkin' about?" Coy roared. "I never bought no pig from him." Still inclined to amuse his friends, he looked at them and said, "Perley, here, says I bought a sow from Rooster." They guffawed in appreciation of his humor again. "I don't know nothin' about no sow."

"I think it's comin' back to you now," Perley continued. "At least, you remember that it was a sow you bought. You remember shootin' it in the head and leavin' it for Rooster to deliver, right?" By this time, all three were staring openmouthed, wondering if they were looking at a crazy man. "Good," Perley went on. "Now you remember. Well, we brought you your sow. Her name's Sally, and Rooster hopes you enjoy her."

Convinced of his insanity now, Coy blurted. "You're crazy as hell. You say you brought me a hog? I don't see no hog."

"That's a fact, Coy," Shorty echoed. "We don't see no hog."

"She's outside layin' across your saddle," Perley said. "We didn't think you'd want us to bring it in here in the saloon. So you got your pig, all we need now is for you to pay the bill, and that'll be fifty dollars. Then we'll leave and let you get back to playin' with your knives."

"Fifty dollars!" Coy exploded. "For that damn little runty sow? The hell you say!" He stopped then when he realized that he had as much as confessed to having shot Rooster's hog. His outburst was followed by a long period of silence as his two partners waited to see what he was going to say next.

"It might seem a little high," Perley went right on. "But the pig had to be delivered here to you at your headquarters, and there was a little cleanup fee for the decorations on Rooster's cabin. All things considered, it seems like a fair price."

Feeling as if he had been backed into a corner, Coy resorted to what he knew best. He lowered his head like a bull and charged.

With no desire to meet the enraged brute head-on, Perley took a fighting stance and crouched as if to repel the attack, confident that, though smaller, he was faster. Just before the moment of impact, he took a step to the side and stuck out his foot, causing Coy to crash headfirst into the bar. The collision with the counter was so severe that it caused it to rock back an inch or two and knocked over a bottle of whiskey on top that sent the bartender, Jimmy McGee, scrambling to catch it before it hit the floor. The contact between Perley's foot and Coy's ankle was enough to cause Perley to spin around, almost in a complete circle. As he spun, he saw Shorty Thompson reach for the .44 strapped to his leg. With no time to think, Perley's reflexes took command and Shorty's pistol fell to the floor and he dropped to his knee, holding his shoulder. Whit Berry slowly released his pistol, which was halfway out of the holster, and let it sink back down when he saw Perley's .44 aimed at him, waiting.

"Now, there wasn't any cause for that," Perley said to Shorty and Whit, since Coy seemed to have knocked himself out on the bar. He paused to kick Shorty's weapon out of his reach. "Rooster, here, is in the business of raisin' pigs, and when a man shoots his sow, he's out of business. I'm sure Coy never thought about that when he shot that sow. And when he thinks about it, he'll most likely agree that he needs to pay for that pig. So here's what we need to do." He pointed to Whit. "Since your partner's shoulder hurts, you dig into Coy's pockets and see if you can come up with that fifty dollars he owes Rooster." When Whit hesitated, Perley said, "He ain't gonna know who took his money. When his head's clear, you can just tell him I took it." Whit went right to a vest pocket on the shaken man and pulled out a roll of money and offered it to Perley. "It looks like he can afford that pig," Perley said. "You just count off fifty dollars and put the rest back in his pocket. We ain't lookin' to rob anybody. We're just doin' business. His pig's on his saddle, waitin' for him." He took the money from Whit and handed it to Rooster. "It's been interestin' doin' business with you gentlemen, but Rooster is out of the business of sellin' sows, in case you might be thinkin' about buyin' another one. I'm sorry about that bullet in your shoulder. You might wanna have a doctor take a look at it, if there's a doctor around here. Anyway, I hope it heals up real quick." With a nod of his head, he motioned for Rooster to head for the door, and he backed slowly after him. "I hope this will be the end of any business we have to talk about."

Regaining his bravado once it became clear that Perley was not inclined to do further harm, Shorty winced painfully and gasped, "This ain't the end of it, not by a helluva lot."

"I'm right sorry to hear that, I know I feel like we're all square now," Perley said and backed on out the door. Outside, he found Rooster already in the saddle, anxious to get away from the saloon. He was about to step up on his horse but hesitated when he saw someone coming from the sheriff's office, so he paused in case he was coming in response to the shot fired.

"Rooster, I heard a shot," Ben Pylant called out, genuinely sorry to hear yet another gunshot from the saloon. "What's goin' on? Any trouble? Who's this you got with you?"

Perley wasn't sure he was the sheriff until his morning coat fell open far enough to expose the star on his vest. Otherwise, Perley would have taken him for a lawyer, or maybe a deacon of the church. "This, here, is Perley Gates," Rooster said, "and he fired that shot you heard 'cause if he hadn't, he might be layin' dead in the saloon right now."

"Did anybody get shot?" Pylant asked.

"That no-account, Shorty Thompson, got shot in the shoulder 'cause he pulled on Perley, but Perley beat him to the draw." He looked at Perley and grinned. "By a long ways," he added.

Perley could only describe the look on the sheriff's face as worried when he heard Rooster's report. He didn't say anything for a long moment, obviously trying to decide if there was some action required of him. When he finally spoke, it came more in the form of a complaint. "Dag-nab-it, Rooster, I've told you before not to aggravate those three jaspers. It just makes 'em more rowdy."

That was too much for Perley. "Sheriff, I just shot a man in there because he was fixin' to shoot me. Is that what you call rowdy? In most towns I've been in, that's more like attempted murder."

"Just a little tussle that caused Shorty to try to keep that damn gunslinger from killin' Coy Dawkins." The remark came from Whit Berry, who was standing in the doorway now, listening to their conversation. "You oughta see poor Coy, scraped half his forehead off."

247

"He done that to hisself!" Rooster exclaimed.

"Coy's still settin' on the floor in there. Sez his head's broke," Whit said. "And Shorty's got a bullet in his shoulder. Seems to me you oughta be throwin' that gunslinger in jail."

Obviously reluctant to take any action, Pylant hesitated. "Well, as long as nobody got killed, I reckon we can just let it go as long as everybody sez it's over," he finally decreed. He paused again when he noticed the dead pig lying on Coy's saddle. Afraid that might open a new can of worms, he ignored it. And hoping to change the subject, he asked instead, "Rooster, whose horse is that you're settin' on?" Rooster puffed up immediately and informed him that it was his, then went on to tell him about the events that led to his acquiring the horse. When Rooster was finished, Pylant turned his attention once again to Perley. "You gonna be in town a while?"

"Nope," Perley answered. "I'll be on my way back to Lamar County, most likely tomorrow mornin'."

That bit of news seemed to brighten the sheriff's demeanor somewhat. "Well, that's good," he said. "You stayin' out at Rooster's?" Perley said that he was. "Good," Pylant replied, then quickly added, "Not that you ain't welcome in Bison Gap, just good that you ought not have any more run-ins with Coy and his friends. We need to keep the peace in town."

"Hah!" Whit Berry scoffed, still standing at the door listening. He remained there until Perley climbed into the saddle and followed Rooster across the little bridge to the road.

"Where you been?" Shorty wailed at Whit when he came back into the saloon. "I've gotta get some doctorin' quick. My shoulder's still bleedin' and it hurts like hell."

"Quit your bellyachin'," Whit replied. "There ain't no doctor in this town." He turned to Jimmy McGee. "Is there?"

"Nope, no doctor," McGee answered, "but Floyd over at the barbershop can take that bullet outta your shoulder. He's got the instruments to do all kinds of doctorin'. He can most likely do somethin' to make Coy feel better, too." He was hoping the three of them would vacate the saloon, since their presence discouraged his regular customers, all but putting him out of business.

"How 'bout it, big'un?" Whit asked Coy, who was able to sit up now, although he was still on the floor in front of the bar.

"You wanna go see the barber?"

"Hell, no!" Coy blurted. "I don't need no haircut!"

Whit snorted contemptuously. "Maybe not, but you sure got your bell rung."

Feeling like he was coming to his senses again, he demanded, "Where is that slippery cuss? I'm fixin' to rip his head off." He rolled over on his hands and knees, then with great effort, slowly raised his tremendous bulk up from the floor and stood there, steadying himself on the bar.

Whit watched, mindful of the effort it took, and commented, "Well, you're gonna have to move a little faster'n that. He's already gone." When Coy began to rock back and forth from one foot to the other, his head back as if about to howl like a wolf, Whit knew he was about to explode from his frustration. "Take it easy," he said. "I know where to find him. He's stayin' with Rooster. I heard him tell that sarsaparilla-sippin' sheriff he was." That served to calm Coy down to some extent, so Whit went on. "We'll take Shorty to the barbershop to get him fixed up, maybe fix you up, too. Then we'll go call on this gunslinger and finish our business with him tonight. You think you can walk yet?" Whit asked. Coy said he could. "All right, let's take Shorty to the barbershop before he closes."

Outside, when they went to untie their horses, Coy stopped short, forgetting the cause of his head-on collision with the bar. "What the hell . . . ?" he started. "What the hell is that on my saddle?"

"That's that sow you bought," Whit said, chuckling. In spite of his pain, Shorty had to laugh, too, even harder when Coy pulled the pig from his saddle and flung it on the saloon porch, all one hundred and ten pounds of it.

Floyd Jenkins got up from the table where he was enjoying a cup of coffee and went through his shop to see who was banging on his front door. The shade with the *Closed* sign on it was drawn, but he could see the three men on his front step when he peeked around the edge of it. His first impulse was to ignore the knocking, since he was closed for supper. His second thought was, if it was the three men he thought it was, they would probably break the door down. So he opened up. "Evenin', gentlemen. I'm closed for supper. Can you come back in the mornin'?"

"If we come back in the mornin', he's liable to bleed to death," Whit said, pointing to Shorty. "And if that happened, then it'd

251

be your turn to bleed to death. You get what I mean?"

"Yes, sir," Floyd immediately replied. "Of course, I'm always open to care for the sick and wounded. Just bring him right on in here and let him lay down on the table. Let me just set this cup of coffee aside." He looked up at Coy, who was seeming to hover over him. "What about your face?"

"What about my face?" Coy shot back angrily.

"I was just wondering if you wanted that fixed, too." Floyd said in defense.

"Never mind my face. You just dig that bullet outta his shoulder, so we can get the hell outta here."

"Right you are, sir," Floyd replied and immediately started his preparations.

While Floyd began his probe for the bullet, Whit started sniffing the air. "Is the little woman back there in the kitchen, cookin' up supper?"

"I'm not married," Floyd answered. "That's a pot of beans I'm cooking for supper."

"I'll help you get rid of 'em," Whit said and went to the kitchen. "I hope you've got some biscuits or cornbread to go with 'em," he called out on his way through the kitchen door.

"Help yourself," Floyd mumbled under his breath when Whit and Coy went in the kitchen door.

"What did you say?" Shorty asked.

"Nothin'. I was just tellin' myself to heat up some water to clean that wound up before I get started probin' around in it." He went into the kitchen to the pump and pumped some water into a bucket. Coy and Whit were already busy eating his supper. When he placed the water bucket on the stove, he found his pot of beans almost empty. "Well, I see you found the beans without no trouble," he commented.

"There ain't no biscuits," Coy complained.

"I reckon you shoulda et at The Buffalo Hump," Floyd remarked.

"Hell, they'da charged us for it," Whit said. "You make pretty good beans, just didn't make enough of 'em." He stuffed another spoonful into his mouth. "You done with Shorty?"

"Ain't even started yet," Floyd replied. "Gotta get some water hot first."

"Any coffee left in that pot?" Whit asked.

When Perley and Rooster returned from town, they found that the wagons had been moved about thirty yards up the creek from

253

the cabin. Possum and Tom had pulled them up side by side, just as they had when anticipating trouble before. At the same time Shorty Thompson was being treated for his gunshot wound by Floyd Jenkins, a discussion of some concern was going on at Rooster's cabin. The men were doing most of the talking, but the two women were hanging on every word. After hearing what had happened in the saloon, there was great concern that the incident might bring more trouble than the dead sow was worth. Perley admitted that his actions may have brought on a new confrontation with the three saddle tramps, but he was convinced that, if somebody didn't stand up to them, they would soon run roughshod over the whole town. And the sow was important enough to Rooster that compensation was necessary.

"He's right," Possum said. "And it's pretty plain to see that the sheriff ain't wantin' to get in their way. A decent sheriff woulda run those coyotes outta town long before we ever got here. So, bad luck or not, it looks like we're the ones who've got the job of standin' in their way."

"At least you found out what the situation is in Bison Gap," Perley pointed out, "in spite of the rosy picture Mayor Wheeler painted. So, you ain't sunk any money in the town yet, and you can still decide if you wanna stay here or go somewhere else."

"What you say is true," Emma spoke up then, "but I believe Mr. Wheeler is right when he talks about the potential of Bison Gap. And it is an opportunity to get a good foothold on the town while it's still in the growin' stages. If we get rid of these trouble-makers, maybe we can discourage others like them from lightin' here. It wouldn't be long before the town would grow big enough, so three brawlin' saddle tramps couldn't cower the whole town."

They all paid attention while she spoke her mind. When she was finished, Tom Parker was the first to react. "Emma's right. It's likely to be the same wherever we go, so I think we oughta be willin' to fight for our stake in this town. I'm for stayin'." Rachael got up, walked over to stand beside him, and hooked her arm inside his to show her support for her husband.

"Well, I reckon we're stayin'," Possum concluded, "so that settles that. Now, what we've gotta get ready for is a visit from those three coyotes. I'm pretty sure we're gonna have one. They don't sound like the kind to take a whippin' like Perley gave 'em and just walk away."

It did not escape Emma's attention that Possum had said, *we're* staying. She didn't bring it to his attention, but she couldn't help wondering if he was planning to stay here in Bison Gap with them. From the beginning, the two of them had an understanding that he was going to take her to her sister's house, and then he would be on his way to wherever he decided to go. The possibility of his staying with them brought her thoughts back to the proposed hotel. If he decided to go into that project with her, they could build a fine hotel. She had all but made up her mind that she had no desire to return to a farm, but she also knew that she had made a promise to Tom and Rachael. They had given up their farm in Butcher Bottom on the strength of her guarantee that she would buy them a farm somewhere else. Perhaps she could still do that and take on the challenge of the hotel, if Possum went into business with her. Her thoughts were brought back to the present situation when she heard Perley talking about setting up a night watch.

"How do you think they'll try it?" Tom asked. "Just ride in here shootin' like a bunch of wild Injuns?"

"They might at that," Perley answered. "But I think they're more likely to come sneakin' around here in the middle of the night, when they think everybody's gone to bed. I reckon it's me they want, on account of what happened in the saloon. I'm guessin' the fellow I shot is the fastest with a gun, since he beat the other one by a long way, but he's got a slug in his right shoulder, and that's his gun hand. So the most he's gonna be doin' is watchin'.

"You reckon we oughta go see the sheriff," Possum wondered, "see if he wants to help?"

"I'm afraid it's too late for that," Perley replied. "I doubt if he'd get involved, anyway. As long as it ain't in town, he figures it ain't his problem." As soon as he said it, another thought occurred to him. "Instead of gettin' ready for a shoot-out and taking a chance on one of you folks gettin' shot, it'd be more civilized if they were just arrested and put in jail. Bison Gap has got a jail, hasn't it?"

"Sure does," Rooster said. "We got a dandy jail. It don't get used much, but it's got iron cells with locks on the doors and everythin'. But how you gonna get Ben Pylant to go arrest them fellers?"

"I'll arrest 'em, myself," Perley said. "I'm the one that caused all this trouble, so it's my responsibility to keep it away from you folks." Back to Rooster, he asked, "Where does the sheriff live?" Rooster said Pylant had a room in the back of the office. "Good," Perley went on, "so he's there all the time."

"I don't know, Perley . . ." Possum shook his head, not convinced Perley was making sense.

"You and Tom are gonna have to get everybody under cover and get ready for anything that comes in here tonight, in case they get by me," Perley went on. "I expect you'll have better protection in this cabin than you would in the wagons. We've got plenty of guns and ammunition, thanks to the deacons, so give everybody a rifle." He noticed six-year-old Alice staring wide-eyed at him. "Except Alice, give her a big switch." He winked at the child. "If I'm lucky, they'll never get this far. But if they do, they don't know how many of us are here. I'm the only one they've ever seen with Rooster, so I'm thinkin' if they hit this cabin, you'll answer 'em with enough firepower to discourage anything they had in mind."

"Most likely," Possum agreed, "but I don't see why you don't just hole up here, too, and give us another shooter to answer 'em, 'stead of riskin' your neck runnin' around out there in the dark."

"Like I said," Perley replied, "I think it'd

be better if we could throw 'em in jail, maybe let the town have a part in givin' 'em a trial. Maybe that would let them and anybody else know that Bison Gap ain't a welcome place for outlaws and saddle tramps."

Possum shook his head slowly and shrugged. "Me and Tom and Rooster will take care of the women and children. You just be careful you don't get yourself shot."

"I'll be careful," Perley said as he turned and went to his packs to get a coil of rope, then hurried to his horse.

Behind him, standing in the door listening, Rachael turned to Emma and commented. "That's the craziest thing I've ever heard. He'll be lucky if he doesn't get shot."

"Yes," Emma said, "he does a lotta crazy things, but he always seems to land on his feet, just like a cat."

When he reached the big bay gelding, Perley apologized. "Sorry, partner, we've got some more work to do tonight." As was his usual custom, Buck made no comment.

"We shoulda made Shorty come with us," Whit complained as they made their way along the creek in the dark, following a narrow trail that was rutted with gullies and roots. "This damn trail is hard enough to follow in the daytime when you can see what the hell's in front of you." He was beginning to suspect that Shorty wasn't as ailing as he claimed when he begged off to stay in the tent they had been camping in.

"We don't need Shorty," Coy replied, his voice gruff and determined. "He wouldn't be no good to us, anyway, bellyachin' about that shoulder. When we get to Rooster's shack, I'm gonna burn it down, with him in it, if he won't come out. I hope that damn gunslinger is still with him, and this time, we'll shoot him on sight."

They continued, following the narrow path through the trees that grew beside the creek as the darkness seemed to deepen by the minute, with no sign of a cabin until Whit exclaimed. "I see a light through those trees in that patch up ahead. I thought for a minute we'd done passed that little path that leads to it. Maybe we'd best be careful till we get a little closer," Whit cautioned when his horse whinnied, sensing other horses near.

"What for?" Coy scoffed. "Hell, we can't see four feet in front of us. They sure ain't gonna be able to see us in these trees." He was right in assuming that, because neither of them could see the lone man on the bay horse, watching them pass by no more than fifteen yards away. They were still unaware of his presence when Perley guided Buck out on the tiny trail behind them, after he was sure there were only two of them. The big one, called Coy, was following his partner.

Had it been his intention to murder them, it could not have been easier as they plodded along, still unsuspecting in the dark. But he was committed to capturing them if he could. Shooting someone in the back was against his nature at any rate. As they approached a small open spot in the trees, Perley looked up to notice a large oak with a stout limb extending over the trail. It gave him an idea. He took the coil of rope he had gotten from his packs and shook it out to fashion a loop. Born and raised on a cattle ranch, it was a good time to make use of his roping skills. Moving Buck up a little closer to the big man on the gray, Perley started whirling his lasso round and round over his head. When he released it, the loop dropped over Coy's shoulders and was drawn up tight, pinning his arms to his sides. It happened so fast and so suddenly that Coy didn't know what was happening. By the time he did, he was helpless to do anything about it, finding himself in midair when his horse went out from under him.

Well trained in working cattle, Buck knew his job. He planted his feet and braced to keep the rope taut. Perley backed him up, dragging a bellowing Coy, his feet flailing, back along the path for several yards until he reached the big oak. Just as he would a roped steer, Perley jumped from the saddle and ran to secure the big man. "Buck!" he commanded, and the bay stepped forward to allow some slack in the rope. Perley made quick use of it to further secure Coy, who was still in too much shock to fully realize what was happening to him. While he was still in that state, Perley untied the other end of his rope from his saddle horn and threw it over the oak limb. Moving quickly, he retied the rope on the saddle horn and backed the horse, pulling Coy up off the ground. At last aware, the infuriated bully began to shout and struggle as his feet dangled several feet above the ground.

Up ahead in the darkness of the trail, Whit was startled at first by the sudden bellowing behind him, thinking Coy was under attack. His first impulse was to kick his horse hard to escape whatever had ambushed them. Even in a state of panic, he knew it was too dangerous to attempt to gallop, so he pulled his horse back after a short dash and turned him off the path and down the creek bank.

Out of the saddle then, he got down under the bank and waited to defend himself. Perley could not know what action Whit was taking, only that he had not come back to see what had happened to Coy. He took advantage of the time to untie the rope from his saddle horn again and loop it around a small tree trunk, satisfied that Coy's weight was enough to keep the rope too tight around him to permit him to wiggle free.

At this point, Perley decided his best bet was to simply take cover and wait to see what Whit was going to do. It figured that he would eventually come back to look for his partner, since Coy was yelling for him to come back to help him between fits of cursing. So he led Buck down by the side of the creek where he would be out of the way, if any shooting started. Then he went back and sat down beside a tree where he could see his *catch* hanging from the limb, but Coy could not see him. He thought it best to keep him in the dark for the time being.

After another ten minutes or so, Coy gave his vocal cords a rest and swung quietly for a while, thinking he had somehow sprung a trap someone had rigged. Maybe, he thought, Whit would soon realize he wasn't behind him anymore and come back to help him. Farther up the creek, Whit crouched and listened. Then he heard the sound of horse's hooves on the path above him. He could see the vague shape of a horse, half hidden by the brush between them. Very cautiously, he called out. "Coy? What the hell happened back there?" When there was no reply, he cocked his pistol and changed his position, trying to get a better look through the bushes. Then he realized it was Coy's horse, but Coy was not in the saddle. He made his way back up from the creek to the path and peered back the way he had come. He couldn't see more than a few yards. The thought crossed his mind that the oaf of a man had fallen off his horse. "The big dumb cow," he muttered. Since there had been no gunfire, nor sounds of anything like an attack of any kind, he decided it must have been something Coy did to cause him to fall off his horse. Shaking his head, he climbed back on his horse, grabbed the gray's reins, and started back down the path, half expecting to meet Coy on foot. Short of that, he thought he might find him with a broken leg or arm and that was what all the yelling was about.

He started back the way he had come, pausing a few seconds when he came to another path that forked off from the one he was on. Looking down that path, he could see the light again and it occurred to him that it was the path to Rooster's cabin. In his haste before, he had been too intent upon escaping to notice it when he went past. Concerned then that Rooster and his fast-gun friend might have heard Coy yelling, he hurried his horse along, only to yank back on the reins a few yards farther. *What the hell?* he thought when he saw a dark form floating in the air before him. He remained there, uncertain whether he should approach it or not. After another few moments, the form spoke. "Well, are you gonna get me down from here or not?"

"Well, I'll be damned," Whit muttered. "What the hell are you doin' up there?"

"What does it look like I'm doin', you damn fool? Cut me down from here."

Whit stepped down from his horse, since there seemed to be no one else around, he walked up to his dangling partner and stood looking at him as if truly amazed. "How did you get hung up there?"

"I don't know," Coy snapped, his patience for his partner's lack of urgency wearing thin. "Musta run into a snare or somethin'. I don't know why you didn't get caught in it. Quit jawin' and cut me down!"

"Lemme see what it's tied to," Whit said and started to walk around him, but froze when he heard the clicking of a cocking hammer and felt the barrel of the pistol against the back of his neck, at the same time feeling his Colt .44 being lifted out of his holster.

"Now, I want you to sit down, Injun style, with your legs crossed under you," Perley said. "And please don't make any sudden moves. This Colt of mine has a hair trigger, and sometimes it goes off just lookin' at it hard." Whit crossed his feet and sat down. "Now, put your hands behind your back."

Aware now who his captor was, Whit protested. "You ain't got no call to ambush folks ridin' on this trail. We was just mindin' our own business, wasn't botherin' nobody."

"Is that a fact? Where were you goin'?" When Whit gave no answer, pausing to think of one, Perley repeated, "Cross your hands behind your back." Whit reluctantly thrust his hands behind his back. Perley quickly slipped a loop of rope over his wrists and drew it up tight, then bound them securely. Then he pulled Whit over on his side, and with the other end of the short piece of rope, bound his ankles. Once he had his prisoners secure, he tied their horses in the trees, then he stepped back to consider his situation. He had caught them, now what was he going to do with them, one tied hand and foot, the other hanging in a tree? *I need a little help,* he told himself. "You fellows just make yourselves comfortable and I'll be right back."

He went back to the creek to get his horse, then he rode back up the trail until he reached the path to Rooster's cabin. As a precaution against getting shot by someone in the cabin, he stopped a short way down the path and yelled. "Hey, Possum! It's me, Perley! I'm comin' in." When he heard Possum tell him to come on, he rode up to the cabin to meet Possum and Tom and Rooster coming out to meet him. "I'm gonna need some help," Perley said. "I've got a couple of polecats waitin' back there lookin' for a ride to town."

Not at all sure Perley was making sense, Possum asked. "What the hell are you talkin' about? Did you see those jaspers?"

"That's what I'm tryin' to tell you," Perley answered. "I caught 'em, but I'm gonna need help takin' 'em to jail. I think it's best to hitch up one of the wagons and haul 'em into town, instead of lettin' 'em ride their horses. That way, one of you can drive the wagon, and the other one can guard the prisoners. And I'll ride behind and keep an eye on 'em and lead their horses."

Once they understood what he intended, Tom said, "I'll take my wagon. On that rough trail, we don't wanna take a chance on that crazy wheel fallin' offa Emma's wagon." He hurried to hitch up his horses. While they waited for him, Possum tried to get more details about what Perley had done. He was still finding it hard to believe even while he and Tom followed Perley back in the wagon. Not wanting to miss the excitement, Rooster jumped on the back of the wagon as well.

They found Perley's prisoners none the worse for wear, but not too happy with their predicament. Both men had done their best to escape their bonds, but to no avail. Coy had flailed his legs until he was nearly exhausted but had only succeeded to work the ropes up an inch or two. Whit was about ten feet from where Perley had left him, having rolled over and over until he was stopped at the base of the oak that Coy was swinging from. "I told you I wouldn't make you wait too long," Perley greeted them. "I brought help and a wagon to take you to jail."

"Well, I'll be . . ." Rooster started when he saw the two outlaws, in spite of Perley's account of the confrontation when he came back to the cabin. His reaction brought an angry snarl from Coy. "I wonder where the other one is," Rooster said, "the one you shot."

"You better worry about him," Coy warned. "When he finds out about this, you're as good as dead."

Perley checked the rope pinning Coy's arms to his sides and commented. "I can see where you managed to sink a little bit. I bet if I left you here all night, you might get that loop up to your elbows and you could get your hands free." Coy responded with a feeble kick with one foot, whereupon Perley quickly slipped a small loop over the foot, pulled it tight, then wrapped the rope around the other foot, tying his ankles together. The swift move caused the helpless brute to roar his anger in a release of fiery profanity. "Back that wagon under him," Perley said to Tom. When he did, Perley climbed up into the wagon, and using the same technique he had used on Coy's feet, tied his hands behind his back. "All right, Rooster, you can untie that rope around the tree." When Rooster untied it, Coy was left standing in the wagon bed with his feet tied together. Perley gave his shoulder a shove and Coy fell heavily, much like a huge tree that had been sawed down. The major difference was the lack of such extreme profanity when a tree is felled.

With Coy loaded and ready for transport, Perley's attention was turned to Whit, lying next to the base of the tree. Perley paused to stand over him for a moment to consider the distance the bound man had moved while he had left him. "I'm kinda curious," he asked him. "Did you think you could climb that tree with your hands and feet tied like that?"

"You go to hell" was all Whit had to offer, so Perley nodded to Tom, and the two of them picked up Whit and threw him in the wagon with his partner.

Ready to roll, Tom climbed up on the wagon seat and took the reins. Possum sat beside him holding a shotgun and Rooster sat on the tailgate. With Perley on Buck behind them, leading the two horses, they started back down the narrow trail, heading for town.

CHAPTER 13

Sheriff Ben Pylant, having finished his late supper, walked out of his office to stand in the front doorway. He looked across the open space between his office and The Buffalo Hump to see if there was anything going on at the saloon. He was relieved to see that three horses he had come to recognize were not at the hitching rail. He was very much aware of the lack of respect some of the citizens of Bison Gap held for him, especially Henry Lawrence, who owned the saloon. In light of that, he thought it a good time to make another appearance at the saloon to make a show of following up on the incidents that had happened earlier. "Good idea," he decided aloud. "I'll go have myself a drink." He pulled the door shut and walked over to The Buffalo Hump, taking a closer look at the two horses at the hitching rail as he passed by. Satisfied that neither of them was the big gray Coy Dawkins rode, he walked on in the door.

Jimmy McGee looked toward the door when he heard someone come in. "Well, good evenin', Sheriff," he announced grandly. "If you're lookin' for those three drifters who have run off damn near all my business, you're too late. They've done gone."

"I just wanted to make sure everything was peaceful," Pylant replied, as he took a good look at the two men sitting at a table with a bottle. They both looked up when they heard Jimmy announce the sheriff's entrance and, seeing it was Pylant, returned to their conversation. "As long as there's no more problems, I might as well have a drink." Jimmy poured him a shot of whiskey, and Pylant spent some time telling him that it was luck on the part of the three trouble-makers that they had left town. "I was get-tin' ready to crack down on them."

"Is that right?" Jimmy replied, making an effort not to be sarcastic. "They just went someplace else. I don't think they left town for good, so I expect we'll see 'em in here again. You can crack down on 'em then." He was enjoying the sudden pale look on Pylant's face when Dick Hoover, the post-master, came in the door, looking for the sheriff.

"Ben," Hoover exclaimed, "somebody pulled up a wagon at the jail and they're lookin' for you. That fellow who shot one of those three drifters is with 'em."

Pylant looked like he had just swallowed something rancid, but he nevertheless responded. The two men sitting at the table followed him out the door. Curious as well, Jimmy went to the door to watch, unable to leave the saloon unattended.

"Howdy, Ben," Rooster called out cheerfully. "We brought you some visitors for your little hotel, here." He hopped down from the tailgate and walked around to meet the sheriff. "I reckon you remember Perley Gates, and these two fellers is Possum Smith and Tom Parker. They're fixin' to set their roots in Bison Gap and they helped me protect my cabin from them two pig-killers in the wagon."

"He's crazy!" Whit shouted. "Me and Coy was ridin' along the river, lookin' for a place to camp, and that damned hired gun Rooster brought in here ambushed us."

"That's right," Coy charged. "We was ridin' along peaceful as you please and he jumped us in the dark. He's already shot Shorty Thompson."

Pylant was caught between a rock and a harder rock. He didn't want anything to do with the two troublemakers in the back of the wagon. To make matters worse, they were joined then by Henry Lawrence, the owner, and Mayor Ralph Wheeler. A few minutes later, Dick Hoover, the postmaster, arrived on the scene. It was soon apparent that the principal citizens of the town were fed up with the inability of their law-enforcement officer to protect their community from lawless men like Dawkins and his friends.

"I'm sure I speak for everyone in town when I say I'm glad to see you've finally arrested those two hoodlums," the mayor said when he saw the two trussed-up outlaws in the wagon. "After all that has happened in Bison Gap today, topped off by the malicious murder of poor Fred Brooks, we had concluded that we needed a stronger man in the office of the sheriff. But I'm happy to see you've made a move to stop this lawlessness."

Rooster started to correct Wheeler's false impression, but Perley quickly stopped him. "Let the sheriff arrest them," he whispered. "It's better that way." Possum nodded his agreement.

Pylant looked first at Perley, then back at the mayor, not sure if he was about to blunder into the exposure of his lack of action in the whole affair. He went ahead with it, anyway. "Well, there was some uncertainty on my part about the arrest, since we don't have a judge to try criminals. But I reckon we could hold 'em until the Texas Rangers can send somebody to transport 'em to trial."

"That sounds like a good plan to me," Henry Lawrence remarked. "We have to do something about men like these. I got so I was afraid to go into my own saloon."

"Or just hang 'em and save the time," Rooster suggested, standing by the side of the wagon.

"We're hoping to build this town into a law-abiding respectable town, Rooster," Wheeler informed him. "I'm hoping we don't turn the town into one run by vigilantes."

Lying close to the side Rooster was standing by, Coy muttered loud enough for him to hear. "If I get loose from here, I'm gonna remember you said that." Rooster took a step away from the wagon.

Finally, someone thought to wonder about another issue. "What about the other fellow, the one who got shot?" Dick Hoover asked. "Where is he?"

"Yeah, where is he?" Horace Brooks demanded as he joined the impromptu meeting in front of the jail. "He's the son of a bitch who shot my boy." He walked straight up to the wagon and slapped Coy on the back of his head. "Where is he?"

"Kiss my ass," Coy responded and Horace hit him again before Wheeler stepped in.

"I know how you feel, Horace, but that ain't gonna do any good for you or the town," Wheeler said. He turned back to the sheriff. "What we need to do now is put these two in jail, then we can worry about the other one."

"He's gone back to their camp, wherever that is," Floyd Jenkins said as he walked up, after seeing the gathering in front of the jail.

"What the hell happened to you?" Dick Hoover asked when he saw the bruises and cuts all over Floyd's face and neck.

"I took the bullet outta the other fellow's shoulder," Floyd said, "and this is the way they paid me for it, this and eatin' up all my supper."

"Where is that camp?" Wheeler asked.

"Like I said, I don't know, but I expect it's on Oak Creek somewhere, north or south, I don't know. They didn't say. All he said was he wasn't goin' with them to Rooster's, he was goin' back to camp," Floyd said. "Let me go back to my shop and get a razor and I'll work on these two bastards till I find out."

"Let's haul them outta there and carry them into the jail," Wheeler said. When Perley and Possum stepped forward to help, Wheeler said, "I didn't know you fellows were gonna get involved this deep in the town's problem. It's not a very good way to welcome strangers who are interested in settling here. I know Sheriff Pylant was in town all day, so I reckon you fellows and Rooster are the ones who captured these two. I want to thank you for your help."

"We didn't catch 'em," Rooster was quick to correct him. He pointed to Perley. "He done it all by hisself. All me and Possum did was help him haul 'em into town."

"You did?" Wheeler asked. "All by yourself?" He took another look at the two men lying in the wagon, one of them the size of two men. "And you're the fellow that shot the other one in the saloon, right?" Perley declined to answer, preferring not to advertise it. He had an idea that Wheeler might be looking to replace his sheriff. So, instead of responding to the question, Perley stepped forward and took hold of Coy's boots.

Once the two prisoners were carried into the cell room, they were laid on the floor until an inspection was completed to make sure the cells were secure. They had been used only a few times to let drunks sleep it off and never really tested. Possum and Perley helped and found that the jail was more than adequate. Rooster commented to Perley that most folks knew there was nothing wrong with the jail, they just didn't have a sheriff who could fill it. "When are you gonna untie us?" Coy grumbled. "You gonna keep us tied up all night?"

"Keep your shirt on," Henry Lawrence responded. Turning back to Pylant, he continued their discussion on feeding the prisoners. "I suppose we'll still honor our agreement we had when we built this jail. I'll have my cook fix two meals a day for them. Ida ain't gonna like it, but she'll do it."

Overhearing, Coy complained again. "You gotta untie us and get us some supper."

"You've done had your supper, you big hog," Floyd barked at him. "You ate all my beans."

"Yeah, and they weren't worth a crap," Whit offered. "You can't hold us in this damn jail. Neither one of us shot that young feller. The man who shot him has done gone from this place."

"Maybe he pulled the trigger," Henry

Lawrence said, "but you were all part of it. My bartender told me the whole story, how you set that poor boy up so you could kill him. For no damn reason other than to entertain yourselves. Jimmy said Fred never reached for his gun and even told you he wasn't gonna pull it, no matter what. No, you're guilty all right, and you oughta hang for it."

"It sounds to me like we're wastin' time talkin' about sendin' for the Rangers," Horace Brooks said. "Henry's right, we need a hangin'." He looked at Wheeler. "If you're so damn worried about havin' a respectable town, then I say have a trial for this scum. Make up a jury. You can be the judge, then when the jury hears the evidence, we can hang 'em." There was immediate agreement among those gathered there, so much so that Wheeler found it hard to argue and finally gave in. He insisted upon one stipulation, that an effort would be made to find a fair jury. It was decided then that they would interview possible jurors during the following two days, then the trial would be held in The Buffalo Hump. With the prisoners secure, most of the group retired to the saloon to continue the discussion of the events of the day, and possibly Bison Gap's first serious step toward being a legitimate town. Perley, Tom, Possum, and Rooster headed back down the creek.

When the men returned to the cabin, they discovered that the women had been involved in a serious discussion of their own. In short, Emma had made up her mind that she was not interested in playing the role of the typical pioneer woman, cooking and cleaning, working in the fields, and having children. She decided that she had the money and the opportunity in this fledgling town to become part of the business of the town. And while the men were in town, she persuaded Rachael to join her in that endeavor. It was not an easy proposition to sell her sister on, for it was not generally the woman's role to support the family. The woman's place was in the home, subservient to her husband, especially to a girl raised in Butcher Bottom. But Rachael soon became quite excited about the possibility. A major obstacle, however, would most likely come in the form of Rachael's husband. All Tom knew was farming, and it would remain to be seen how he would react to their grand plan.

Eager to hear what had taken place in town, both women and the girls ran out to meet the men when they heard the wagon coming down the path to the cabin. "They put 'em in the jailhouse!" Rooster called out before Tom pulled the wagon to a stop. He and Possum informed the women of the meeting of most of the town's tradespeople in front of the jail while Perley pulled his saddle off his horse. A fresh pot of coffee was deemed necessary before the discussion was finished, which Rachael was happy to prepare. In summary, it was felt that the town had serious intent to grow strong and healthy. In view of that, Emma felt it the opportune time to inform them of her and Rachael's decision to go into the hotel business. The initial reaction was one the women expected.

Tom was the first. "I swear, Rachael, we don't know nothin' about runnin' a hotel."

Emma answered for her sister. "What is there to learn? Folks comin' to town need a place to sleep, so you rent 'em a room. It's as simple as that."

"Is that so?" Tom replied. "Maybe those folks might be hungry. Are you gonna feed 'em?"

"In the hotel dinin' room," Rachael answered. "That's gonna be my job. I'm gonna be runnin' the hotel dinin' room."

"Maybe you forgot you've got a family to take care of," Tom insisted. "And you're gonna be cookin' for folks in the hotel?" He pointed a finger at the baby now in Emma's arms. "What about little Daniel Seaton Slocum, Jr.? How you gonna run a hotel with a baby that ain't even walkin' yet?"

"I expect we're gonna hire us a good cook," Emma answered him. "Rachael's gonna be too busy managing the dinin' room to do the cookin'. And don't you worry, I'll take care of business and my baby, too, if I have to carry Danny around on my back like a papoose."

"Well, what in the world would I be doin'?" Tom asked, frustrated to this point by what he considered an impossible undertaking. "I don't know nothin' about workin' a hotel."

Entertained by the debate, Rooster answered his question. "You'd be settin' on the front porch, countin' the money." Everyone laughed but Tom.

Seeing his obvious concern about his position as head of the family, Rachael said, "You'll be free to do what you want. Nobody's better at workin' the land, and a good hotel is gonna need to supply its own meat and vegetables."

As the discussion continued long after the coffeepot was empty, Possum listened with increasing interest. Finally, after Alice and

Melva had fallen asleep on a pallet Rooster laid in the corner for them, and the grown-ups were beginning to yawn, he made an announcement that injected new interest in the project. "Danged if I don't believe you women mighta come up with a dandy idea." He cocked his head and gave Emma a big smile. "The word might get around fast about a hotel run by two women and one of 'em totin' a baby on her hip. If you're lookin' for a partner, I'll throw my money in it, too." That was enough to almost blow the roof off.

It had been Emma's fervent wish, but she had been convinced that Possum would take his share of the money and return to Dodge City or Wichita. She walked over to him and extended her hand. "Put her there, partner! Won't nothin' stop us now!"

He shook her hand and gave her another wide grin. "I sure as hell don't know nothin' about runnin' a hotel, so you'll be the one makin' the decisions." He saw by her big smile that that was the way she preferred it. "We'll go see Ralph Wheeler in the mornin' and take a look at them plans he's got for the buildin'."

Perley was an interested spectator to the evening's discussion and wasn't surprised when Possum threw in with Emma on the financing. It was a good investment for a man like Possum with a small fortune he didn't know what to do with. The two women were determined, and he, like Possum, felt they could make a successful go of it. If the venture was a success, it could provide a reasonable income for the partners, and that was probably all Possum was looking for.

About two miles south of Bison Gap, past the long turn in the creek, Shorty Thompson sat by the fire before the small tent he and his two partners used for a camp. It was late, well past midnight, and he had expected Coy and Whit back before then. He wouldn't worry for some time yet, however. They might end up burning Rooster's cabin to the ground, if they were unsuccessful in catching Rooster and his gunman friend, Perley Gates, outside and it became a standoff. He hoped they could save the cabin. It would be a helluva lot better camp than this old tent. He had thought about riding with them, but his shoulder was aching something fierce, and he didn't like the idea of lying around somewhere in the dark, waiting for them to come out of the cabin.

He picked up a stick and poked around in the fire with it to keep the wood in the flame, and he thought about Perley Gates, and he wondered if he was really that fast. He tried to re-create the moment in his mind, and it seemed that was all it was, one moment. *When Coy went head-on into that counter, he spun that fellow around. I went for my gun, and he pulled his and shot me before I raised mine to fire.* "Maybe he already had his gun out before he spun around," he muttered. "That musta been it, and he just got off a lucky shot, likely didn't even know he squeezed the trigger." He reached with his left hand to pull his .44 from his holster, then placed it in his right hand, testing the weight of it. It served to tell him that it was going to be some time before his shoulder would be healed to the point where he could use that arm again. "Perley Gates," he announced to the fire before him. "If Coy and Whit don't send you to hell tonight, you ain't seen the last of me."

He awoke with a start, started to push himself up, then exclaimed sharply when the pain in his shoulder reminded him of his wound. "Damn," he muttered, realizing it was approaching daylight. Thinking his partners had just left him to sleep sitting by the fire, he rolled over on one hand and his knees, then holding his wounded arm up, did a three-legged crawl to the tent. "What the hell?" He wondered when he looked in to find no one there. He got to his feet and looked all around him. "Whit! Coy!" He shouted out, but there was no answer. Then he looked toward the creek and saw that their two horses were not there with his. *They didn't make it back!* Not sure what to do, he remained standing in front of the tent for several long moments, looking all around him as if expecting to see them showing up. "It don't mean they were ambushed or shot," he said aloud. "Maybe they shot those two jaspers, and they stayed in the cabin all night. Those bastards, I bet that's what they did." That seemed a reasonable assumption, so he decided that was the case. "They stayed there and divided up everything they found between 'em, no doubt," he snuffed. "Ain't nothin' to do but wait till they get back." Satisfied they would show up when they were ready, he started to make himself some breakfast. "It ain't so easy with just one hand," he mumbled when he sliced some bacon to fry.

Morning faded into afternoon with still no sign of Whit and Coy. And when the afternoon wore on with still no appearance, he finally decided that things had not gone well last night, and they were not coming back. The question now was what to do. With one arm out of business, he needed his partners. There was no telling how long he would have to lay low, waiting for his shoulder to heal. It would help a helluva lot if he knew for sure if he was on his own or not. *In the meantime,* he thought, *I've gotta be able to protect myself.* So, after he had eaten some breakfast, he drew his .44 with his left hand and proceeded to take some target practice on a tree near the creek. "Not bad," he said when he hit the tree somewhere with every shot. Clutching that little bit of confidence, he decided to go see if he could find out what happened to his partners. It took some time to saddle his horse, but after a great deal of frustration, he finally got it done.

His plan was to ride around the town and pick up the Oak Creek trail on the other side and follow it until he got to Rooster Crabb's cabin. As he neared the town, however, his curiosity triggered a notion to take a look, just to see if anything was going on. If, for example, Coy and Whit had somehow managed to get themselves ambushed by Perley Gates, he might see their bodies on display like some towns were inclined to do. It was a practice that was supposed to discourage outlaws from breaking the law, but all it did was encourage outlaws not to get caught. There was plenty of cover in the trees on the south end of town, near the stable, so he figured he could get close enough to see down the street.

There was no one around the front of the stable, so he rode as close as he thought it safe, then dismounted and made his way to within thirty yards of it. As he had figured, he could see the length of the short street, as well as the jail and The Buffalo Hump across the creek. He was relieved when he failed to see two coffins propped up in front of any of the businesses. That didn't mean his friends weren't dead, but it was a positive sign. *Now go to Rooster's cabin,* he thought. About to turn away, he paused when a horse whinnied in the corral next to the stable. He looked at the horse but shifted his gaze to another one when he realized it looked like the gray that Coy rode. If it was Coy's, it would have an eight-inch scar on its left croup where a bullet had grazed it during a chase by a sheriff's posse. He stared at the horse until it finally turned its tail to him and he froze when he saw the scar. *It is Coy's horse!* He then scanned the other horses, looking for Whit's sorrel. It was not as easily distinguished as Coy's, but he saw one that looked an awful lot like

Whit's. *They're in jail,* he realized, knowing there was no other reason their horses would likely be in the corral.

"Well, I can't go sashayin' up to the jail and ask the sheriff if they're in there," he mumbled. He didn't feel like he wanted to try it on his own with just one good arm. He needed Coy and Whit, so he decided to circle back and cross the creek. He could come up behind the jail and look at the back of it to see if he could get to a window and maybe pass a gun in to them. That didn't seem too risky, so he decided to wait until dark to try.

CHAPTER 14

It was an interesting day for the citizens of Bison Gap. The seldom-used jail held two dangerous outlaws awaiting the town's first trial by jury, and jury selection was already underway. In addition to that, rumor had circulated the little settlement that there might be a new hotel in the planning stages. And to make it even more interesting, rumor had it that two women were to be the proprietors. As for Emma and Possum, it was no longer a rumor. After their meeting with the mayor, they approved the plans he had already had drawn up for the building, and Henry Lawrence agreed to contact the carpenter who had built The Buffalo Hump.

The whole affair seemed the most unlikely thing to happen from Perley's perspective. His brothers would find it hard to believe his simple gesture to escort a young widowed mother and a friend of her late husband could turn out to have such significance for the town of Bison Gap. On the other hand, they might not, since a lot of things Perley got involved in turned up the unexpected. Even now, when he had ridden with the man and woman to their destination, he was not free to return to the business of the Triple-G cattle ranch. Ready to bid farewell to Emma and Possum, he was persuaded to wait a couple of days more, this time by Ralph Wheeler and some of the other businessmen of the town. The reason was his role in the capture of Coy Dawkins and Whit Berry, making him a key witness in their trial. Reluctantly, he agreed to stay until the trial was settled. It was far too late to catch up with the cattle drive to Ogallala, anyway, so he wasn't opposed to spending a couple more days in town.

When word got out around the county of the activity stirred up in Bison Gap, the little town saw a small influx of strangers. One such stranger was a tall, lean man named Eli Ballenger who rode into town on a dark Morgan horse in the early afternoon. He tied the Morgan at the hitching rail in front of the saloon and went in to have a drink. "Howdy," Jimmy McGee greeted him when he walked up to the bar. "Whaddle it be?"

291

"I'll have a glass of beer, if you've got it," Ballenger replied, reaching in his vest pocket for a coin.

"Yes, sir," Jimmy said. "I've got beer today, but if business keeps up like it has been, I won't have any tomorrow."

"Is that a fact? Well, I'll drink it today, then," Ballenger said with a chuckle. "Never been to Bison Gap before. Are you sayin' it ain't usually this busy?" Jimmy said that was the case, then proceeded to tell him why there were so many strangers in town. When he had finished, Ballenger asked him to tell him more about the new hotel.

"I hear it's gonna be a first-class hotel," Jimmy said.

"Gonna be run by two women, you say?"

"That's a fact," Jimmy answered. "There's a feller who can tell you all about it." He pointed to Possum, sitting at a side table, having a drink with Horace Brooks. "He came here with the two women who're gonna run it."

"You don't say," Ballenger said. "I think I'll go over and say howdy." He picked up his beer and walked over to the table. When Possum and Horace paused in their conversation and looked at him, he said, "Don't mean to interrupt your discussion, gentlemen. Just thought I'd say howdy." Both men returned his howdy and continued to stare up at him, waiting to see if he had more to say. "I'm just passin' through Bison Gap, lookin' for places to invest in towns that look like they have good growth potential. Of course, I've agreed not to say who I'm workin' for, but the bartender over there told me I've just missed the chance to invest in a new hotel."

"Well, now, that's just too bad, I reckon," Possum said with a great big grin. "I just came from a meetin' with the mayor, and we signed a contract and put some money down. Gonna build a jim-dandy hotel, right across from the saloon."

"Is that a fact?" Ballenger replied. "I'm just a dollar short and a day late, I reckon. Good for you. Looks like a good place for a hotel, but I'll have to tell the folks I'm workin' for that the town will have to grow some before it'll need another hotel. I hope it goes well for you. I 'preciate the information. Let me buy you two gentlemen a drink." He signaled Jimmy to come over to the table. "Give my friends here another of whatever they were drinkin'."

"Why, thank you kindly," Possum said. "Set down and join us."

"Much obliged," Ballenger said and pulled a chair back. "I believe I will." Possum went on to tell him about their plans and assured him that he was just an investor and would have no role at all in the operation of Bison House, as the women had decided to call it. It was a pleasant conversation that ended only when Perley came in, looking for Possum. Possum introduced him to Ballenger, but the friendly stranger took his leave, saying he had a long ride ahead of him.

"Where did he say he was headin'?" Perley asked.

"I don't know," Possum replied. "I don't know if he did say." He looked at Horace but Horace just shrugged.

"Well," Perley started, dismissing the subject of the stranger, "I'm glad I caught both of you here. Horace, I'm gonna leave my horses with you, Buck and my packhorse, till this trial is over, then I'll be on my way. How much will you charge me to sleep in the stall with Buck?"

"Hell, Perley, I won't charge you nothin'." Horace said. "If you're boardin' your horses, that's enough."

"Ain't you comin' back to Rooster's?" Possum asked, genuinely concerned. "Where you gonna eat?"

"Right here," Perley said. "Jimmy said Ida Wicks will feed me."

"Damn, I don't know, Perley," he looked over his shoulder to make sure no one could hear him. "Ida's cookin' might be all right for them two in the jailhouse, but you might be lookin' for a bellyache."

Perley laughed. "I'll risk it. I think it's best that I stay here in town, so they can find me real quick if they want me to testify. Then when it's over, I'll head straight out north. I've been gone a good while, and I'd best get back to the Triple-G."

Possum's face was etched with disappointment. "Damn, Perley," he said. "I've done got used to havin' you around." Then he thought of something else. "What about all them horses you drove down here from Butcher Bottom? You've gotta do somethin' with them."

"I thought about that, and I decided to give 'em to Tom. He's still thinkin' about farmin' or ranchin', and he could use those horses if he decides to raise cattle, or trade 'em if he doesn't."

"I expect Emma's gonna be sorry you ain't comin' back tonight," Possum said. "We just kinda thought you would. I know Alice ain't gonna like it a-tall. She says she's gonna marry you when she gets growed up." They both chuckled at that.

"Tell her I'll come back to see her when

she turns sixteen, if I ain't too feeble to ride."

"I ain't tellin' her no such thing," Possum laughed. "You'd best be careful what you promise that young'un."

Perley and Possum shook hands, and Possum climbed on his horse and headed up the creek to Rooster's cabin while Perley and Horace went down the street, leading Perley's horses.

In spite of Possum's condemnation of Ida Wicks's cooking, Perley enjoyed a heaping plate of what she called Prairie Stew. He found he couldn't identify everything that was in it, but when it was all mixed together, the taste was good. There were biscuits, too, and honey to go with them, so he retired to the stable a contented man. It was already dark when he pushed Buck's rump out of the way so he could get to his blanket in the corner of the stall. The hay his blanket was spread on smelled fresh and sweet. He was sure Horace had made a special effort to fork fresh hay in the stall as soon as he came back from the saloon. A lot had happened in the last couple of days, so he was ready for some sleep. He surrendered to it without a fight when it came, not knowing nor caring about anything else that happened in the town.

While Perley slept, a dark figure moved quickly through the trees behind the jail, stopping every few yards to stop and listen to the sounds of the town closing up for the night. When the only building left with lights on was the saloon, the figure parted from the shadows of the trees to hurry to the back of the jail. His arm still in a sling, Shorty stopped and knelt down on the ground when he found he was about to tap on a glass window. Confused for a moment, he realized then that the sheriff's living quarters were in the rear of the building. *Where the hell are the cells?* He wondered. There were no lamps burning in the windows, so he hoped that meant the sheriff wasn't there or was already in bed. To be safe, he employed his three-legged crawl underneath the glass windows until past them. On his feet again, he peeked in the window and decided the sheriff was not there. There was no telling when he might be back, so now a sense of urgency was added to what he was attempting. He eased his body around the corner then and found what he was looking for. High up the wall, he saw two small, barred windows, probably only a foot or so below the ceiling inside the jail cell. Staring up at the tiny windows, he saw what appeared to be a screen to keep the bugs out. That could be a problem, he thought, depending on how strong the screen was. He paused to take another look around him. Confident there was no one, he tried to attract his partners' attention. "Psst," he sounded, "psst, psst."

Inside the cell, lying on one of two cots in the small enclosure, Coy Dawkins, annoyed, asked, "Is that you makin' that damn noise?"

"What noise?" Whit Berry answered, half asleep. "I ain't makin' no noise."

"Psst, psst, psst."

"There you go again," Coy charged. "Now say you didn't make no noise. You tryin' to make it sound like there's a snake or somethin' in here?"

"Damn it, Coy, I told you I ain't makin' no noise. Maybe there is a snake in here, 'cause I heard it that time, but it sounded like it came from the outside." Both men got up from their cots.

Outside, Shorty was growing impatient with his lack of results, so he whispered loudly, "Coy!"

"It's Shorty!" Whit exclaimed and looked up at the window too high to see out of. "Gimme a lift," he said to Coy, who couldn't see out of the window, either, even at his height. So Coy stooped down to let Whit climb on his shoulders. When he stood up straight, he banged Whit's head on the ceiling, causing him to emit a stifled curse.

"What'd you call me?" Coy demanded.

"It's Shorty!" Whit repeated. "I can't see you, you're standin' too close to the wall." Shorty looked around him again, afraid he might be seen, then took a couple of steps away from the wall. "Now I see you!" Whit exclaimed. "I knew ol' Shorty wouldn't run out on us," he said to Coy. Back to Shorty then, he said, "You gotta get us outta here. They're talkin' about hangin' us."

"How the hell did you get throwed in jail?" Shorty asked. "I thought you was goin' to Rooster's place."

"We run into a little trouble," Whit said, and went on to relate their experiences on the trail to Rooster's.

"That's sorry news all right," Shorty said. "Good thing I didn't go with you. But there ain't much I can do with just one arm, and it bein' my left one. You're gonna have to get yourselves out. I brought you a pistol, if I can figure out how to get it through that window. I can't reach up that high, and it looks like there's a screen on it."

"There is," Whit said. "Lemme see how

stout it is." With just enough space between the bars to force his arm through, he poked at the screen until he managed to loosen it to the point where he could get his arm all the way out. "Throw that pistol up and I'll catch it," he said. For the next fifteen minutes, he attempted to catch the weapon when Shorty tossed it up to the window time after time, but it was not as easily done as they imagined. Shorty was not very accurate using his left arm, and Whit was restrained by the bars in the window from moving his arm to catch it. Coy began to get tired of standing there with Whit on his shoulders and started cursing both of them. He was just about to dump Whit on the floor when Whit finally caught hold of the barrel of the Colt hand gun. "I got it!" Whit exclaimed.

"Not so loud!" Coy cautioned. "You'll wake the sheriff up."

"The sheriff ain't in there," Shorty said.

"He ain't?" Coy replied. "Then why the hell didn't you just come in the door instead of playin' catch with the damn gun?"

" 'Cause I forgot to bring my key for the padlock on the door," Shorty replied sarcastically. "It's up to you and Whit now. You've got the gun, so you can jump him when he comes back. Then we'll have to get your horses outta the stable."

"Right," Coy said. "Wonder where the sheriff is. Reckon when he'll be back?"

"How the hell would I know?" Shorty answered. "Whenever it is, you jump him. I'll be watchin' from those trees back there. Then we'll go to the stable and get the horses and get outta this town."

"I'm gonna find Mr. Perley Gates," Coy said. "I owe him somethin'."

"Get out of jail first," Whit told him. "Then worry about Perley Gates."

Sheriff Ben Pylant prepared to leave the meeting of the town council Mayor Wheeler had called for at his store after closing time. "I reckon I know what I'm supposed to do, so I'm gonna go on back to the jail now — make sure my prisoners are all right." Wheeler had called for the meeting to make sure everyone knew their part in the trial of the two outlaws. That included Dick Hoover, who had reluctantly agreed to represent the two defendants.

"Your job is gonna mostly be to guard the prisoners and make sure they don't get outta hand," Wheeler said. "I reckon we didn't need to tell you that, but I 'preciate you sitting in on the meeting. Have your prisoners ready for trial at two o'clock tomorrow afternoon."

Pylant assured him that he would, making an effort to impress the council with a confident attitude, even though he felt queasy inside with the dread of dealing with the dangerous twosome. He hoped the trial would move swiftly and the hanging would be done. He didn't feel comfortable with the two in his jail, and the worst part was he suspected they knew it. These were the thoughts spinning around his brain as he walked across the bridge over the creek in front of the saloon. He was tempted to stop in before going to his office, maybe have a drink or two, then maybe by the time he went to the jail, Coy and Whit would both be asleep. But a couple of drinks usually made him sleepy, and he didn't plan to sleep that night. In fact, he had decided he would sit up in his office all night with his chair facing the cell-room door, and a rifle and shotgun loaded and laying on the desk before him. He could catch up on his sleep tomorrow night, after Dawkins and Berry were dead. So he passed on by The Buffalo Hump and proceeded to the office with its one lamp burning on his desk.

As a precaution, he stepped up on the stoop very carefully, so as not to make any noise, then paused in front of the door to listen to any sound that might suggest something was wrong. There was none, so he inserted the key in the padlock on the door and unlocked it. He opened the door to find everything just as he had left it two hours before. He released a little sigh of relief and walked on inside, moving as quietly as he possibly could, in order not to awaken his prisoners. His first priority was to take the key to the gun rack from his desk drawer and take the Winchester rifle and a twelve-gauge shotgun from it. He put two shells in the shotgun and checked the rifle to make sure it had a loaded magazine. Then he cranked a cartridge into the chamber and laid it on the desk in front of him. That done, he sat down and faced the cell-room door.

"He's back," Coy whispered when he heard the sound of the rifle cocking on the other side of the door. He and Whit both sat up on their cots.

"All right, lay back down there and start to do some groanin'," Whit said. When Coy was curled up on his cot, Whit called out. "Sheriff!" There was no response from the other side of the door. "Sheriff!" Whit called again and kept calling until Pylant could ignore it no longer.

Finally, the door opened and a lantern was

thrust through it, followed by the sheriff. "What are you yellin' about?" Pylant asked. "Go to sleep."

"I can't sleep, Sheriff," Whit complained. "It's Coy. He's got sick on somethin' and he's keepin' me awake."

"He wasn't makin' any noise," Pylant countered. "I didn't hear him. I didn't hear anything till you started hollerin' for me to come in here."

"It ain't the noise he's makin'," Whit complained. "It's the damn smell. He's gone plum rotten inside, and he's filled that slop bucket up with it."

"I don't smell anything," Pylant insisted.

"You ain't in here with that damn bucket under your nose."

"Well, I ain't about to come in there just to smell it."

"I ain't askin' you to come in here," Whit said, holding his nose. "Just let me put that bucket outside the cell, so I can get back to sleep." At that point, Coy turned over and pretended to vomit into the bucket beside his cot. "There he goes again," Whit complained. "He's about filled it up. All I want is to swap this bucket for that one in that other cell and you won't hear no more outta me tonight."

"I still can't smell anything," Pylant insisted.

"You will if we set it outside this cell," Whit insisted as well. "I ain't tryin' to pull no tricks, Sheriff. I just wanna get some sleep before they hang us tomorrow."

Pylant hesitated, not sure what to do, but Coy sounded pretty sick. Finally, he said, "All right, I'll swap slop buckets with you, but I don't want any funny business from you. I'll have a gun on you the whole time."

"Fair enough," Whit said. "It won't take but a minute, and then you can go back to your office." He walked over beside Coy, and holding his nose again, he reached down and picked up the bucket, making a show of doing it very carefully, as if trying to prevent it from tipping over.

Convinced by Whit's performance that it was a sincere complaint, Pylant went into the other cell and picked up the empty bucket. "All right," he ordered, "I'm gonna put this bucket right outside that cell door. When I unlock it, you put that bucket right beside it and take the empty one back inside your cell. Any wrong move you make, I'm gonna shoot you. You understand?"

"Yes, sir, I do," Whit answered, "and I surely do thank you for your kindness."

Pylant placed the empty bucket just outside the door as he had said he would. Then he drew his pistol and held it on Whit as he turned the key in the lock. He took a quick step to the side, to avoid any possibility that Whit might try to suddenly swing the door wide in an attempt to hit him with it. Whit pushed the door only wide enough to put his bucket beside the empty one. After no show of sudden moves from his prisoner, Pylant bent down to pick up the bucket, his pistol held back to prevent Whit having any chance to reach for it. He paused, puzzled when he looked in the bucket. "I still don't smell anything," he said. Then: "There ain't anything in this bucket."

The words had not fully left his mouth when he felt the cold steel of the gun barrel pressed against the top of his head. "It's gonna be full of your brains if you don't drop that gun right now," Whit promised. Pylant froze, stunned. "Drop it, I said, or I'm gonna put a bullet right through your head." Pylant dropped the gun, quivering in terror. Whit swung the cell door open. "Git in here!" The terrified man did as he was ordered, almost stumbling over one of the buckets in the process. "Set down on that cot and keep your mouth shut if you wanna live."

"Why in the hell didn't you just shoot him

when you had that gun on his head?" Coy asked.

" 'Cause I didn't want nobody in town to hear a gunshot." Whit replied, annoyed that he had to explain it to him. "We're got some work to do before we get outta this town. Go in the office and see if you can find somethin' to tie him up with." He turned back to Pylant, who was cowering on the cot. "Make no mistake about it, Sheriff, if I hear a peep outta you, I'll shoot you deader'n hell."

Coy came back in a few minutes. "I found some rope."

"Good," Whit said. "Let's tie him up." They bound his hands and feet together. "Rip off a piece of that blanket," Whit ordered then, and they used it for a gag. When they were through, they lifted him up to lay on the cot. "Now, you just lay there and take a little nap, and somebody'll most likely come find you in the mornin'. I don't reckon you'll have to get up to pee. Looks like you already done that." His comment got a big laugh from Coy.

Lying helpless on the cot, Ben Pylant was silently giving thanks that his life had been spared, although he was not sure he would ever fully recover from the fright he had experienced mere minutes before. He could hear the two outlaws on the other side of the wall, ransacking his office, looking for their weapons and anything else of use they might find. In a short while, the noise stopped and he assumed they had found what they were looking for. He felt his pulse quicken again as he lay there, listening, hoping the door would not suddenly fly open again and they would return to kill him. Long minutes passed before he finally believed they had gone. He relaxed, only then realizing every muscle in his body was tense. *I don't expect I'll have to resign,* he thought, *I reckon I'm already fired.*

CHAPTER 15

Perley shifted over to sleep on his other side, having been awakened from a sound sleep by Buck's questioning whinny. He lay there for a few minutes, listening, and realized Buck wasn't answering another horse's whinny. He had heard someone moving in the stable, most likely Horace Brooks came back from the house for some reason, something he forgot, maybe. He lay there half-awake for a few moments more, still hearing sounds of movement on the other side of the stalls, more sounds than Horace was likely to be making in the middle of the night. Suddenly alert, it occurred to him that someone might be stealing horses. He sat up, more alert, and it struck him that there was not a lantern lit in the whole stable. Compelled to see what was going on, he got up and strapped on his gun belt, just in case, then slipped out of the stall into the alleyway. The activity was taking place at the other end of the short alleyway, and there was just enough moonlight through the gate at the end for him to see a figure coming out of a stall, leading a horse, followed by a second man. A third figure emerged from the tack room door, carrying a saddle. *This doesn't look right,* Perley thought and moved a little closer.

Too occupied with their endeavor, the three men were unaware they were being watched. Perley hesitated, undecided if he was witnessing a robbery or some bona fide customers who were getting an early start. He wasn't sure what time it was, maybe it was closer to sunup than he thought, and he'd best just go back to his stall before he startled them. He turned back, but before he took a step, he heard one of them say, "Coy, bring me that saddle." Wide awake now, Perley turned back to take another look, thinking that surely he was mistaken. But Coy was not that common a name, so he inched up along the stalls and slipped inside an empty one next to the one the men had just come from. All three men were out in the alleyway now, with two horses. Perley peered over the rail. There was no doubt after a closer look, it was Coy Dawkins and Whit Berry, and the third figure, his arm in a sling, was Shorty

Thompson. And they were mere moments away from riding out of the stable.

Perley pulled his Colt from his holster and eased out of the vacant stall to stand in the alleyway. "You boys are out kinda late, ain'tcha?" The reaction on their part to his calm question was, in effect, the same as if he had thrown a stick of dynamite in their midst. All three were startled. "I wouldn't," Perley warned when Whit started to go for his gun. Whit changed his mind when he saw Perley's .44 already covering them. Shorty, already hampered by the loss of his right arm, made no attempt. Coy, however, reacted as he usually did, and started to charge Perley, but had taken only two steps when Perley shot him in the foot. He howled in pain and dropped to the ground. "All right, now we're gonna get rid of those gun belts. With your left hand, unbuckle your belt and let it drop. That goes for you, too, Coy."

Shorty and Whit did as he instructed, but Coy complained. "You shot me, you son of a bitch. I can't drop my belt, I'm on the ground, I can't get up."

"Help him up," Perley said to Whit and Shorty.

"Perley Gates," Shorty snarled defiantly. "I shoulda known. What if we can't pick him up?"

"Then I reckon I'll have to shoot both of you in the leg, so you don't go runnin' off before I get some help to haul you back to the jail." He cocked his Colt again and aimed it at Whit. "I'll start with you."

"Hold on, damn it!" Whit blurted. "We'll get him up. Come on, Shorty, he's crazy enough to do it." They struggled to lift the oversized brute to stand on one foot, with Whit doing most of the work because of Shorty's bad shoulder.

Once Coy was up and supported by Whit, Perley said, "Now Shorty, you reach over and unbuckle his gun belt, and please don't get any ideas about that gun in his holster. I don't wanna put another bullet in you unless I just have to."

"You son of a bitch," Shorty growled, but he did as he was told.

When Coy's belt fell to the floor of the alleyway, Perley said, "All right, we're gonna walk right on out of the stable now." Seeing no choice but to obey, they reluctantly walked a limping Coy Dawkins out to the front of the stable, where Perley was happy to find Horace Brooks, his shotgun in hand, waiting for them.

"I wasn't sure what was gonna come ridin' outta my stable," Horace exclaimed when he saw Perley marching the three outlaws out. "I heard the shot, so I came runnin', but I wasn't about to go chargin' into that dark stable."

"I don't blame you for that," Perley said. "I could use your help walkin' these jaspers back to the jail. I don't know if the sheriff's all right or not." He looked at Whit. "How 'bout it, are we gonna find the sheriff dead?"

"No, but I wish to hell we'da shot him, seein' as how you folks are set on hangin' us, anyway," Whit answered.

"They ain't had your trial yet," Perley said. "Maybe they won't hang you."

"Shit." Shorty scoffed.

Back to Horace then, Perley said, "Help me walk them over to the jail, and we'll see if the sheriff's all right." For the prisoners' benefit, he gave Horace some further instructions. "Keep that shotgun trained on 'em, and if they try to run, shoot 'em from the belt down. We don't wanna kill 'em, since they might have to hang 'em after the trial."

"If that one with his arm in the sling even thinks about runnin'," Horace said, "I'll sure as hell cut down on him, but I ain't promisin' I'll hit him in the legs. He's the son of a bitch who killed my boy."

"I understand how you feel," Perley said,

"and I don't blame you. But you have to give him credit, he was gone from here, but he was thoughtful enough to come back for the hangin'."

They walked the prisoners back across the creek to the sheriff's office and jail, picking up a few spectators who had been in the saloon and heard the shot. When they got there, Perley told Horace to go inside to see if Ben Pylant was in there. "I'll keep my eye on these three while you see if he's all right."

In a couple of minutes time, Perley heard Horace yell. "I found him! Looks all right, he's tied up, but he's all right. I'm untyin' him. Gimme a minute and you can put 'em back in the cell."

A few minutes more saw Horace and Pylant standing in the front door. The sheriff was holding a rifle. "You can bring 'em on inside," Pylant said. He and Horace took a couple of steps back from the door to give them room.

Perley marched them inside and as they filed past Pylant in the office, standing with his rifle ready, Whit gave him a mocking smile. "Evenin', Sheriff," he said. "I hate to spoil your little nap." Following behind him, Coy laughed, as he hobbled along with his arm on Shorty's shoulder for support.

Pylant was doing his best not to show the

314

humiliation he felt for having been taken so easily by the two escapees. "Take 'em right on through that door to the cell room," he directed. "There ain't but two cots in each cell, so you can put one of 'em in the other cell." He only watched while Perley put them in the cells and Horace locked the doors.

"I'm gonna need some doctorin'," Coy protested. "That son of a bitch shot me in the foot. I need that barbershop feller to look at it."

"What for?" Horace replied. "They're gonna hang you tomorrow. You ain't gonna be worryin' about your foot." He closed the door behind him and tossed the cell door key on Pylant's desk. He looked at the large clock on the wall behind the sheriff's desk. "Dang, it's almost time to get up. I've got my chores to do."

"They got a gun in there, somehow," Pylant blurted, causing Perley and Horace to give him puzzled looks. "I don't know how they got it. There wasn't any way I could have known they had a gun." It was obvious then that he felt the need to excuse himself from blame for letting the prisoners get the jump on him.

"I reckon somebody passed it in to 'em," Perley said. "They have any visitors?" Even as he asked, he couldn't imagine them having had any visitors. When Pylant shook his head, Perley said the obvious. "I reckon the other one, Shorty, passed it through the window."

"Yeah," Pylant said, thoughtfully. "I didn't think about that."

Perley glanced at Horace, who was waiting to catch his eye. There was no need to say anything, they were both thinking the same thing. This incident had hit the sheriff pretty hard. He was losing his grip on a job that most of the town suspected him unable to hold before this test. "You go ahead and get to your chores," Perley said to Horace. "I think there ain't much use for me to go back to the stable now. I think I'll hang around here with the sheriff till breakfast. That all right with you, Sheriff?"

"Yes, that would be all right," Pylant said at once, a strong hint of relief in his tone. "I'll make us a pot of coffee."

"That's a dandy idea," Perley said. "I could sure use a cup."

The news of the attempted jailbreak spread fast and early around the little town. It brought the mayor and the other members of the town council to the jail early as well. Perley was still there when they arrived, and he helped Pylant assure His Honor that the prisoners were still incarcerated, although one of them had a gunshot wound in his foot, the result of a bad decision on his part. Perley was also quick to point out that the trial court now had all three of the outlaws to try, which surely must be looked upon as a bonus. In view of this one close call, it was decided to get the trial started earlier than the two o'clock originally scheduled. When all the facts of the night just passed were assembled, the town council realized that there would have been no trial save for the simple fact that Perley was sleeping in the stable that night. Wheeler and the others knew that Pylant would have to be replaced as sheriff. The problem was there were no other candidates, but Wheeler decided to take that matter up with the others after they got the trial over with. So they assembled the jury that had been selected and began the trial at ten o'clock that morning. As expected, it was a short trial, even though Dick Hoover made a commendable attempt to defend his clients, and it came as no surprise that the verdict was guilty, and the sentence was hanging.

After the trial, three ropes were tied to the limb of a large oak tree beside the creek. The three condemned men were unceremoniously carted out on a wagon to their rendezvous with the noose, and the whole town turned out to watch. That is, except two. Never one to enjoy the spectacle of a public hanging, Perley passed it up to enjoy a cup of coffee and a piece of Ida Wicks's special apple pie. Ida, like Perley, had little interest in watching a hanging.

The responsibility for burying the bodies was passed to Floyd Jenkins. He reluctantly accepted it only after Ralph Wheeler promised he would be paid the same fee they would pay an undertaker, if they had one. Since Floyd was the closest thing the town had to a doctor, it seemed the logical choice. "I'll take on the undertakin' job as long as the town council pays the bill," he told Wheeler, "but my services stop as soon as the merchants stop supportin' the council."

"Fair enough," Wheeler responded. "Now, we need to address the situation with our town marshal. Anybody seen Perley Gates? I didn't see him at the hanging."

"He came in the saloon," Jimmy McGee said. "He walked in just as I was lockin' up to go to the hangin'. I told him Ida was still there and he could come on in, if coffee was all he was lookin' for. He might still be there. I'm goin' back right now to open up again."

"I'll go with you," Wheeler said.

Wheeler found Perley still sitting at a table with Ida Wicks, passing idle conversation, with Ida doing most of the talking about what that part of Texas was like when she was a girl. Perley was glad to see the mayor walk right up to the table and pull a chair back. Ida saw that as a signal to retreat to the kitchen. "I hope you and Ida have been discussing the future of Bison Gap, and what we can do to develop it," Wheeler joked.

Perley laughed and said, "I suspect she's as ignorant on that subject as I am. At least, if she ain't, she never brought it up."

"Your friends, Emma Slocum and Possum Smith, have closed the deal to build the hotel," Wheeler said. "What we need right now is a town marshal."

"You've got a sheriff," Perley said. "Ain't that enough?"

"Ben Pylant came to me right after the hanging and resigned his job," Wheeler said. "I reckon he knew he wasn't up to handling the job, and I respect him for owning up to it. We need a man who can think and react, one who can handle a gun with the best of the outlaws."

"I reckon," Perley said. Aware then of the intense look on Wheeler's face as he gazed, unblinking, into his eyes, Perley responded quickly. "Oh, no, not me," he insisted. "I ain't ever had any hankerin' to be a lawman. I'm fixin' to head back to Lamar County in the mornin'. I'm just waitin' to have a drink with Possum before I go."

"You've already got friends settling here," Wheeler countered, "and you're making new ones every day with the way you handle trouble. We're building a real town here. You could do worse."

"I suppose you're right about that, if I was interested in that line of work. But I ain't. I was born and raised in the cattle business, and I expect that's where I belong. But I 'preciate the offer."

His refusal was obviously sincere, and Wheeler had to accept it as final, but there was still the problem of no law-enforcement officer. "I understand your position," Wheeler said. "So now, I guess I'll just try to ask you for a favor to help the town — and your friends who have just committed to investing here. Possum tells me you've already been gone too long to catch up with that herd of cattle you were driving to market in Ogallala. So, how about taking the marshal's job temporarily for a short time to give me and the council time to find a man?"

Perley didn't know what to say. Wheeler was right in saying he had the time to help the town, but he felt a responsibility to head back home to at least help out there. Perley wished Possum hadn't told Wheeler that he was too late to catch the herd. "How long is a short time?" Perley finally asked.

"Well, I'd say a week or three," Wheeler answered. "I need to have time to contact some people I know who might want to come on this adventure with us."

"I swear, Mr. Mayor, I don't know," Perley hedged. "I ain't so sure I'd make much of a sheriff, not even for a short time." It was his nature to avoid trouble if at all possible, not to go looking for it.

"Let me tell you this," Wheeler continued. "We got along for a long time with Ben Pylant as sheriff, and that's because there's never any real trouble in Bison Gap, so he was all right in the job. When some real trouble finally hit us, Ben wasn't up to it. And that's all we would expect from you, just to be there if real trouble hit us again before we find a permanent lawman. I promise you we won't dally. We'll go to work tomorrow to find us a man. You can move your stuff into the sheriff's office tomorrow.

Ben said he'd move out tonight. Whaddaya say? Will you help us?"

"I reckon," Perley finally said, "but only for a week or two." The mayor seemed so desperate that he didn't have the heart to turn him down.

"Good man!" Wheeler said and extended his hand. "I knew you were made of the right stuff. The town appreciates it." He reached into his coat pocket, pulled out a key, and gave it to Perley. "Here's a key to the lock on the office door. Ben said he'd leave the other one in the desk drawer."

Possum and Rooster walked in the saloon at that moment. Seeing Perley and Wheeler at the table, they hurried over to join them. "I was afraid you mighta decided to go ahead and start out when I didn't see you at the hangin'," Possum said.

"I reckon I'll be stayin' here a little longer'n I thought," Perley said.

"Perley's agreed to take the job of marshal," Wheeler said.

"Temporary marshal," Perley corrected, "only for a week or two."

Possum's face lit up and a broad smile parted his whiskers. "That's a mighty fine idea," he said. "You gonna stay out at Rooster's place with us? Emma will be tickled to hear you ain't gone."

"No, I'll be bunkin' in the sheriff's office. If I'm gonna be playin' sheriff, I reckon I'd best be in town, so they can find me. But I'll sure be seein' Emma and the rest of you while I'm here."

"Well, I'll let you boys have that drink you were talking about," Wheeler said. "I've got to go tell Henry the good news." He hurried off then to tell the owner of the saloon that Perley had agreed to stay for a while. He didn't tell Perley, but he had not given up on persuading him to stay on permanently.

As Wheeler had promised, things were pretty quiet around Bison Gap after their first official hanging. Perley's days were spent doing little more than making himself known to all the merchants and townsfolk. A stranger in town might think him an odd choice for town marshal, or sheriff, as most of the people called him, because of his polite, almost shy, unassuming manner. But they had not seen, nor heard of, the lightning-like reactions that sent a slug into Shorty Thompson's shoulder before that notorious gunman could clear leather — nor the unassisted arrest of all three of the dangerous outlaws.

During the week after the trial, Perley

found time to visit the folks he had jour-
neyed with from Butcher Bottom, much to
Alice and Melva Parker's delight. And
Possum spent about half of his time visiting
the sheriff's office. It was a pleasant time in
the little town, although there was a storm
building on a ranch some eighty miles away.

Margaret Cross opened the door to the
study and held it open for a few moments
before entering. "Come on in, Margaret,"
Zachary Slocum said. "I ain't asleep, I just
closed my eyes for a few minutes."
   She entered the room then and walked
over beside his chair to pick up his empty
coffee cup on the table beside it. "Zachary,"
she called him by his first name when there
were only the two of them. In the presence
of others, family included, she always called
him Mr. Slocum. "Zachary," she repeated
to make sure he really was alert. "Mr. Eli
Ballenger has asked to see you. Shall I show
him in?"
   Slocum was immediately receptive. "Yes,
yes," he answered, "show him in." He got
up from the chair and turned to receive
him. In less than a minute, Margaret returned. A tall thin man followed her. At the
door, she stepped aside and held the door
open. When he walked into the room, she

left, closing the door behind her. "Mr. Ballenger," Slocum greeted him, "I hope you have something worthwhile to report. It's been a week."

"I found them," Ballenger stated. "They're in a little town called Bison Gap, about eighty miles south of here."

"Have they still got the baby with them?"

"Yes, sir, the baby is with them," Ballenger said. "And he's strong and healthy, according to what one of the men who brought the woman down there from Butcher Bottom told me the other day."

"How long are they gonna be there in Bison Gap? Did he tell you that?" Slocum was anxious to know, afraid they would disappear again.

"They aren't going anywhere," Ballenger stated calmly. "The woman and the man they called Possum are planning to build a hotel in the town."

"A hotel?" Slocum exclaimed. "Where the hell did that Gypsy bitch get enough money to build a hotel? Are you sure about that?"

"I'm sure," Ballenger stated positively.

"Damn," Slocum swore as he tried to digest that unlikely possibility. "She didn't have a penny to her name when my son married her. Where did she get that kind of money? Damn Gypsy, she most likely stole it."

"I don't know," Ballenger answered, not really interested in where the woman got her money. Impatient to get on with his report, he told Slocum that Emma was living with her sister and her sister's husband, as well as the man he identified as Possum, in a couple of tents about a mile from town.

"What about the other one who was with 'em, the one called Perley Gates?"

"When I left Bison Gap, Perley Gates was planning to leave the next day to return to Lamar County, so I suppose he's out of the picture. I can't tell you that for sure, because I didn't see him leave. From what I was able to learn, however, he had no interest in their business beyond seeing them safely to Bison Gap."

"Are you gonna be ready to go after my grandson?" Slocum asked, then remembering Margaret's advice, added, "And the bitch that gave him birth?"

"As I told you in the beginning," Ballenger reminded him, "I can find them for you. I've finished the job you paid me for." He read the anxiety in Slocum's eyes. His men were driving cattle up into Kansas and would not likely be back for a month or more. "I can put you in touch with two men who will pick up the woman and her child for you. They can come here first. You can make your deal with them, and for another one hundred dollars, I'll take them to the target and make sure they go after the right woman and child." He could see that Slocum was not entirely comfortable with his proposition, so he offered another plan. "Or, if you'd rather, I can handle it all for you, so you don't have to actually meet the two men."

"I prefer they didn't come here to the ranch," Slocum said. "I prefer to only have contact with you and you handle the arrangements with them."

"Fair enough, I'll take care of everything.

"What will they cost me?" Slocum asked.

"Four hundred," Ballenger answered, "Two hundred each. If you decide you want to use them, I'll ride back to Bison Gap and wait there for them to arrive. You'll never see them. I'll arrange to meet them at a place where they can be handed over, then I'll deliver the woman and child here to the Lazy-S." When Slocum hesitated before committing, Ballenger said, "I've used them before. They're very dependable."

"All right," Slocum said. "Go ahead and put it in action. I'll pay you what I paid you for finding the child." He went to the small safe built into the corner of a huge desk and counted out five hundred dollars. "There's one more thing. I'm sending my son with you to meet your two men before you get back here with the woman and my grandson. I want you to come here first, then the two of you can ride down to Comanche Run. He'll make sure everything is like you say. Then you and he can bring the baby and his mother back here. Do you have any problem with that?"

"No, sir," Ballenger said, "I have no problem with that. That's as good a plan as any. It'll be as you wish. You're paying for it."

"Do you know where Comanche Run is?" Slocum asked. "Not everybody does."

"As a matter of fact, I do," Ballenger said when he took the money. "It's about fifteen miles south of here, right on your southern boundary, if I remember correctly."

"That's right," Slocum replied, a sly smile on his face. He didn't think Ballenger would know.

"I'll be in Bison Gap day after tomorrow," Ballenger said then. "I would estimate the delivery of your package within a week. Good day to you, sir." He passed Margaret on his way to the front door and tipped his hat but said nothing.

"He found them?" She asked when she went into the study, and he nodded in reply. "Are you ready to eat something now?" Again, he nodded. "I'll set it on the table." She turned around and went to the kitchen without further comment. She knew that he was well aware of her negative feelings on the matter of abducting his late son's child.

CHAPTER 16

Eli Ballenger walked into The Buffalo Hump shortly after noon and went to the bar. Jimmy McGee remembered him from his recent visit to Bison Gap and gave him a friendly greeting. "Back to see us, are you? The last time you were here, we had us a big trial goin' on. I'm afraid there ain't nothin' that excitin' goin' on now. What brings you back to town?"

"Jimmy, right?" Ballenger asked. When Jimmy said that was correct, Ballenger continued. "I'm on my way back north, so I thought I'd stop by your friendly little town for a drink and maybe find something to eat. If I remember right, this is the only place in town that serves food, right?"

"That's a fact," Jimmy replied, "but it won't be much longer. We're fixin' to have us a hotel with a regular dinin' room."

"I heard something about that the last time I was here." He turned to look over

330

the few customers in the saloon. His gaze stopped at a table where two men were seated, eating. "That looks like the fellow I was talking to when I was here — said he was one of the investors in the hotel."

"That's right," Jimmy said. "That's Possum Smith. Nobody would ever think Possum had that kind of money, would they?"

"Who's the fellow sitting with him?"

"That's Perley Gates. He's the sheriff now," Jimmy answered.

"You don't say," Ballenger replied. "I remember seeing him now, but he was talking about leaving the day I was here. And now, he's the sheriff? What changed his mind?" He wondered if he might be anyone to worry about.

"He ain't really changed his mind. He's just takin' the job temporarily till the mayor and his council can find somebody permanent."

"Is that a fact?" Ballenger replied. "I think I'll go over and say howdy to Possum. How about telling your cook to fix me a plate?" He tossed his drink back and walked over to the table.

Possum looked up when Ballenger approached the table. "Well, howdy, stranger, I didn't think we'd see you back in town. You thinkin' about buildin' another hotel to give us some competition?"

Ballenger laughed. "I don't think so. Like I told you last time, the town ain't big enough for two hotels yet. I just stopped in to eat some dinner." He returned Perley's nod of greeting. "That grub doesn't look that bad. I've ordered a plate, myself."

"That right?" Possum responded. "Well, set down and join me and Perley."

"Why, thank you, I believe I will, if you don't mind." He pulled a chair back and sat down. He paused while Ida Wicks set a plate down for him and asked if he wanted coffee. When she left to fetch it, he continued. "Jimmy says you're the sheriff now," he said to Perley.

"Just for a little while," Perley said, "till they hire one."

"Have you had a lot of experience in law enforcement?" Ballenger asked.

"No, not a bit," Perley answered, "never had the slightest interest in it." When Ballenger asked how he happened to take the job, Perley answered, " 'Cause there wasn't anybody else. They just don't want the sheriff's office or the jail to be vacant while they're lookin' to fill the position. There ain't any real need for one right now, except for drunks who need a place to sleep it off."

Satisfied that Perley would not likely be in

the way of his two kidnappers, Ballenger felt even better about the planned abduction. He even permitted himself to enjoy his dinner with the two of them. Perley Gates seemed to be as harmless as his name implied. A more friendly and mild-mannered young man Ballenger couldn't imagine. He certainly seemed to offer no threat to his plans. He sat, listening to Possum's predictions of a successful hotel operation, and his admiration for the gumption of the two women who proposed to pull it off, until he heard the sound of the one o'clock train rounding the bend of Oak Creek. "Well, I suppose I'd best be getting along," he said. "I certainly enjoyed the conversation." He stopped at the bar to pay Jimmy, then went out the door.

Leaving the saloon, he walked across the little bridge to the main street and across that to the railroad depot as the train screeched to a stop. No passengers got off, but the doors of a stock car back near the caboose opened and a ramp was hauled out. As Ballenger watched, Joe Cutter and Waylon Logan each led a horse off the train. Seeing him waiting there, they led the horses directly to him. "Eli," Waylon acknowledged. "Understand you've got a little work for us."

"That's right, something that should be easy to handle."

"Your telegram said you needed us to do some trappin'," Joe said. "What kinda trappin' you thinkin' about?"

"I just need you to pick up a woman with a little baby and carry her north of here to a place called Comanche Run. Shouldn't take you more'n two, two and a half days' ride from here."

"That sounds easy enough," Waylon said. "What's the hard part?" He knew there was one, else Ballenger wouldn't have called for them.

"The hard part is she doesn't want to go," Ballenger said.

"Kidnappin'," Logan responded. "Damned if we ain't done about everything there is to break the law, but we ain't never done no kidnappin'. Have we, Joe?" Cutter answered with no more than an indifferent snort. "Where we gotta go to get this woman? Has she got a husband?"

"We don't know nothin' about takin' care of a baby," Cutter protested before Ballenger could answer.

"You don't have to take care of the baby, idiot," Ballenger said. "The woman will be taking care of her baby. She doesn't have a husband, and she's staying in a tent a mile

334

from town. There's an old codger that has a cabin where she's camped and there's only one man you'll have to worry about. He's the only young man there. He's married to the woman's sister. There's one other one," he said, thinking of Possum. "He's an old coot, too, and it looked to me like he's staying in the cabin with the other one. If you do it right, you should be able to go in and take the woman without the two in the cabin even knowing it."

"If it's gonna be that easy, why didn't you do it, yourself 'stead of sendin' for us?" Joe Cutter asked.

"Because that's not my line of work," Ballenger answered. "That's your line of work. If you don't want to do it, I'll give it to somebody else."

"We're here, ain't we?" Waylon said. "How much is it worth to ya?"

"Hundred-fifty apiece," Ballenger said, "I brought you a packhorse and another horse for her to ride. In addition to the money, you can keep the horses when you deliver the package."

Logan looked at Cutter and he nodded. "All right," Logan said. "We'll do it. What's so special about this woman?" Ballenger told them where she was to be taken and why. After they heard the full explanation,

335

Logan commented. "Damn, Joe, it almost sounds like we're doin' a righteous thing here, takin' a grandbaby home to his grandpa." They both laughed at the thought. "From the way you tell it," he said to Ballenger, "it sounds to me like Grandpa don't really give a damn about the woman. He just wants the baby."

"That's about the size of it," Ballenger said, "but Slocum is hiring you to bring him the woman, so that's part of the deal. He needs her to take care of the baby. Now, do we understand each other?" They both nodded. "Good. We'll go down to the stable and get my horses."

"How 'bout we get us a drink and maybe somethin' to eat," Joe Cutter said. "We've been shut up in that stock car with the horses for four hours. I was about ready to start eatin' some of that hay."

"I think it'll be better for you if we just go pick up my horses and get outta town," Ballenger replied. "There's no sense in you two being seen around town. The less people who see you, the less people can give the sheriff your description. In a little town like this, folks would remember two strangers. There's a bottle of whiskey and some beef jerky in with the other supplies I brought for you. Wait till we get outta town and you can eat that. Maybe that'll hold you till we make camp. Then you can scout their camp out while it's still daylight."

Cutter and Logan sat on their horses near the trees behind the stable while Ballenger got the horses from Horace Brooks. "You leavin' town again?" Horace asked when Ballenger walked in. "When you left 'em here this mornin', I thought you might be with us a while."

"I've got business to attend to up north of here," Ballenger answered, "and I wanted to have my horses fed and watered." He threw his saddle back on the Morgan gelding and Horace picked up the other saddle that had been on one of the other two horses Ballenger brought in that morning. "Much obliged," Ballenger said when Horace threw the saddle on the horse.

"What happened to the fellow who was settin' this saddle?" Horace asked, thinking it looked like a cheap little saddle.

Ballenger smiled at him and said, "There wasn't anybody sitting in it. It came with the horse, so I figured I might as well keep it." He climbed on the Morgan.

Horace handed him the reins to the other two horses. "Might be a little easier to rig you up a lead rope for 'em," Horace said.

"I won't be ridin' far today," Ballenger

said, "so I'll just hold the reins. He nudged the Morgan with his heels before Horace thought of any more questions.

Cutter and Logan waited until he rode up to them and handed off the reins of the two spare horses. Then he led them around the back of the town before coming back to the creek again. A short ride brought them to the path that led to Rooster's cabin. He pulled up there to describe the layout of the two wagons and the two tents, telling them that after they ate something he would take them to a better spot where they could see for themselves. All his careful preparation caused Waylon Logan to comment. "If there ain't nobody to worry about but the husband of that woman's sister, seems to me we oughta just ride in there and take the woman — shoot the husband if he gets in the way — and be done with it."

His comment was met with an impatient look from Ballenger. "You boys haven't gone Comanche on me, have you? I contacted you two because you've always done good work for me in the past. This job has to be done quickly and with as little fuss as possible. Like I told you, you should be able to go in, pick up the woman, and get out without anybody getting killed. If you look the place over good and go in at the right time, you stand a better chance of getting away before anybody has a chance to get on your trail. The town's a mile away, and they've only got a temporary sheriff there now. I doubt he'll even involve himself in a chase."

"We get the message," Joe Cutter was quick to reassure him. "Nobody'll get shot unless it comes down to them or us."

"All right, then," Ballenger said. "Let's go up the creek a little way. I picked out a good spot for you to camp where we can leave the extra horses while we scout their camp."

"Ain't you gonna camp with us?" Waylon asked.

"No," Ballenger replied. "After I show you their camp, it'll be up to you to get the package and deliver it to the meeting place. I'll go on to Comanche Run to make sure your money is there when you get there. You know where Comanche Run is, right?"

"Sure," Waylon answered. "Don't everybody?"

"Well, Brent Slocum and I will meet you there. "That's Slocum's son. He'll ride on to the ranch headquarters with me to take the package from there. Do you know where Comanche Run is?" Ballenger asked him again, to be sure.

"Hell, yeah," Waylon replied. "I shot a

man there one time. He tried to welch on some money he owed me. You sure old man Zachary Slocum will pay us the hundred and fifty you said?"

"I'm sure," Ballenger said. "I'll get it from him. And if he tries to come up short on it, I promise you, I'll pay you myself." That seemed to satisfy him. The truth of the matter was Ballenger got the money from Slocum before he rode down to Bison Gap. The amount he quoted for their part, and Slocum paid him, was four hundred dollars, or two hundred each, but Ballenger took a cut of the money to offset the cost of the supplies and extra horses. When all three seemed satisfied with the deal, Ballenger led them to the spot he had picked out for their camp.

"I swear," Cutter saw fit to comment, as he looked through the packs Ballenger brought, "you weren't lyin' when you said you had enough supplies to get us there." He held up a can for Logan to see. "Lookee here, we even got some canned milk to feed the baby. I reckon that's in case his mama's gone dry." He returned his attention to the packs again. "There's plenty of jerky and side meat for the grown-ups, too." He paused when he pulled out a large gunnysack. "What's this sack for?"

"Just for whatever you might need it for," Ballenger replied, "in case you want to throw a sack over her head to make it easier to carry her."

Joe chuckled and shook his head. "I gotta hand it to ya, Ballenger, you don't never leave anythin' undone."

After the two had eaten something and had a couple of drinks from the bottle he supplied, Ballenger led them to a long, low ridge about three quarters of a mile away. The ridge was thick with oak trees and offered an ideal place to scout the two small tents pitched in a pasture on either side of a pair of wagons. It was exactly as Ballenger had described, and now they were able to see the actual setup and their best access to the tents. Ballenger pointed out the tent that housed the woman and her baby. "There's two wagons between that tent and the one where the sister and her husband and their two children are staying. Make sure you remember which one your target is in. It's smaller than the other one." He had no sooner said that than Emma came out of the tent with some items of clothing and proceeded to drop them in a washtub. "That's your target," Ballenger said.

Thinking they had seen all they needed to

see at this time, they looked then to deter-
mine which way they would run after abducting the woman and her baby. "Right
straight out the end of that pasture and
through the gap in the ridge," Waylon suggested. "We'd be headed in the direction we
need to be in." Joe agreed, and with that
settled, they were satisfied that they had
seen all they needed to see. Waylon pointed
his forefinger like a gun and fired an imagi-
nary shot at the tent.

"How you take the woman is up to you,"
Ballenger reminded them, "but be damn
sure you don't hurt that baby, or none of us
will get paid." He was immediately assured
that they understood. "When are you going
to do it?" Ballenger asked.

"Well, it'll be easiest to wait till they've all
gone to bed," Cutter said. "Ain't that what
you think, Waylon?" Logan agreed.

"All right, then," Ballenger said. "I'll see
you at Comanche Run with your money."
That was all he said. He climbed on his
horse and started down the back of the
ridge, heading north, leaving them to return
to the camp they had set up.

"Sure thing, Perley," John Payne, the blacksmith said, "I'll shoe ol' Buck, here, and
take him back to the stable for you."

"I'd appreciate it, John," Perley said. "He might not need 'em real bad yet, but I noticed they're gettin' that way. So I figured I'd go ahead and get it done while I've got the chance." With that off his mind, he walked back to the sheriff's office, surprised to see Possum's horse tied up at the rail. He walked in to find his friend sitting at his chair with his feet propped on the desk.

"You always leave the door unlocked?" Possum greeted him. "There ain't no tellin' who you might find waitin' for you."

"I hadn't really thought about that till right now," Perley joked. "But I can see now that it was a foolish thing to do. You're right, I'm liable to find any kind of riffraff in here." They both had a chuckle, then he asked, "What are you still doin' in town? I thought you went back out to Rooster's after we ate."

"I did," Possum replied. "But I had to come back again to bring Emma into town. She said she was supposed to meet with Ralph Wheeler for something to do with the hotel, and I'm supposed to be there, too."

"That so? Where's Emma now?"

"She's lookin' at some material for a dress at Wheeler's store. Cora invited me and Emma to supper, but I told her I had to meet you and I'd be back for the meetin' right after supper." He made a face and said, "I don't feel easy settin' at the mayor's table to eat. I'm liable to do somethin' to embarrass Emma."

Perley had to laugh. "Well, if you're hungry, I reckon we can take a chance on Ida Wicks's food again."

"Might be better'n what Emma gets at Cora Wheeler's table," Possum said. "And Ida don't care if you pick your teeth at the table."

"I expect we'd best go on over to the saloon if you're supposed to go back for a meetin' with the mayor," Perley suggested. "Don't want you to miss anything important."

"It wouldn't make much difference if I was there or not, except for my signature. Emma knows what she wants, and she makes all the decisions. I swear, Perley, that is one smart woman. She gets right into it with the mayor and them carpenters he lined up to build the hotel. And I don't know nothin' about it." He paused to think about that, then added, "And I don't wanna know anything about it."

He and Possum were the only two customers in The Buffalo Hump who had come for supper, but there were a half-dozen more to keep Jimmy McGee busy pouring whiskey.

344

"I expect I'd best get up to the store to see if they're havin' their meetin' yet," Possum said. "I swear, Perley, you oughta stay here and take the sheriff's job permanently and make me your deputy. You've said, yourself, that you ain't all that fond of tendin' cattle."

"How 'bout you takin' the job as sheriff and hire me as your deputy?" Perley answered.

"That'ud work, too, I reckon," Possum joked. "Reckon how ol' Wheeler would like that?" He was joking, but he dearly wished there was some way to keep Perley from leaving.

"You'd better get goin'," Perley said. "You're liable to be goin' home after dark, if you don't get that meetin' started."

"Ain't no problem," Possum shrugged. "The mayor said it was just a short meeting for me and Emma to sign some kinda papers."

They parted then, Possum to his meeting with his business partner, Perley to the stable to see how Buck liked his new shoes. When he left the stable, he decided to play his role as sheriff and take a little walk up and down Main Street, just to make sure nothing was on fire or some drunk couldn't find his way home. When he walked by

Wheeler's Merchandise, he noticed the lights were still on and Possum and Emma's horses were still tied out front. *The big-time hotel operators Emma and Possum are still at it,* he thought. *Better wind it up, it's already getting dark.* It was a narrow little trail along the creek to Rooster's cabin, and it could be difficult in the dark. Coy Dawkins and Whit Berry had found that to be true.

CHAPTER 17

As soon as darkness started to set in, Joe Cutter and Waylon Logan saddled up and prepared to leave their temporary campsite before a hard dark set in. They decided to take no chances on finding their way back to that spot on the ridge overlooking Rooster Crabb's pasture. They had no trouble retracing their tracks of the afternoon, however, and soon were watching the wagon camp and the two tents. The plan was to give the camp time to go to bed, then slip into the camp and cut into the back of the smaller tent. By going in that way, they figured they would less likely be seen by anyone in the other tent. Once they were in the back of the tent, one of them would grab the woman, the other would pick up the baby. The success of the abduction would depend on the element of surprise and their ability to keep the woman from waking everyone else. If they failed in that endeavor, they would shoot anyone who tried to stop them, in spite of their promise to Ballenger.

The first good sign for them was the fact that the camp went to bed early. From their perch on the ridge, they saw the woman go in and out of the smaller tent several times, often going in the larger tent. Finally, after the camp seemed to settle, she went back into the smaller tent and stayed for a longer time. "She's in for good," Waylon decided. Joe agreed, so they moved their horses down the ridge on the other side of the wagons for quick access to them when they made their move. Under cover of the now-heavier darkness, the two kidnappers made their way into the quiet camp. Cutter, being the stronger, as well as the bigger, was to grab the woman, while Logan would snatch the baby up and also act as the rear guard, in case the other woman's husband came to her rescue.

"You ready?" Waylon asked. Joe said that he was, and shook out the burlap bag, which he had decided to yank over the woman's head. They advanced toward the outermost wagon and stopped there to listen before continuing on to the back of the smaller tent. Cutter drew his knife to cut the rear of the tent, but before he made the first thrust, they suddenly heard the baby start to cry.

"Damn!" Waylon murmured under his breath, and they both froze, expecting the whole camp to rouse as if it was a warning signal.

They were still standing frozen when the woman came out of the tent, holding the baby, unaware of the two confused intruders behind her. With no option apparent to him, Cutter suddenly acted. He moved up behind her and snatched the burlap bag over her head and shoulders, even while she still held the infant close to her breast. In almost one motion, he picked her up on his shoulder and moved as quickly as he could toward the trees at the foot of the ridge and the horses waiting there. Behind him, Waylon hurriedly watched the other tent, his pistol in hand, prepared to shoot the first person to emerge. In a state of shock, the woman could not breathe for several long moments, confused by what had happened. When she realized what was taking place, she started to cry out, but was only able to utter the first alarm before Logan grabbed the bag to find her mouth and held his hand over it until they were into the trees. "Keep walkin'" he said. "I'll lead the horses till we get a little ways away from that camp."

When they thought it was safe to stop, Logan walked back for several yards where he could see the camp. There was no sign of anyone coming to her rescue. "I swear, woman, you folks are pretty heavy sleepers, ain'tcha?"

Totally in shock, she could not answer for a long few moments. When she could, her first words were for the baby, which she had somehow managed to hold on to. "The baby!" she cried and tried to wrestle the bag up off him.

"Lady," Waylon's gruff voice warned her, "if you keep your mouth shut, won't nobody hurt you or that baby. I'll lift this sack so you can see if the baby's all right, but you make a noise, and I'll bust your nose for you. You understand?"

"Who are you?" she demanded. "What do you want?"

"Do you understand?" He demanded again and grabbed her by the throat.

"Yes, yes," she cried. "I understand!" He pulled the sack up over her head and she frantically examined the infant.

"Is he okay?" Cutter asked her.

"Yes, he's okay. Let me go now. I have nothing of value to give you. My husband will come after you, if you don't let me go."

Waylon grinned. "You ain't got no husband, lady. We ain't that dumb. I'm gonna tell you like it is. We've been hired to deliver you and your baby to a man who's wantin' his grandson, and you took him away. It's gonna take a couple of days to get there, but if you behave yourself and don't give us no trouble, it won't be that hard on you. We brought you a horse to ride and we're got food for you."

"We've even got canned milk for the baby, in case you ain't got none anymore," Joe said.

Purely dumbfounded, but beginning to understand what was happening to her, Rachael tried to calm herself. "You've made a mistake. This is not my baby."

"Is that so?" Cutter said. "Well, you'd best hold on to him like he was, because if you drop him, I'm liable to get pretty nasty." He grabbed her arm and pulled her to him, picked her and the baby up, and plopped her down in the saddle of the horse they had brought for her. She started to scream, but he slapped her hard across her face. "I told you, damn it."

"You've gotta listen to me," she pleaded. "You've got the wrong person. This is not my baby. I'm just takin' care of him for my sister. You need to let us go." She continued pleading with them while they led her horse farther and farther away from her family. "Look, I'll bet the man you're working for is Zachary Slocum, and this is his grandson. And the baby's mother is Emma Slocum. Isn't that right?" There was no answer from either of her abductors. "You have to believe me. My name is Rachael Parker. Emma's my sister."

Beyond the lower end of the ridge now, the two men climbed into their saddles. "Save your breath and take care of that young'un. He's more important than you are, so if you let anything happen to him, I'll put a bullet in your head, and me and Waylon will just ride on back to Fort Worth."

Her dismay now becoming panic, she pleaded once more. "I'm right about Slocum and his grandson, ain't I? I'm not lying to you. He's gonna be mad when he finds out you took the wrong person."

"Lady, why in the hell wouldn't you know who's after you? All that talkin' you're doin' just makes me sure you're the woman callin' herself Emma Slocum. Now shut the hell up, I'm tired of hearin' your mouth." He nudged his horse and broke into a lope through a narrow pass, his way lighted now by a huge full moon rising over the low hills to the east.

Riding in line between Cutter and Logan, she began to cry, devastated by the freak accident of her capture. Riding farther and farther from her husband and daughters, who might not even realize that she was gone, she was not sure if she would ever see them again.

Possum and Emma arrived at the camp to find her brother-in-law and her two nieces in a state of panic, having just then realized that Rachael and the baby were missing. "They've been taken!" Tom cried. "It's my fault. I didn't even know it was happening. It's my fault," he repeated over and over. "I was asleep, and I heard the baby cry, but it was for just a little bit. Rachael was gone, but I knew she was in your tent looking after the baby. He didn't cry anymore after that first time, then he quit, so I thought Rachael quieted him. Oh, God, if I had only gotten up to see if she was all right, but I swear I never thought there was anything wrong." He looked at Emma, who was stunned, still trying to accept what her brain was receiving. Tom turned from her to Possum. "They've got my wife," he pleaded. "We've got to go after her!"

"My baby!" Emma finally cried out in anguish. "They found us!" There was no doubt in her mind that whoever kidnapped her son was sent by Zachary Slocum.

Shocked as much as anyone, Possum could only stare at the scene of despair before him. With Tom's wailing confession of guilt, Emma's sobbing, and both of the little girls' bawling, he couldn't make himself think what to do. Finally, his mind started working again, and he took charge of the tragedy. "You're most likely right, Emma. It figures that Slocum sent somebody down here to find us. And if that's the case, they're takin' the child to the Lazy-S. We can go straight to the Lazy-S, but it's two or two and a half days' ride from here. It'd be best if we could catch up with 'em before they got back to the Lazy-S. Trouble is, we'd have to pick up their trail where they left here, and that ain't gonna be too easy in the dark." He shook his head, knowing he needed help, and the kind of help he needed wasn't the kind he might get from Tom. For starters, he didn't know how many kidnappers there were. "I'm goin' back to town to get Perley," he stated. "We can't do nothin' till it gets light enough to see which way they went."

"But they'll just have that much more head start if we wait till then," Tom protested.

"We'll just have to ride like hell to make it up," Possum replied. "One thing for sure, if we just go ridin' off without followin' their trail, we might as well just head on to the Lazy-S headquarters, and there ain't no tellin' how many we'd be up against there."

"I don't know." Tom shook his head, devastated. "Maybe you're right, but I can't help thinkin' about Rachael. If they came for the baby, why did they take Rachael?"

"Because they thought Rachael was me," Emma stated. "He told me he wanted me to go with him to take care of my baby the first time they came after Danny."

"I expect that's right," Possum agreed, "and they most likely didn't bring nobody to take care of a baby. I'm goin' to get Perley. We need him." He climbed back on his horse and headed back to town, leaving them to deal with their grief.

Perley was roused from a sound sleep by Possum pounding on the office door, but he became instantly alert when Possum explained the reason for his late-night visit. The next person to be awakened was Horace Brooks, who met Perley and Possum at his door with his shotgun in hand. When they explained, he pulled his boots on and ran next door to unlock the stable, and Perley hurriedly saddled Buck. In only a few minutes' time, Perley and Possum left the stable with a wish of "Good luck" from Horace.

After the short ride back to the pasture behind Rooster's cabin, they found the scene pretty much as it had been when Possum left to fetch Perley. Emma's eyes were red and swollen from crying, and Tom was doing his best to console his daughters while fighting his own despair. It struck Perley much the same as a funeral, and they turned at once to him to answer their prayers. "Let's just see what we can do," he said, not really sure, himself. Rooster, having heard the commotion, was there holding a lantern, so Perley said, "Lemme borrow that lantern and see if we can figure out what happened."

Rooster gave him the lantern, and Perley took it to Emma's tent to examine the grass in front of it. The grass was pretty high overall in the pasture, but it was beaten down from Emma going in and out of her tent. Beyond the front of the tent, however, there were signs of more recent traffic leading away from the tent. "Look at this right here," Rooster said, pointing to a patch of grass a few feet farther along that stood out in the moonlight. Perley brought the lantern closer and discovered a larger area of disturbed grass than that which a single person might make just walking. "Right here is where they grabbed 'em," Rooster declared. He hurried ahead then, looking for more tracks in the grass. It wasn't easy, for the leaves of grass were recovering rapidly, but the grass was high enough to give the trackers the general direction the kidnappers took when they left the camp.

When they looked in the direction indicated, Perley said, "Looks like they mighta been headed across the pasture toward that gap near the end of that ridge." Possum and Rooster agreed.

"There's a little stream on the other side of that gap in the ridge," Rooster said. "At least there is this time of year. Most of the time it dries up when the middle of the summer gets here. You might be able to pick up some tracks there." They continued in the direction they had agreed on, across the pasture. Before coming to the gap in the ridge, they reached some smaller trees and discovered evidence of horses in the form of fresh droppings. It was natural to assume the kidnappers had left their horses there while they went into the camp on foot.

They continued on to the gap, and beyond, to the stream. As Rooster had predicted, it was only a few inches deep, but there was a bare, sandy area on each side of it. And even without the lantern, the moon-light shone bright enough to plainly see the hoofprints where the horses had crossed. "I make it four horses," Perley announced. "What do you think?" Possum and Rooster concurred. "Looks to me like there was two of 'em, and they brought a horse for Emma and a packhorse." Again, there was agreement. "So, I reckon we'll start out after 'em as quick as we can. That is, as long as we can pick up their tracks. Wise to wait till mornin', but I'm for startin' now. Who's goin' with me?"

"Hell," Possum replied, "you know I am."

"Me, too," Rooster volunteered.

"Somebody needs to stay with Emma and the girls," Perley said. "I expect that leaves you, Tom."

Accompanying them as a silent spectator to that point, Tom spoke up then. "The hell I will! That's my wife they've run off with. I'm damn sure goin' with you." He left very little doubt about his intentions. So Possum reluctantly decided he would stay with Emma and the girls, since Rooster knew the country better than any of them. Emma was more satisfied with that arrangement, since Possum had been looking after her ever since they left Kansas.

Thinking of the small herd of horses he

had driven down from Butcher Bottom, Perley proposed a plan for the chase. "Whaddaya think about each one of us leadin' a spare horse and switch over on it when we tire the first one out. We might make up a little time on 'em and hope they didn't get too far ahead tonight. They've gotta be slowed down some with a woman and baby with 'em."

"That might be worth a try," Possum said. "So you'd best get busy saddling up."

They got ready to ride, first rounding up the horses and selecting their spares, fitting the extra horses with bridles only. Perley pulled his saddle off Buck and threw it on a roan. With plans to release the first horse after tiring it out, he chose to end up with Buck for the balance of the chase. Traveling as light as possible, they took some jerky in their saddlebags for food. When all was ready, they filed out of the camp, each man leading his extra horse, with Possum and Emma wishing them good luck and the little girls waving good-bye.

Leaving the little stream, they rode along a narrow valley the tracks led to. It seemed like a natural trail to follow, so they continued until it ended at a line of low hills. Then it was necessary to find some sign to point the way from there. As the moon traveled farther across the Texas sky, it became more difficult to strike a sign, forcing them to dismount to search on foot. They were about ready to declare the search off until daylight when Perley almost stepped on some fresh droppings. The thought shot through his mind of his brother John. Had he been there, he would have reminded Perley of his oft-repeated phrase of his propensity for stepping in a cow pie. *This time, it wasn't bad luck,* he thought, for it told him that the men they were after had turned abruptly to follow a narrow ravine up a hill. At the top, he found another ravine leading down to an expanse of flat prairie with sparsely scattered trees. It was on this prairie that the hunt ended for the night with the lack of any visible sign.

It was a grim camp that night, absent the usual lighthearted banter that would normally be present with three men around a campfire. There was coffee, thanks to Rooster thinking to get his battered coffeepot from his cabin, along with some coffee to brew in it. There was naturally talk about the possibility of not being able to find their trail in the morning, and what they would do in that event. Perley had to assure Tom that he planned to go to the Lazy-S should that happen. He figured

Zachary Slocum was crazy, but not an outright evil man, and surely he would release Rachael when he found out she was not his grandson's mother. He didn't express it, but he was just as determined to return the baby to his real mother.

Sunrise brought them out of their bedrolls and back to the search for tracks. Water became a crucial factor at that point because they had been forced to make a dry camp, so it was with some relief when the morning light revealed a line of low trees and shrubs stretching across the prairie about half a mile away. They decided to head for it, hoping that in addition to watering the horses, they might find evidence that the party they followed had passed that way. It seemed to be in the same general direction they had been traveling. When they reached the creek, there were no tracks, nor did they really expect to find any. That would have been a real piece of good luck. "What do we do now?" Tom asked, his patience nearing the breaking point.

"Well, after the horses get a drink, we'll split up and scout this creek in both directions before we decide they didn't come this way," Perley said. "Rooster, I'll take downstream, if you'll go upstream. Tom, you can go with either one of us, or you can stay here, whatever you want." Tom decided to go with Rooster, so they split up and started scouting the creek bank.

Perley had gone no more than half a mile when he heard Rooster yelling. He turned to see him galloping toward him shouting something he couldn't understand, but he figured he must have found some tracks. "We found where they was!" Rooster shouted. "They musta made camp here last night. There's ashes of a fire, and I could see where they slept." Perley was quick to turn his horse around and follow Rooster back. When they came to the spot, Tom was waiting for them. "You was dead-on when you said they came this way," Rooster exclaimed. Perley didn't admit that he was just guessing. After they came out on the prairie, he had no idea which way they had gone. "And those ashes are still warm," Rooster went on. "I'd say we ain't that far behind 'em, after all."

Perley looked the campsite over and came to the same conclusion Rooster had. The ashes were still warm, and there were fairly fresh droppings their horses had left behind. Clear hoofprints led out of the camp, heading north, following the creek. "Rooster, you know this country. Where does this trail beside the creek go? The way these two men are goin', it almost looks like they were lookin' to strike this trail." He pointed at the tracks. "Now, it looks like they're followin' the trail."

"There ain't nothin' up that way," Rooster answered. "This trail ends at Comanche Run. That's an old waterin' hole the Comanches used to camp at. It's where a clear spring runs into this creek. Nothin' there but a burnt-up piece of cabin a feller tried to use for a tradin' post. The Comanches killed him and set his cabin on fire."

Perley looked over at Tom. "Comanche Run," he repeated. "I'm bettin' that's where these two are figurin' on campin' tonight. So, if it was up to me, I'd say let's forget about tryin' to scout every track on the trail and head straight to Comanche Run as fast as we can." Back to Rooster then, he asked, "How far is it from here?"

"I don't know, close to forty miles, I reckon."

"Forty miles," Perley said. "We can make it up there tonight if we swap horses about halfway. Whaddaya say, Tom?"

Tom didn't hesitate. "I say let's go for it. I think you're right, and if you ain't, we'll just go on to the Lazy-S."

CHAPTER 18

After their second day of traveling, Rachael's abductors made camp at the place they called Comanche Run. It was still fairly early in the evening, but they gave her the impression that this was a planned stop. She knew it for sure when Joe Cutter commented, "Ain't nobody here. I thought he was gonna be here when we got here."

"Can't you do somethin' to stop that baby from squallin'?" Waylon Logan complained. Then, answering Cutter's remark, he said, "He'll be here when he gets here." He turned back to glare at Rachael.

Tired in addition to being frightened, she had not closed her eyes all night long the night before. When they had camped, they made her cook the bacon and jerky they had brought. When it was time for bed, they realized they had not decided on the best way to restrain her for the night. If they tied her up, hands and foot, as they would have if it was just her to worry about, that would keep her from running off during the night. But as Logan had pointed out, "How's she gonna take care of that baby, if she's all tied up? You gonna take care of him?"

"Hell, no," Cutter had answered. It was going to be a problem for them, and they couldn't think of a solution.

"I'll give you my word that I won't try to escape, and you won't have to tie me up," she had suggested, which brought a hearty laugh from both of her kidnappers. In the end, they decided the only way was to have her and the baby sleep on the blanket between them. To restrain her further, her ankle was tied with a rope around Logan's ankle. They felt confident that if she tried to get up during the night, one of them would be awakened. To her discomfort, they didn't give her much room, so she could barely move without touching one of them. Consequently, she had been afraid to go to sleep. During the long night, she had been constantly on guard for the seemingly casual hand that strayed toward her. Her only defense had been to give the baby a little pinch whenever she felt an exploring hand, causing the baby to cry, which resulted in a string of profanity from Cutter, Logan, or both.

"He needs more milk," she said.

Joe Cutter got a can of milk from the packs and opened it with his heavy skinning knife. "Here's the damn milk," he said and handed her the can.

She took the can and backed quickly away from him. She picked the baby up then and went over to sit near the fire. She reached under her skirt and tore off a piece of her petticoat, then, using it as a wick, she poked it in the hole in the can. When it had soaked up some of the milk, she pressed it on the baby's lips. He stopped crying and took the milk. Terrified when they had stopped the night before by the creek, she could not stop herself from shaking, which seemed to have amused the cruel pair. It had inspired them to make lewd remarks and threaten to do any number of crude things to her. She believed the only hope she had of surviving the night without being violated was to say that she was the baby's mother, so she did.

Logan walked up to the fire and stood over her, watching her feed the baby. "Maybe you weren't lyin', maybe you really are dried up."

"What if she was tellin' the truth when we first got her?" Cutter wondered. "What if she really ain't the real mama?"

Logan looked back at Rachael. "Then I

reckon we'll kill her and keep the baby. Then you can feed him with that rag."

It was a little past sunset, with still no sign of the party the two kidnappers were supposed to meet. In a few minutes after the last glimpse of the sun dropped below the horizon, it was as if some great being had suddenly blown out a lantern, leaving the prairie deep in darkness, waiting for the moon's appearance. "Dump the rest of that coffee and make us a fresh pot," Logan ordered Rachael. She laid the baby on her blanket and went to the spring to fill the pot. When she straightened up again, she froze when she saw the dark outlines of two men on horseback watching her.

"Cutter? Logan?" A deep voice rang out.

In a panic, Logan and Cutter scrambled away from the firelight, grabbing their rifles as they rolled over on the ground to take up firing positions. "Who is it?" Logan demanded.

"Take it easy," the voice returned. "Who do you think it is?" Ballenger said sarcastically. "Just wanted to make sure it's you — we're coming in."

"You coulda fooled me," Logan informed him. "I thought it was some fool lookin' to get shot — come ridin' up outta the dark like that."

The two riders walked their horses into the firelight. "I see the woman," Ballenger said. "Where's the baby?"

"Yonder on the blanket," Logan answered and pointed, "safe and sound. Where's the money?"

"Have you ever known me not to honor any deal between us?" Ballenger asked. "I've got your money. Any trouble?"

"Nah, no trouble, I just wanna get this cryin' young'un off my hands." Remembering the coffee then, he said, "We was fixin' to make us a fresh pot of coffee. Step down and have some." He looked toward the spring, where Rachael was still standing terrified. "Get on back here and get that coffeepot on." He and Cutter watched as Ballenger and his companion dismounted and walked up closer to the fire. "Who's this you got with you?" Logan asked.

"This is Mr. Brent Slocum," Ballenger replied. "I told you he'd be riding along to make sure everything went all right."

Brent said nothing for a couple of minutes but continued to stare at Rachael. Finally, he spoke. "Who's the woman?"

His question caused Cutter and Logan to look at each other, astonished, before Cutter answered. "She's the baby's mama. You said bring the baby's mama, so we brung her."

Brent looked at Ballenger and said, "That's not Emma Wise. I don't know who she is, but she's sure as hell not Emma Wise. I've met my brother's wife, and this woman is not her."

"I told them that!" Rachael blurted. "But they wouldn't believe me."

There followed a pocket of silence when everyone was stunned speechless, broken by the sudden crying of the baby. "Take care of him," Ballenger ordered Rachael. She put the coffeepot down and picked up the baby. He turned to Brent. "Are you sure she's not the baby's mother? I never saw her up close, but she sure as hell looks like the woman I saw carrying the baby before."

"I told you I was sure," Brent replied, then another doubt entered his mind. "She might be that baby's mother, and if she is, then the baby is not my nephew. And that means my father needs to get the money back that's already been paid for this farce."

"Now, hold on, Brent," Ballenger said, "we'll get this straightened out."

Realizing their payday was in jeopardy, Logan and Cutter immediately got their hackles up. "I don't know what you two are tryin' to pull here," Cutter charged. "We took the baby that was in the tent Ballenger pointed out, and we took the woman that came outta the tent with him." He pointed his finger at Ballenger. "You said you'd been watchin' that camp and there weren't but one baby there, so that's the right baby. Maybe she ain't the mama, but he's the baby you're supposed to pay us to get."

"He's right about the baby," Ballenger said. "There was only one baby there, so he's gotta be the right one."

"I don't know," Brent responded. "Maybe after you left, these two jaspers picked up some easier baby." He was not convinced, and he felt he was going to have to be before he accepted the infant. In the meantime, he still didn't know where the woman came from.

The woman in question was still in a fearful haze, wondering what would become of her and the baby. Out of fear for her safety, she backed slowly away from the fire as they continued to argue. It struck her that no one seemed to notice her movements, intent as they were upon resolving the mix-up. She continued to back up, slowly easing away from the firelight. Still no one noticed that she was gradually fading into the darkness, so she continued to back away, praying that the baby would not give her exit away by crying. She was convinced that, no matter

370

how the argument turned out, it was not going to go well for her. Determined not to stay there to find out, she decided she would not have another chance to run. It was a desperate decision, but to stay was ultimately to die. Of that she was convinced, so she continued to back away from the camp until she was suddenly stopped by an arm around her waist and a hand clamped tightly over her mouth. "Don't make a sound. It's me, Perley."

She almost collapsed, her emotions overpowering her, but he kept her from falling. "Hang on, Rachael, I'm gonna get you somewhere safe. Tom's waitin' right behind me. If we're lucky, we can ride on outta here before they even know you're gone." He walked her back to the shell of the old cabin where Tom, Rooster, and the horses waited, and she hurried into the arms of her anxious husband. It was at that moment that young Daniel Seaton Slocum, Jr. decided to tell the world that he was dissatisfied with the way he was being treated. Utilizing the full power of his healthy lungs, he let out a wail like that of a coyote pup.

As if a fire alarm bell had rung, the fireside discussion ceased immediately as the participants realized Rachael and the baby were no longer there. It was Waylon Logan who said the obvious. "She's gone!" He exclaimed. "She's run off with the young'un."

"Oh, hell," Perley exclaimed. "There goes our luck. Get outta here!" He and Tom helped Rachael up into the saddle, then Tom climbed up behind her."

"What are you gonna do?" Rooster blurted as he climbed up on his horse.

"Rooster, you lead 'em back the way we came," Perley said. "I'm gonna see if I can delay 'em enough so you can put some distance behind you."

"You be careful." Rooster said. "Don't do nothin' foolish."

"I ain't gonna charge 'em, if that's what you mean. You just run, and when the horses get tired, find someplace to protect yourself. I'll try to find you later. Now, get goin'."

Rooster took off with Tom right behind him. Perley moved Buck around behind one of the walls still standing on the old cabin where he might be protected from gunfire. Then he turned his full attention to the excited group of men some fifty yards away at the campfire. He wasn't sure how best to delay them but decided it best not to let them know he was there until he was forced to stop them when they went after Rachael and the baby. While he watched, his rifle and pistol ready, they appeared to be arguing still but the two men who had actually kidnapped Rachael were shouting for her to come back to the fire. The name they continued to call her by was Emma.

After a few minutes of this, with no results, Ballenger had had enough. "She can't be far, carrying that baby. Get some limbs off that fire and use them as torches. She's probably hiding somewhere close by." He then grabbed one, himself, and started walking in the direction he thought he had heard the baby's cry. Holding the torch close to him, it cast a light on his face, and even at that distance, Perley thought he had seen the man before. He would have to be closer to be sure where it was, however.

With no desire to kill anyone unless he was given no choice, he brought his rifle up to his shoulder and aimed very carefully before slowly squeezing the trigger. Ballenger was stunned for a moment when the flaming portion of his torch was clipped off. Thinking it a near miss, he immediately dropped to the ground. *Huh,* Perley thought when he saw the broken piece of the torch fly off, *I didn't know I was that good a shot.*

The shot caused a riotous scramble for safety among the four conspirators as they sought cover from the attack. Hoping to make them think he was not acting alone, Perley ran a dozen yards to his left and fired another shot. He couldn't clearly see any of them now, since they plunged into the safety outside the firelight. His second shot was aimed at the coffeepot sitting beside the fire, sending it up in the air about a foot. Without hesitating, he got up and ran back to his right, about a dozen yards past the spot where he had taken the first shot. Alert to the fact they were under attack, there were four return shots fired at the spot of his second shot, this time, having seen his muzzle flash. As he ran to his next location, he saw their muzzle flashes and that's where he aimed his third shot, again moving as soon as he pulled the trigger.

He stared hard into the darkness to make sure none of the four had slipped out of whatever cover they had found against his attack. He was sure that, so far, no one had tried to counterattack. When the full moon of the night suddenly popped up over the horizon, he knew that his siege wouldn't last much longer. At least he was confident that he had bought a little time for Rooster and Tom. It was time to make his own departure. From now on, there would be no more harassment shots, if he had to shoot again, it would be to stop them.

■ ■ ■ ■

"You see anything, Joe?" Logan asked, as they hugged the ground behind the log they had taken for cover.

"Not a damn thing," Cutter replied. He looked over at the other two behind the log. "How 'bout you?"

"Nothing," Ballenger answered. "I think they got what they came for and now they're gone." It had been fully a half hour since any shots had been fired in their direction. With the moon now fairly high over the prairie, the dark outline of the burned-out cabin was clearly distinguished from the trees around it. After giving it more thought, Ballenger suddenly got to his feet.

"You damn fool," Cutter barked. "You lookin' to get shot?"

"No, I'm not," Ballenger stated calmly. "There's nobody here and we've been played for a bunch of fools." He walked out to the remains of the fire, stood there, and looked around him. "It was just one man. He ran back and forth between shots to make us think we were surrounded. Think about it. If there were more than one, why didn't any of them shoot at the same time?" He reached down, picked up the coffeepot, and looked at the hole in it. "He's a helluva shot, too."

"Because he hit the damn coffeepot?" Logan scoffed. "Hell, he hit the coffeepot when he was tryin' to shoot at us."

"He hit the coffeepot because he was aiming at the coffeepot," Ballenger insisted. "His first shot was that stick of wood I was using as a torch. He clipped it right in two. That wasn't a miss. He wasn't trying to kill me." He paused before he continued. "And that tells me he's weak. He hasn't got the guts to kill a man."

"All that may be true," Brent Slocum spoke up then. "But the fact of the matter is the woman and child you were paid to deliver got away."

"Who was paid?" Logan demanded. "We ain't been paid! It's your damn fault she got away. Me and Joe did what we was hired to do, we got the woman and the baby and brought 'em here, just like you said. It was you two, doin' all that arguin' about her bein' the right woman or not, that gave her the chance to run. Our deal was to bring her and that baby here and you was to pay us our money."

"Well, we're just wasting time right now," Ballenger said. "We've got one man to kill before we get the baby back, and we need to catch him before he gets them back to Bison Gap. If you want your money, we'll have to get that baby, and to hell with the woman. With four of us, there shouldn't be any trouble taking that one man down."

"Three of you," Brent was quick to correct him. "I'll not be a part of it. When you get the baby back, bring him to the Lazy-S."

"Very well," Ballenger said. "I still like the odds." He looked at Cutter and Logan. "You still want to earn that money?"

"Oh, we're goin', whether you pay us or not," Cutter answered. "That son of a bitch ain't gettin' away with takin' potshots at us."

"Good," Ballenger said, "let's get going then." They hurriedly threw their saddles on their horses and left Brent Slocum to watch them disappear into the night.

CHAPTER 19

With the light of a full moon shining down on the trail along the creek, Perley held Buck to a comfortable lope, one the big bay could maintain for a good while. It was questionable whether or not he could catch up with Rooster and the others. From Comanche Run, it was a two-day ride back to Rooster's cabin under normal conditions. They were going to have to stop somewhere to rest the horses, just as he was. If Rooster found a good place to stop, where they would not be easily seen, there was a good possibility he might not see them. A lot of good he would be to them if he rode past them in the middle of the night. With that in mind, he decided he'd best not ride too far before he picked a spot to stop the pursuit. But that would not be critical for a little while yet, so he urged Buck on.

When he thought it was time, he reined Buck back to a slower pace and began to look closely at the patches of trees and bushes along the creek, trying to judge each spot for its potential for a defensive stand. None stood out until he came to a place where the creek split to go on both sides of a small island, only big enough to contain three trees, one of which had fallen. With a thick growth of laurel bushes on two sides of it, it looked to be an ideal ambush site, as well as a good choice to stand off an assault. "That might do just fine," he told the bay gelding and pulled him up while he surveyed the surroundings. Once he made up his mind, he moved quickly then to prepare for the pursuit he knew was sure to follow him. Guiding Buck into the water, he crossed over the little island and dismounted between the two trees still standing. Then he gathered dead limbs and leaves from the fallen tree and built a fire behind it. When he was satisfied his fire would burn for some time yet, he climbed back on Buck and crossed the other fork of the creek to the opposite bank. Riding back in the direction from which he had just come, he picked his spot. About forty yards from the little island, he came to a low mound of laurel bushes. The mound was high enough to hide Buck from the trail across the creek and gave him a good platform to fire from.

Satisfied, he let Buck drink from the creek until he had slaked his thirst, then he led him around the mound and tied him there.

With the same thoughts in his mind that Perley had when he loped along the creek trail, Ballenger scanned the banks of the creek as he and his two partners hurried to catch up with him. He knew that Perley would eventually have to rest his horse, just as the three of them would. At best, he felt Perley had no more than a thirty-minute head start, and they pushed their horses hard to try to make up that time. There had been some thoughts back there at Comanche Run of leaving the responsibility for catching up with the fleeing woman and child with Cutter and Logan. But he felt quite a bit of fascination for the cocky sniper who had danced back and forth to pin them down while the woman fled. He seemed worthy of his challenge. A crack shot, no doubt about that, but why did he hesitate when he could have killed two or more of them had he so chosen? It took a conscienceless killer to do that, a professional killer like himself. Ballenger prided himself in his reputation as the fastest and the best, and he felt bound to test the mettle of this man. In spite of his eagerness to catch him,

however, he was not willing to take unnecessary chances, so he let Logan and Cutter
ride ahead of him. His thoughts were interrupted then by an alert from Waylon Logan.

"Yonder," Logan said, and when Ballenger
pulled up beside him, he pointed to a thin
line of smoke drifting up from what appeared to be an island in the middle of the
creek. "Looks like a log layin' across there.
Wonder if he's got the woman with him?"

"The damn fool built a fire," Cutter
remarked. "I reckon we can thank him for
that."

Ballenger was not sure, almost disappointed that the man he had become so
fascinated with would build a fire to give
away his hiding place. Maybe, he thought,
the woman is with him and she had to do
something for the baby that required a fire.
"We'd best be careful," he warned.

"We can get a little closer and see if we
can't smoke him outta there," Logan said.
That seemed to make sense, so they followed him to a stand of little pines about
fifty yards from the island. There they left
their horses and split up, each one making
his way to a position to fire on the island.
Ballenger's last remark to them before they
split was to remind them that, if the baby
was hit, there would be no payday for

381

anybody. "With all the squawlin' that young'un done, it'd give me some satisfaction to put a bullet in him," Logan saw fit to remark.

From his position behind the mound, Perley watched the three men scatter in the moonlight and move in closer to the island. As soon as the first one was set behind a tree, he opened up on the log, sending pieces of bark flying. Perley waited until the other two got set and they started shooting as well. Now after moving in closer, all three were actually between him and the island. He brought his rifle to his shoulder, laid the front sight on the one closest to him, and squeezed off one round. Joe Cutter cried out in pain when the .44 slug caught him behind the right shoulder and he dropped to the ground. Seeing one of the other two get up from his position in a clump of berry bushes and run into the trees on the bank, Perley figured he was trying to get a shot behind the log. So he left his position on the mound and ran down the opposite bank until he was even with the log on the island. He got there at the same time Waylon Logan reached a point on the opposite side of the creek. Able to see behind the log then, Logan saw that there was no one there at the fire. "Hey! There ain't no . . ." was as far as he got before the bullet from Perley's rifle impacted with his chest and dropped him to the ground.

By moving to intercept Logan, Perley was now in a position where he wasn't sure where the third party was. He moved back to the mound, his main concern to make sure Buck was all right. When he looked toward the spot where he had seen the third man position himself, he was no longer there. He considered his choices — try to work his way through the trees on the other bank, looking for the third man, or call it a day and go after Rooster and the others. He had shot two of the three and the other one was either hiding or stalking him now. As he thought that, he unconsciously looked all around him. There was one more place to look for him, so he untied Buck from the tree limb and led him to the little clump of pines where the three men had left their horses.

The horses were still there, three of them, tied to the pine limbs. He made a quick decision. He wasn't sure where the third man was, but at least he could leave him on foot, so he gathered up the horses' reins and climbed up into the saddle. It was an awkward situation, but the horses didn't resist as he held a handful of reins and nudged Buck forward. It was a good decision not to take the time to rig up a lead rope, for he heard the snap of a bullet as it passed close to his head. He was gone before he heard the report of the rifle that shot it. Asking Buck for speed, he galloped down the creek trail, lying low on Buck's neck as a second shot passed overhead. *Too far for accuracy,* he thought. *My luck's holding up.* He figured he had galloped for over a mile when he felt some of the reins slipping from his hand. He reined Buck back to a lope, but one of the horses was now free. Perley didn't stop to try to catch him again. The horse followed him for another quarter of a mile before pulling up to a stop. Perley pushed on for what he guessed to be about ten miles before stopping for the night, his horses tired as well as his hand.

Fully a dozen miles behind him, Ballenger stood, perplexed as he returned to the place he had first taken cover. He was feeling the sting of his second defeat at the hands of the unknown gunman, when he saw him galloping away, leading their horses, leaving him on foot. He was even more determined to face him now on an even playing field where no one held any advantage over the other. That was the real test. He was not as sure of his opinion before, that the man was too weak to kill. That would only be determined when he was staring death in the face, instead of shooting at someone who couldn't see him.

Standing out in the middle of the trail, he looked to his right to see the body of Waylon Logan on the creek bank, lined up with the log lying between the two trees on the island. Beyond Logan's body, he could see the small fire dying out. There was no reason to check on Logan. He could tell he was dead from where he stood. Disgusted with the way the chase had gone, he decided to go back and see how badly Cutter was hurt. He found him a few feet from where he had been hit. He was alive, but in considerable pain, although the wound was not life-threatening.

Cutter looked up at Ballenger and groaned. "Did you get him?"

"No, he got away and he took our horses with him," Ballenger said.

"What about Waylon?" Cutter asked.

"Dead," Ballenger answered. "How bad are you hurt?"

"Pretty bad, I think," Cutter replied and groaned when he tried to prop himself up against a tree. "I gotta get to a doctor. I'm bleedin' a helluva lot."

"Well, unless you think you can walk about eighty miles, you're not gonna see one. We don't have a horse. And not only that, we don't have any food or anything else."

"That don't sound too good," Cutter groaned.

"No, it doesn't." He started to say more about the hopelessness of their situation but stopped short when something moving in the dark shadows caught his eye. Without having to think about it, he whipped his handgun out, ready to fire. "Well, I'll be . . . ," he started and returned his pistol to its holster. "Salvation," he announced dramatically. "The horses got loose. Come here, boy," he coaxed. "Come here." The horse did not come to him, but it remained standing in the shadows. Slowly, so as not to spook the horse, Ballenger walked up to it, speaking calmly to it as he approached. He took hold of the reins and stroked the horse's neck for a few minutes, looking for the others, but there was only the one horse. He led it back to Cutter.

"Glory be," Cutter exclaimed. "That's ol' Sam! That's my horse. Did you find your'n?"

"No, this was the only one. I don't know what happened to the others, whether he turned them loose or not, but I think if your horse came back, the others probably would have, too. So what I think happened is your horse just happened to pull away."

"We ain't got but one horse? We're gonna have to ride double."

"No, I don't think we'll have to do that," Ballenger said. In a fraction of a second, his six-gun was in his hand and looking at Cutter's chest.

"What the hell?" Cutter gasped.

"No hard feelings, I just don't like to ride double," Ballenger said. He squeezed the trigger when Cutter tried to come up from the ground, his shot slamming the terrified man in the chest. He cocked the hammer and aimed the pistol at Cutter's head, but there was no need for another shot.

A few miles south of the bend in the creek where Perley had stopped for the night, Rooster stood at the edge of the trail staring back in the darkness as if expecting Perley to show up at any minute. "You want some more of this coffee?" Tom called out to him from the small fire they had thought it safe to build.

"A bit," Rooster replied and walked back to join Tom and Rachael by the campfire. He seemed more concerned about the safety of Perley than either of them did. Had he ridden with the unassuming young man as they had, he might have understood their feeling that whatever Perley got into, he would always land on his feet. "I figured he might catch up with us by now," Rooster said as Rachael drained the last of the pot into his cup.

"If there's one thing I've learned about Perley Gates," Tom said. "He knows how to take care of himself. Ain't that right, Rachael?" She said that it was. "I wouldn't be surprised if he didn't ride right on by us," Tom continued. "We're hid pretty good here."

"Maybe so," Rooster said, "but I think I'll stay awake tonight, just in case they got by him and they're still comin' after us."

"I'll split it up with you," Tom said. "Ain't no use in you havin' to stay awake all night."

It was close to suppertime when Possum heard the call from the other side of the pasture. He squinted against the sun on its way down to see who was calling. After a minute, when he was sure, he turned toward the campfire. "Emma, your family's come home!"

"Where?" She exclaimed, almost dropping her ladle in the pot of boiling soup in her excitement. In an instant, she was standing beside him, staring out across the pasture as well. "Thank the Good Lord in heaven," she said, watching the three horses approaching, then uttered, "Where's Perley? I don't see Perley."

Her comment reflected his concern as well. "He mighta hung back a-ways, just to make sure nobody was followin' 'em. I reckon they'll tell us."

"They're gonna be hungry," Emma said. "It's a good thing this soup is almost done." She stood there nervously rubbing her hands together as if anxious to have her baby in her arms. Finding it impossible to wait until they rode into camp, she hurried out to meet them before they reached the wagons parked there. She reached up and took the child Rachael happily handed her. "Welcome home, all of you."

"Where's Perley?" Possum asked when no one volunteered. There was an awkward pause in the greetings, as no one of the three wanted to confess that they didn't know.

"I don't know." Rooster started to take the responsibility, since no one else volunteered, but he suddenly hesitated. A wide smile broke out on his face and he continued. "But I expect that might be him yonder." They all turned to see the lone rider at the far edge of the pasture, leading a string of three horses.

The celebration started all over again, Emma fed the baby, and pretty soon Emma and Rachael were ladling out the soup and passing the biscuits Emma had baked for supper, hoping that there might be plenty of people to eat them. Possum and Emma wanted to know every detail of the rescue and Rooster, Tom, and Rachael were just as eager to hear what had happened when Perley had stayed behind. Of special interest to Possum was the string of horses Perley brought back with him. Two of them were saddled, one of which was a Morgan with an expensive saddle. The other was one of the spare horses he picked up on his way back.

"I noticed you came back ridin' bareback," Possum said to Tom.

"That's right. Rachael was ridin' my horse. We rode double outta that camp, then this mornin' we run up on one of those extra horses we took with us." He looked at Perley. "So you picked one of 'em up, too. Maybe the other one will show up here one day."

"I wouldn't be surprised," Perley said.

"Who else might show up?" Emma asked him. Her question caused everyone else to stop talking and look to him for the answer.

He was reluctant to go into much detail, but he shrugged and said, "I don't think you have to worry about those two who came in here and took Rachael and the baby. One of 'em's dead for sure and the other one is bad wounded. There were two other fellows that met 'em at that spring."

"Comanche Run," Rooster inserted.

"Anyway, there were two other men there to meet 'em." That was as far as he got again before Rachael interrupted.

"One of the two was Brent Slocum," she said. "I heard the other man call him that, but I didn't hear him call the man who came with him by name. What happened to those two?"

"One of 'em came after me," Perley said, "but the other one didn't. I don't know where he went." He went on to tell them that he had stolen all the horses belonging to the three who chased him. "One of 'em pulled free after I rode a good ways, so I reckon there's a possibility that third fellow found him. But he'da had to walk pretty far before he did."

"Tell you the truth," Rooster said, "I thought you'da caught up with us before you did. I was a little worried till you showed up tonight."

Perley shrugged, then explained. "I decided to hang back a while, just to make sure that other fellow was on foot."

"Sounds to me like you've been pretty busy," Possum said. "I doubt we'll get any more visits right away. But as long as Zachary Slocum thinks he's gotta have his grandson to raise, we're gonna have to be extra careful. He knows where the baby is now, and he's liable to send somebody else to try to grab him."

"Might be better if you moved into the cabin," Rooster suggested. "I can sleep in the barn." When Emma started to object, he insisted. "I end up sleepin' out there half the time anyway, 'specially when I've been into my corn whiskey."

"That sounds like a good idea to me," Possum said. Perley nodded his agreement. "There's room in that cabin for Rachael and the girls, too," Possum continued. "It'd be a lot easier to keep 'em all safe." He glanced at Tom. "I reckon Rachael could come out to the wagon to visit you, if she felt a need to." Tom's face flushed while everybody laughed at his embarrassment.

"I think it's a good idea," Rachael said, looking at her husband. "And it won't be for long, honey," she teased. "When Emma and Possum build their hotel, I'm sure we'll find a permanent place to live, maybe in the hotel."

Perley rode down the street in Bison Gap, leading the dark Morgan gelding with the expensive saddle. Passing Wheeler's Merchandise, he stopped when Ralph Wheeler came out on the porch and hailed him. "Perley," the mayor exclaimed. "I'm mighty glad to see you back in town."

"Why," Perley asked. "Is anything wrong?"

"Well, there was a little trouble at The Buffalo Hump last night. I just don't like to have the town without law enforcement."

"I had something I had to take care of," Perley said. "Didn't Horace tell you I was gonna be gone for a little while?"

"Yes, but I thought you'd be back the next morning, I didn't know he meant you'd be gone this long."

Perley shrugged. "I didn't know, myself, how long it was gonna take, so there wasn't any way Horace coulda known." He was already feeling the restriction of the town marshal's job, and it was a sign to him that he could never take it on permanently, even had he given that possibility any thought. "What was the trouble at The Buffalo Hump?"

"Some Mexican cowhand from a ranch

south of here somewhere started raising hell because Jimmy didn't have any tequila. He fired a couple of shots through the window, ran everybody out, and from what I've heard, just took up residence at one of the tables for the night. It cost Henry Lawrence a night's business, because the Mexican effectively closed the saloon. That's why we need a sheriff here in town."

"You do remember that I'm just helpin' you till you get a full-time sheriff, or marshal, whatever you wanna call him, don't you?" Perley asked. "I had to stop a kidnapping aimed at one of the new investors in your town. And I'd think that was important to you."

"Oh, it is, it is," Wheeler quickly responded. "I just wanted to let you know we're glad to see you back. Is Emma all right?"

"Yeah, she's all right, and her baby, and her sister, too," Perley replied, thinking the mayor's concern for them was a little belated. "Well, I'd better go see if the jail's still standin', I reckon." He nudged Buck and continued on down the street to the stable.

Horace Brooks met him at the front of the stable. "Good mornin', Perley, I see you got back all right. Where'd you get the horse?"

"It's a long story," Perley said. "It sorta followed me home. I wanna put him up in your stable and see if his owner comes to pick him up." He stepped down from Buck. "Give both of 'em a portion of grain." He was about to ask about his other horse at the stable when they heard a shot fired back up the street. He reacted at once, but Horace stopped him.

"That ain't nothin' but that crazy Mexican," Horace said. When Perley looked confused, Horace asked, "Didn't anybody tell you about the Mexican?"

"The mayor stopped me on my way in to town. He told me some drunk cowhand had took up residence in the saloon, but he didn't say he was still in there this mornin'."

"He's been there all night," Horace said. "I reckon Henry and Jimmy were hopin' he'd pass out and they could tie him up, but he just sits there, darin' anybody to come in the place. That's the first shot I've heard this mornin', though. Hell, I feel sorry for his horse, tied up at the rail all night, no water, no grain."

"Damn," Perley swore, "that is bad. I reckon I'd better go get him outta there. Is Jimmy still in there?" Horace said that he thought he was.

Perley took the coil of rope from his saddle and walked across the little bridge to the saloon where a lone horse was tied at the rail. He stepped up on the porch, and standing to the side of the door, pushed it open far enough to peek inside. He saw the drunken cowhand seated at a table in the middle of the saloon, facing the door. Since he was slumped in the chair, Perley thought he might have finally passed out, so he opened the door a little wider. Now, he could see Jimmy McGee slumped over on the bar, dead or asleep, he couldn't tell. He was about to push on in when the cowhand suddenly raised his pistol from the table and sent a bullet into the door a few feet from Perley's head. Perley jumped back away from the door. *That doesn't look like I'm gonna get any breakfast anytime soon,* he thought. He had planned to eat there this morning. Now he hoped Ida Wicks was not trapped inside.

He hurried around to the back door of the saloon and cautiously tried the door. It was not locked, so he opened it and walked in to find Ida sitting behind the kitchen table, a shotgun on the table before her. She started when he came in, but he put a finger to his lips to quiet her. She nodded her understanding. He tiptoed through the kitchen to the door to the saloon. There he saw the Mexican still sitting in the chair, his back to him. Perley shook out his rope and stepped through the door. The cowhand was alert enough to hear the sound of the rope as Perley twirled it over his head, and he sat up straight to listen. He made a much easier target than Coy Dawkins had on a horse. Perley's lasso dropped over him and was immediately drawn up tight, pulling the Mexican, bound to his chair, over on his back. Unable to reach for his pistol on the table as he went over, he was helpless. Perley made quick work of him, wrapping the rope around and around him until he couldn't move from the chair, all the while screaming insults at Perley in Spanish. Looking at the bar then, he was glad to see Jimmy raise his weary head and stand up. "Are you all right?" Perley asked.

"Boy, you're a sight for sore eyes," Jimmy replied. "Yeah, I'm all right. The son of a bitch threatened to shoot me every time I tried to leave the bar. I'm just tired as hell and I've got to go to the outhouse before I bust."

Behind him, Perley heard Ida Wicks, standing in the kitchen door. "Whooee! Ride 'em, cowboy!"

"Are you all right, Ida?" Perley asked. When she said she was fine, he asked, "Why didn't you just go out the back door?"

"Because I didn't want him comin' in here to tear up my kitchen," she said. "If he'da come in here, I was gonna blow his ass right back in the saloon." Changing the subject without batting an eye, she asked, "You wantin' breakfast this mornin'? It's gonna be a little late."

"Yeah, I'll be back later. I'm gonna take Jimmy's special customer to jail first, but I'm comin' back. Jimmy, I'm gonna borrow your chair. I'll bring it back when I come to eat." He pulled the free end of the rope over his shoulder, hunkered down, and pulled the cowhand, chair and all, out the front door. Outside, he untied the cowhand's horse and looped the end of the rope around the saddle horn. Then he took hold of the horse's bridle and led it toward the jail a short distance away. The Mexican howled in pain as the chair bumped down the steps before hitting the smooth dirt between the saloon and the jail.

By the time he had been dragged over the dirt between the two buildings, the cowhand was in no condition to protest his treatment. He made no move to fight Perley when he was led into one of the cells and locked up.

As soon as his hands were freed, he staggered to the slop bucket and fell on his knees before it. Perley pumped some fresh water and set it inside the cell. "Here," he said, "you're gonna need this." He took a quick look around in the sheriff's office, but it appeared that no one had been in while he was away. He locked the front door then, picked up the chair in one hand, and led the cowhand's horse with the other, stopping at the watering trough before taking the horse to the stable. After the horse was taken care of, he went back to the saloon, where some of the regular customers were already filing in since the threat was gone. Horace went with him, deciding he might as well have breakfast, too.

"I swear, Perley," Horace said. "I wish to hell you'd think about keepin' the marshal's job."

CHAPTER 20

Eli Ballenger was in no mood to fight the late Joe Cutter's ornery gray gelding. The horse seemed inclined to pick its own pace, no matter how hard Ballenger fought to dominate. He attributed it to the fact that Cutter was a huge man and a cruel master, in contrast to his slim, wiry frame. He had thought hard about pursuing the man who had managed to completely destroy this simple kidnapping job. Reason enough was the fact that he had stolen his horse and saddle. He had paid eighty dollars for that saddle and he intended to get it back as well as the Morgan gelding under it. However, there were other matters to take care of. Major among them was his arrangement with Zachary Slocum. Slocum's son was on his way back to tell his father the woman and child had been kidnapped but had managed to escape after they had been brought all the way to the southern boundary of the

Lazy-S ranch. Brent Slocum had clearly not been pleased with the way the operation had been handled, and Ballenger could really not blame him. And now, his reputation depended upon his ability to straighten things out with Slocum, plus the matter of money already paid for the job. With his agents, Cutter and Logan, out of the picture, Ballenger could see no alternative but to go after the child, himself. And that was not to his liking. His business was assassination, and he was the best in the business. Kidnapping babies and their mothers was for lowlifes like the two he had just hired. Unfortunately, he had made a contract to do it. Before anything else, he told himself, he would recover his horse and saddle, and he would find this man who had made fools of them all. And he would kill him.

The woman and child had no doubt returned to Bison Gap, so it stood to reason that the man who stole his horse was there also. So after he searched the bodies of his former partners for anything useful, he wrestled the ornery horse's head back toward Comanche Run to see if their packhorse was still there. If it was gone, he would be hard put to make any kind of camp without a bedroll or supplies. When

401

he reached the camp, he found the pack-horse patiently waiting, along with the horse Rachael had ridden. He was satisfied then that he had the supplies he needed, even though it was not his packhorse or his supplies. He had little choice, since his packhorse was at the Lazy-S, and he was in no mood to defend his failure to deliver the package to Zachary Slocum. With that in mind, he decided it best to let the horses rest, then start out for Bison Gap later that night.

Morning brought the promise of yet another day of cloudless skies and clear warm nights. Ballenger cut some strips of bacon to fry to go with a cup of coffee before starting out on his vengeful task. He had no choice other than to use the coffeepot Cutter and Logan had used. Since he needed no more than a cup or two of coffee, he filled the pot with water just short of the bullet hole and measured an estimated amount of grounds. When he finished his breakfast, he set out again for Bison Gap.

Arriving in the little settlement close to suppertime, he pushed the reluctant gray down the length of the street to the stable at the end. As soon as he pulled up there, he saw what he had come looking for. He had not expected to find his horse so easily.

402

To be sure, he dismounted and walked to the rail of the corral to get a closer look. Any doubts he may have had were immediately dissolved when the horse came over to greet him. "Didn't expect to see you again so soon." The voice came from behind him. "I believe you musta took a likin' to our little town."

Ballenger turned to see Horace Brooks coming out the front door of the stable. "It's an easy town to take a liking to," he said. "I was just passing by when I noticed this Morgan here in the corral. When I took a closer look, I recognized him. That's my horse. He got away from me a couple of days ago, and I've been looking for him ever since. He had my saddle on him, too. How'd he end up in your corral?"

"Perley Gates brought him in," Horace replied. "He said the horse had followed him home and he was gonna leave it at the stable to see if its owner came lookin' for it. He'll most likely be glad you came by."

"Perley Gates?" Ballenger responded, surprised, "the young fellow who's acting as the temporary sheriff?"

"That's the feller," Horace replied

Ballenger was stumped for a moment, thinking back to the unassuming young fellow he had met, sitting at the table in the saloon with Possum Smith. He had to doubt that Perley was the man who had led Joe Cutter and Waylon Logan into an ambush and then stolen the horses. If he had not been careful, he might have been caught in that same ambush. He could not have been so far off in judging a man. Maybe, the man he was looking for turned the Morgan over to the sheriff, and that was how it ended up in Horace's stable. He noticed then that Horace was staring at him as if puzzled, and he realized that he had been lost in thought for a long moment. "That reminds me," he said. "There was something I wanted to talk to the sheriff about. I almost forgot it. You think he's around today? I heard he was out of town for a few days."

"Well, yeah, he was. But like I said, he brought your horse in a couple days ago. Soon as he got back, he had to go in and hog-tie a crazy Mexican who was shootin' up the saloon." He went on to tell Ballenger the whole story of the way Perley roped the cowhand and dragged him over to the jail. When he had finished, Ballenger's opinion of the mild-mannered temporary lawman had rapidly changed. He had underestimated the craftiness of the man, and he was suddenly more determined to test his nerve when there was nothing for Perley to hide behind.

"You think he's at the jail now?" Ballenger asked.

"Most likely. Either there or at The Buffalo Hump eatin' supper."

"Fine, fine," Ballenger said, nodding as he did, his mind creating the scene he was anxious to participate in. "I'll come to get that Morgan when I'm finished with Perley Gates. Just so you'll know it's really my horse, take a look under the fender on that saddle that came with the horse and you'll see my name, Eli Ballenger, etched into the leather." He paused to see if Horace had any reaction to that.

"I reckon that'da be proof enough," Horace said. "I never thought to even take a look to see if the owner's name was on it, because I remembered the horse and you."

"I'll notify Sheriff Gates myself. Don't you worry about that. I'll pay you for the horse's board, even though I didn't bring it here."

"No problem," Horace said. "There ain't no charge."

Ballenger snorted in amusement when he thought of something. "You're not going to be out any money when this is all finished. I'll leave you these two nags I rode in with for your trouble. I'll just pick up the pack-

405

horse when I get my Morgan." He turned and walked away, leaving Horace standing dumbfounded, holding the reins to Joe Cutter's gray, the horse Rachael had ridden, and the packhorse.

When he got to the sheriff's office, he found the door locked with a padlock, so he continued on to the saloon. With no reason to be cautious, for he felt sure Perley had not been close enough to recognize him as one of the four men at Comanche Run, Ballenger walked boldly into The Buffalo Hump. For a few moments, he stood there looking around the room until he spotted Perley sitting by himself, quietly eating his supper. Over at the bar, Jimmy McGee recognized him and called out a "Howdy." Ballenger acknowledged it with one of his own and said, "Pour me a shot of whiskey, rye if you've got it. I'll take it over at the table with the sheriff."

Busy working on a tough piece of beef, Perley was not aware he was going to have a visitor until Ballenger pulled a chair back and sat down. Perley looked up in surprise. "Have a seat," he said, after the fact. "What brings you back to town, Mr. . . ." He paused then, unable to remember the name.

"Ballenger," he reminded him.

"Right," Perley said. "Mr. Ballenger. You

406

just passin' through again?"

"Nope, this time I came here to see you," he said, "about a horse that had been stolen." He smiled, enjoying the puzzled look on Perley's face. "A dark, almost black Morgan gelding." He paused momentarily when Jimmy set his whiskey on the table. "Well, I've been looking for that horse and I found it over at the stable just now. The fellow that owns the stable, what's his name? Harry?"

"Horace," Perley corrected, "Horace Brooks."

"Right. Anyway, Horace said I'd better check with you before I take the horse with me. So what about it, Sheriff? How did you happen to come by that horse?"

"I reckon I'm the one who stole it," Perley admitted, his full attention focused on what Ballenger was saying now. It came to him then that when he saw the four men around the fire at Comanche Run, there had been one split second when he wondered if he hadn't seen one of the men before. But he was too far away to get a good look. "Maybe I oughta be askin' you if you've been to Comanche Run lately," Perley said.

"Why, I don't know," Ballenger said, feeling the confidence that comes with knowing how a conversation will end. "Where is

Comanche Run?"

Certain he was being played now, Perley laid his fork down on the table. "About a two-day ride from here," he said. "So that was you hidin' in the bushes while I ran off with your horse. And now you've come to give yourself up for kidnappin'. Is that right?"

"Kidnapping?" Ballenger laughed. "I told you, somebody stole my horse, and that's what I'm here for. I've never heard of Comanche Run. Maybe what we need to be talking about is the confession you just made about stealing my horse. I don't appreciate you calling me a kidnapper, so I reckon I deserve a public apology for that, and right here in this saloon is a good place to get it." He was gradually talking louder until he reached a point where he was certain everyone in the saloon could hear him. The sudden quiet that had descended over the other customers stood as testimony to that. "I'll have that apology now, Sheriff."

It was finally plain to Perley that Ballenger was baiting him for a face-off right there in the saloon, and it proved to him that there was no doubt that he was the third outlaw in that ambush by the creek. It was also certain that he was part of the kidnapping of Emma's baby and Rachael. It occurred to him that only a professional gunfighter would push him for a showdown to settle the disagreement, confident that it would settle the argument — and would not be considered murder, because it was a duel. "I don't reckon you'll be gettin' an apology," he said. "What you will be gettin' is a cell in the town jail while you're waitin' for the Texas Rangers to transport you to trial."

Ballenger threw his head back and laughed. "You're bluffing, Sheriff. You got no evidence that I was anywhere near this place you call Comanche Run."

"I've got an eyewitness," Perley said.

"Who?" Ballenger demanded.

"Me," Perley said. "I saw you there."

"You're a damn liar," Ballenger roared, finally losing control of his glib manner.

"I'm afraid I'm gonna have to put you under arrest for kidnappin' and attempted murder of an officer of the law," Perley calmly stated.

"Is that so?" Ballenger responded. "And I'm afraid you're gonna have to try to arrest me." He pushed his chair back and stood up. His eyes glued on Perley, he pulled his morning coat off and folded it across the back of the chair. The Colt Peacemaker riding low on his thigh was handy in a black leather quick-draw holster. The crooked smile on his face told Perley he might be in trouble. "We'll settle this question the right way, instead of arguing. Bullets don't argue."

"That's not the way we do things here in Bison Gap," Perley said. "You'd best hand that gun over, and we'll go on over to the jail and let you cool off some. I'll take it easy on you 'cause you were nice enough to come in and confess."

Ballenger was reaching a point of exasperation, anxious to settle with Perley for making shambles of what was supposed to be a simple delivery of a baby, but most of all for the way he had played him for a fool. "Get on your feet, you dumb son of a bitch, or I'll shoot you in that chair."

"Ballenger, my supper's gettin' cold. How 'bout you sittin' back down and let me finish eatin'? Then we can talk it over like civilized men and maybe you'll see this thing the way I see it." When Ballenger could only glare, astonished and seething with anger, Perley said, "I'm just tryin' not to have to kill you."

"You damn coward!" Ballenger blurted. "You're pretty good with a rifle when you're hid and nobody's shooting back at you, aren't you? Let's see how you are when you're face-to-face with somebody who can shoot back. Get up from there or I swear you're a dead man right where you sit." He dropped his hand to rest on the Colt.

"All right, all right," Perley said. "I'm gettin' up." He took another bite out of a biscuit, then slowly got to his feet. "I declare, Ida Wicks bakes the best biscuits in West Texas. You wanna try one before we act like a couple of kids?"

"Damn you!" Ballenger snarled and took a few steps backward as Perley walked out to face him. The only sound in the room was that of customers getting out of their chairs to clear the middle of the room.

"How you wanna do this?" Perley asked, "have somebody count to three or something?"

His question brought a smile to the gunman's face. "We don't need anybody to count. You just draw when you feel lucky."

"You mean you want me to go first?" Perley asked. "That don't hardly seem fair to you."

"I've stood face-to-face like this with eight men," Ballenger said, still grinning as he relished the next few seconds. "You'll be number nine, but you're the dumbest bastard I've ever shot. Now the talking is over. Pull it when you're ready to die."

"When I'm ready?"

"Yes, damn it, when you're ready," Ballenger said. He looked down then, confused to see the hole in his shirt as he stepped backward from the impact. He had not even heard the shot that killed him. His gun still in his holster, he looked at Perley in disbelief as he dropped to his knees, remained there for several seconds, then fell over on his side.

There was not a sound in the barroom for almost a full minute before the first question was quietly asked by someone near the corner of the room. "Did you see it? I never saw it."

"He musta already had his gun out," someone else said. He was immediately answered.

"No, hell, he didn't. It was in his holster when he stood up and faced him."

"I reckon I musta blinked when he drew," another said, " 'Cause I was lookin' right at him and I never saw him reach for it."

To Perley, this was another incident where he had been forced to do something he didn't want to do. He was sorry there were any witnesses to the shooting. He had seen once again that he had been blessed, or cursed, he wasn't sure which, with a hand speed and reflexes he truly didn't understand. He was aware of no conscious thought when it was time to act. Always before, his shots were in reaction to his adversary's offensive move. This time, he drew first, which seemed unfair, but he finally did as Ballenger insisted. He would have to think about that.

"Perley, Perley," he finally heard Jimmy McGee's voice in his ear. "You all right, Perley?"

"What? Oh, yeah, I'm all right." He looked down to see his gun still in his hand, so he quickly holstered it. He looked at Ballenger's body sprawled on its side. "I'm sorry 'bout the mess, but it didn't look like I was gonna be able to avoid it."

Jimmy had a wide grin on his face as he gushed, "I ain't never seen anything like that in my whole life!" He shook his head in disbelief.

"Tell Ida I'm sorry I didn't finish my supper," Perley said. "It was good, just like it always is, although that steak was a little bit tough, but due to the interruption, I just sorta lost my appetite. I don't want her to think I didn't like it. I'll be right here for breakfast in the mornin'."

Jimmy shook his head, amazed by Perley's concern for Ida's feelings after the incident that had just taken place. "Right, I'll tell her," he assured him.

Perley moved the gawkers that had already

gathered over Ballenger's body while he unbuckled the gun belt and relieved the body of any other valuables, including a roll of paper money of considerable size. He was satisfied to find the money. It looked to be ample to pay for the burial with plenty left over to give the town council. One of the spectators volunteered to go get Floyd Jenkins and another one helped Perley carry the body outside, where Perley waited for Floyd. In a short while, he showed up pushing a handcart especially made for the purpose of transporting a body. Already irritated because the job of undertaker had been thrust upon him, he complained that he had been in the middle of his supper. "I know how you feel," Perley said. "I kinda had mine interrupted, too. Has the town council made a deal with you about how much they'll pay you to take care of bodies like this one?"

"Hell, no," Floyd answered. "All they've told me so far is that they're gonna pay me something. I'm already out twenty-five dollars to have John Payne make this buggy for me."

"Well, I reckon you're lucky this fellow is able to pay for his own burial," Perley said. He peeled off some bills from the roll he found in Ballenger's pocket. "Here's twenty-five dollars to pay for your buggy, and twenty more to bury him. Is that satisfactory?"

Floyd was properly surprised. "Well, I'd say so," he responded, aware that Wheeler was considering something in the neighborhood of ten dollars for the burial — and his cart had actually cost him a little over fifteen dollars. "I appreciate it, Perley. It's a pleasure doin' business with you."

Perley helped Floyd load Ballenger's body on the cart and waited there when he saw Ralph Wheeler hurrying down to the saloon, pausing only a few moments to look at Floyd's passenger before continuing. "Mr. Mayor," Perley greeted him.

"I heard about the shooting," Wheeler said. "Who was he?"

"I don't really know, but it's my guess he was a gun for hire. He was part of that kidnappin' of Emma Slocum's baby. And I expect he got paid pretty good to do it, since he's makin' a donation to the Bison Gap city council for things like public burials and meals for jail inmates and so on." He handed the rest of Ballenger's money to the mayor.

Wheeler was almost stunned, having never considered a bonus. "How much is there here?"

"I didn't count it," Perley said.

"I appreciate your honesty," Wheeler said, and assured him it would be used for official town business only. When Perley said he figured as much, Wheeler asked, "I don't suppose there was any chance to just arrest him?"

"Nope. I made the offer, but he didn't take it."

Wheeler left him then, eager to tell Henry Lawrence and Dick Hoover about the donation. Before going back to the jail, Perley took one look back at the saloon where the spectacle of the shooting would be discussed for the rest of the evening.

He walked in the cell room to observe the sad sight of the Mexican cowhand still suffering the effects of a gigantic hangover. He had given the man the option of being released that morning, but he was so sick he wanted to stay there for another night. Perley let him stay, but he told him now that he would have to be on his way in the morning because there was some business he had to attend to. "I don't wanna catch you in that saloon again," Perley warned him.

"No, no, no saloon," the cowhand insisted, making a sour face. "Whiskey no good for Pedro."

"Whiskey no good for anybody, I reckon." It occurred to him that the last job he would ever want on this earth would have to be that of a lawman. He suddenly felt a small case of homesickness.

CHAPTER 21

Once again, they had managed to stop an attempt by Zachary Slocum to kidnap his grandson, this one more professional, supposedly, with the likes of Eli Ballenger and his agents, Joe Cutter and Waylon Logan, to carry out the abduction. Perley was well aware that this did not mean the threat was over, not with a man like Slocum. Any owner of a cattle empire the size of the Lazy-S Ranch might be prone to believe he determined right and wrong as it suited his desires. And Slocum seemed to be self-endowed with absolute power. So what would be next? Would he send his whole crew of cowhands to Bison Gap to take the baby by force — and the mother, too? Or would there be another hired specialist like Eli Ballenger to make the next attempt? Perley was sick of the mess, and he was ready to go home, but he knew that the matter needed to be resolved for good. It was not of his making, but he was involved in it up to his neck. These were friends of his and he did not feel he could desert them at this juncture. These were the thoughts that lay heavy on his mind as he followed the narrow path by Oak Creek on his way to Rooster's cabin.

The weather being pleasant, they were all outside with a table set up between the two wagons that had transported them from Butcher Bottom. Rooster was of course in attendance, never one to miss a feast like the one prepared by Emma and Rachael on this occasion. The baby was sleeping nearby in a rather crude cradle that Tom had put together. There was cause for celebration, Rachael and the baby's safe return, as well as the start of construction on the Bison House Hotel. Possum had been dispatched to town earlier that day to ensure Perley's attendance.

"There he is!" Rooster called out when Perley rode up. "Heard you had a little to-do with some hot-shot gunslinger yesterday."

"Just some sheriff's business," Perley said as he stepped down, not wishing to go into any detail.

"Just some sheriff's business, huh?" Rooster responded. "That ain't what I heard. They're talkin' about a strike of lightnin' hit the saloon. I wish I'da seen it."

"That's just the kinda thing that ain't good to talk about," Perley said. "And that's the reason I'm gettin' myself outta Bison Gap as soon as I can. Talk about a fast gun draws every kind of gunslinger in the country to a town, and that's not what you want for Bison Gap."

"Perley's right," Emma said. "We don't wanna draw those kinds of people to stay in our hotel, do we, Rachael?"

Rachael was quick to agree. "But we aren't trying to get rid of you," she added just as quickly. "I don't know where we'd be right now, if it hadn't been for you."

"I 'preciate it," Perley said, "but I think we all agree it'll be better if I don't hang around." When he saw their solemn faces, he joked, "It ain't the first time I've been asked to leave someplace."

"Fiddle," Emma replied. "I don't believe that. Just ask Alice or Melva."

Perley laughed and said, "Well, you know I'll be back when Alice turns sixteen." She laughed and Perley added, "Ol' Buck might be too feeble by then to tote me."

"Let's eat this supper before it turns stone cold," Rachael ordered, and they sat down at the table. It was never officially declared, but the conversation around the table was definitely of a farewell nature, with lots of talk about the experiences they had shared ever since they started at Doan's Crossing on the Red River.

"Me and Emma was worried about havin' to take care of you," Possum declared. "We thought your brothers just saw an opportunity to get rid of you." They all laughed at that, and Perley claimed that that wasn't far from the truth.

After supper, the talk got around to something of a more serious nature. "We still have Zachary Slocum to worry about," Perley said. "And I reckon this business with him ain't over till he decides he ain't got any right to steal a baby from its mother. I don't know what it's gonna take to get him to give up. Maybe we have to go to the law with the problem, but I think I should go have a talk with him to see if there's any chance he'll voluntarily give up."

Emma listened with intent upon what he was saying and was inspired to ask a question. "I wonder if it would do any good if I went with you? Maybe if he could get to know me a little better, he might be willing for me to raise his grandson." It was a bold suggestion, but after a great deal of discussion followed, everyone agreed that it might make a difference to Slocum if he could change his opinion of Emma as a Gypsy bitch. "With Perley to protect me, I'm not afraid to go," she said, then turned to her sister. "I hope you don't mind takin' care of Danny for me again, but this time don't take him on another trip."

"I ain't promisin' nothin'," Rachael replied, laughing.

"I'll go with you," Possum volunteered, still wanting to be a part of it. By evening's end, it was decided. They would go with Perley to call on Zachary Slocum.

Two and a half days of travel took them to the headquarters of the Lazy-S Ranch. It was easy to find after they got to Comanche Run and followed a trail from there that took them right to the ranch house. Walking their horses across the yard toward the front porch, they were met by a man who came from the barn to intercept them. When they pulled up before him, he said nothing, but looked from one face to another as if trying to identify them. "We've come to talk to Mr. Slocum," Perley said. "Is he here?"

"Sí, Señor Slocum is here. Do you have business with him?"

"Yes, I think we do," Perley answered. "Tell him his daughter-in-law has come to

422

see him." Juan Garcia looked at Emma, clearly confused until Perley said, "Go tell him."

Still confused, Juan shrugged and said, "I tell him." He then went to the front door and knocked.

After a few minutes the door opened, and they could see Juan talking to someone inside. Then Margaret Cross stepped out on the porch, thinking that Juan must have gotten confused. Seeing the two men and the woman, she asked, "What is your business with Mr. Slocum?"

"What he just told you," Perley said. "His daughter-in-law wants to talk to him."

Margaret did not know what to believe, it being so unlikely. She stared hard at Emma for a few seconds before asking, "You're Emma Wise?"

"No, I'm Emma Slocum," she answered defiantly. "Wise was my maiden name."

Margaret was not sure what to do. There was no telling how Zachary would react to such a bold visit. She hesitated but a moment more, then decided, *to hell with it, I'll go get him.* To them, she said, "You can dismount and wait on the porch. I'll go get Mr. Slocum."

They dismounted and stepped up on the wide porch. "Best keep on your toes,"

Possum warned, halfway serious. "He might come out carryin' a shotgun."

After what seemed a long few minutes, the door opened again and Zachary Slocum walked out to stand before them, glaring at each one in order. Though a few years past his physical prime, he still conveyed the image of a powerful man, with forearms like a blacksmith, attached to heavy, wide shoulders. It was little wonder that he was accustomed to king-like obedience from his family and his men. "Have you brought my grandson?" He asked, thinking there could be no other reason for their bold visit to his home.

"No, I have not," Emma spoke before Perley had a chance to. "We've come to tell you that Danny is my son, and he belongs with his mother until he's old enough to decide for himself where his home is. When that time comes, if he wants to go to you, I won't try to stop him. I've also come to tell you how sorry I am that you lost your son when I lost my husband, struck down by an evil man who held no respect for human life. For his evil act, he has paid with his life. Now, I'm askin' you, as a Christian man, to leave me and my baby alone."

When she finished, no one said anything for a long moment, so surprised was everyone by her declaration, especially Perley and Possum. Possum started to say something, but Perley gave him a rough nudge and shook his head, effectively shutting him up. As far as Perley was concerned, Emma pretty much conveyed the message they had come to deliver, and it sounded better coming from the mother. Slocum, suddenly on the defensive, glanced at Margaret, who was still standing in the doorway for support, but she was as stunned as he. The picture they had painted of an ill-bred Gypsy woman did not resemble the confident young woman stating her peace. The wind having been sucked from his rage, Slocum was hard put to deny her claims. "You are denying my grandson the opportunity to grow up on a working ranch where he would have every opportunity to learn and grow," he argued. "He wouldn't have to scratch in the ground for enough food to stay alive."

"Let me answer that one for you, Mr. Slocum," Perley spoke up. "I think you probably don't know that Emma is building a hotel right now in Bison Gap, in a partnership with Mr. Smith, here. I might add that they're payin' for it with cash money. So your grandson ain't hardly gonna be goin' hungry. And the hotel will be operated by someone named Slocum, spreading your name over a wider area of Texas. That can't be bad for you."

"I heard that rumor," Slocum said, "but I didn't believe it. You're sayin' it's true?"

"It's a fact," Possum replied. "The deal's already set with the town council."

Standing behind Margaret in the door now, Brent Slocum listened with more than casual interest. Like Margaret, he was surprised to see his father seeming to be at a loss for words. He stepped out on the porch then. "There has already been too much bloodshed over this matter," he said. Turning to Perley then, he asked, "The two men Eli Ballenger sent, they're dead?"

"They are," Perley answered. "At least one of 'em is and the other one got shot."

"Ballenger?" Brent asked.

"Dead," Perley answered.

Brent turned to face his father and repeated, "There has been enough bloodshed, Papa. Maybe it's time to call off this feud."

Margaret stepped out on the porch then and moved close to Slocum. "Maybe he's right, Zachary," calling him by his given name. "Why don't we invite your daughter-in-law and her friends inside for some coffee and maybe something to eat? I've got a fresh-baked apple pie cooling on the windowsill."

For a moment, the all-powerful master of the Lazy-S, seemed to be lost. Then he looked from Margaret to his son, smiling at him, and he suddenly regained his pride. "By God," he exclaimed, "you're right. You're all right. Come on inside and tell me about this hotel you're building. Brent, go get Raye and the girls. They'll wanna meet your sister-in-law."

Possum looked at Perley, both of them grinning. "Ain't no better way to end a feud than with a slice of apple pie," Possum said.

It was a happy peace party that returned to Rooster's cabin close to suppertime a couple of days after leaving the Lazy-S Ranch. There seemed to be reason to believe Zachary Slocum when he assured them there would be no future attempts to snatch his grandson from the arms of his mother. In fact, he and his son, Brent, had suggested that mother and son might wish to visit the Lazy-S when the boy was old enough to enjoy the operation of a working cattle ranch. Of course, that invitation was always open, depending upon Emma being able to take time away from her management of Bison Gap's hotel.

Supper that night also served as a farewell dinner for Perley, who once again planned to depart for Lamar County the following morning. Never one to enjoy farewells, Perley said his good-byes soon after supper, saying he had some things to take care of that night before leaving Bison Gap in the morning. Perhaps the hardest part, after a hug from both women and both of Rachael's daughters, was a handshake with Possum. Rooster and Tom were both in high spirits over their short relationship with Perley Gates, but Possum seemed genuinely sorrowful. As he had told Perley before, he had gotten used to having him around, and he had still had hopes that he would take the sheriff's job Wheeler offered. Perley told him he could never be a lawman. "I've got family wonderin' where I am," he said. "I'm already gonna catch hell for never comin' back to help drive those cattle to the market. But I wish you and Emma the best of luck with your hotel. I don't see how you can miss."

Early morning found him at the stable, where he settled up with Horace Brooks for boarding his horses and ended up selling Horace one Morgan gelding and saddle for a price too good for Horace to pass up. He gave him Ballenger's packhorse. After saying "so long" to Horace, he headed to

Wheeler's Merchandise to give Ralph the key to the sheriff's office and buy supplies for his trip back to Lamar County and the Triple-G. Wheeler was disappointed to see him go but understood his need to leave. "I've had a fellow lined up for the job in case you didn't take it," Wheeler said. "He's the foreman for a ranch south of here, and I think he'll do a good job."

"You had him lined up all along, I expect," Perley said.

"I was hoping you'd change your mind," Wheeler insisted.

"Well, you've got some good folks here in your little town. I hope it grows like you want it to." With that, he said good-bye to Wheeler, packed his supplies on his sorrel packhorse, and stepped up on Buck. He turned the bay gelding toward the bridge over Oak Creek, the same bridge Rooster had showed him when he and Possum and the others found Bison Gap. Once across the bridge, he turned Buck east for two miles to pick up the trail Possum had led them down, before turning north.

He had not traveled ten miles when he became aware of someone following him. And he began to become a little concerned when each time he paused to take a look back, he discovered the rider was rapidly catching up with him. Just for the sake of being cautious, he decided to pull off the trail when he came to a stream with trees on each side, enough to pull Buck and his packhorse out of sight. He pulled his rifle out and waited. In about fifteen minutes, the rider came splashing across the stream, leading a packhorse behind him. "Possum!" Perley yelled, causing him to almost come out of the saddle when he yanked the reins to turn his horse.

Perley rode out of the trees. "Possum, what is it? What's wrong?" He waited a few moments while Possum righted himself in the saddle.

"Dang, Perley, I took a chance on you takin' the same trail we came down here on. Good thing you did, else I'da never caught you."

"Well, you caught me," Perley said. "What's wrong? What happened?"

"Oh, nothin's wrong, I just wanna go with you," Possum replied.

"Go with me?" Perley responded. "Go with me where?"

"I don't know. Wherever, I reckon. I ain't got no place in mind. I just know I ain't wantin' to set around a hotel twiddlin' my thumbs. I talked it over with Emma last night after you left, and she knows I don't know nothin' about runnin' a hotel. When I brought her down here, I never planned to stay in the first place."

"So you pulled out of your partnership with her?"

"Nah, we're still partners, it's just money she needs from me. She can handle the hotel without me around to get in the way. I'll get my share of the profits. She said I can look at the books anytime I wanna. I figure you need a partner, and I'm hopin' you don't mind if I ride along with you. If you do mind, then I reckon I'll leave you at the Red and I'll go on back to Kansas. Whaddaya say?"

Perley shook his head, astonished. He laughed and replied. "I reckon I could use some company."

ABOUT THE AUTHOR

William W. Johnstone has written nearly three hundred novels of western adventure, military action, chilling suspense, and survival. His bestselling books include *The Family Jensen; The Mountain Man; Flintlock; MacCallister; Savage Texas; Luke Jensen, Bounty Hunter;* and the thrillers *Black Friday, The Doomsday Bunker,* and *Trigger Warning.*

J. A. Johnstone learned from the master, Uncle William W. Johnstone, with whom J.A. has co-written numerous bestselling series including The Mountain Man; Those Jensen Boys; and Preacher, the First Mountain Man.

The employees of Thorndike Press hope you have enjoyed this Large Print book. All our Thorndike, Wheeler, and Kennebec Large Print titles are designed for easy reading, and all our books are made to last. Other Thorndike Press Large Print books are available at your library, through selected bookstores, or directly from us.

For information about titles, please call:
  (800) 223-1244

or visit our website at:
  gale.com/thorndike

To share your comments, please write:
  Publisher
  Thorndike Press
  10 Water St., Suite 310
  Waterville, ME 04901